I0636187

1996

Allyson Norris

Copyright © 2025 by Allyson Norris

All rights reserved. No part of this book may be reproduced, stored in a retrieval system, or transmitted in any form or by any means—electronic, mechanical, photocopying, recording, or otherwise—without the prior written permission of the author, except for brief quotations used in reviews, articles, or academic analysis.

This is a work of fiction. Names, characters, places, and incidents are either products of the author's imagination or used fictitiously. Any resemblance to actual events, locales, or persons, living or dead, is purely coincidental.

Cover design by Allyson Norris
Interior formatting by Draft2Digital
First printing: January 2025
ISBN: 9798218732912

To Deer Creek Camp
Thank you for countless
summers filled with
amazing memories

how to haunt
May 20

It starts with a ghost story.

Chills race down my spine and goosebumps ripple across my arms like bugs playing tag. I try to rub them away but dragging my palms across my skin does not help. Grimacing, my mind flashes back to the brief moments in Quinny's room when I tried to persuade her not to make me come to this stupid party, but like always, Quinny insisted that we had a reputation to uphold. A reputation that mandated idiotic parties like these.

So she coaxed me into trendy jeans and a tank top, tried to tame my hopelessly wild auburn curls, and begged me to wear contacts. Hazel and Jolie let me borrow their makeup since I barely have any of my own—the good kind, full of chemicals that would make my mother freak.

Usually, I roll my eyes but deal with these kinds of events. I only go because it's what Quinny expects of anyone who's friends with her, even though Coach warns us never to get in trouble or our volleyball positions will be in jeopardy.

But it's the last week of school and things have been so crazy, not to mention that my parents have been acting odd lately. With finals and everything else going on, I'd looked forward to a quiet night in, complete with green tea and soft acoustic in the background while I studied.

Music blasts over the speakers while teenagers shout over the throb to be heard. I wave and smile at the passersby, many who enviously stare at me because I have an in with Quinny. It doesn't matter that we're only juniors—Quinny puts every senior girl to shame. She walks through the room effortlessly—Jolie, Hazel and I in her shadow.

It's impossible to tell whose party this is. Bodies are packed like animals in the living room, laughing too loud and causing a spike of dull pain to shoot through my head. I pinch the bridge of my nose. Hazel elbows me and mouths *be cool*.

We follow Quinny outside, where some of our classmates sit around a fire pit, smoke billowing up like a cloud into the dark sky. The wisps remind me of the top of Mom's diffusers all around the house.

"Hey gang." Quinny waggles her fingers at the group we've joined. "What's going on over here?"

"Just telling ghost stories." A boy named Dominic drags a hand through his hair.

My stomach clenches at the words "ghost stories".

"Dom has had some really scary ones," adds Alivia. She pats my hand when I take the open seat beside her. "Hey, Maeve. Excited for volleyball camp this summer?"

Alivia has always been one of the nicest girls. She remembers everything you talk to her about and seems to actually be interested in what you have to say. She's an art girl, not an athlete. But she usually shows up to most of the big school events, including volleyball games. I love chatting with Alivia, but I think Quinny feels threatened by her. Alivia is so likable and has a unique style, something even Quinny can't quite emulate. Unfortunately, she can be a little snappy to Alivia at times because of her jealousy, but Alivia is gracious and everyone else brushes it off because, well, that's just *Quinny*.

"Yes! I think next year will be our best season yet." I stretch my legs out, resting them on the edge of the fire pit and enjoying the way the flames cast heat across my skin. "I'm so excited to watch you guys." Alivia smiles.

I smile back.

"Maeve!" Quinny interrupts. When I glance at her, she wears a tight-lipped smile. "Dom was *just* about to tell us a ghost story. Are you listening?"

Ghost stories. I bite my lip and taste blood. "Um, what if we talk about something else? How do you guys honestly feel about the chem final? I'm kind of panicked if I'm being honest—"

Quinny squints at me. "Maeve?"

Dom cracks his knuckles. "Okay. This story is about a man named John and his wife Elizabeth. They were so in love and John loved showering her with gifts. So he bought her three expensive pieces of jewelry: a pair of earrings, a necklace, and a ring."

Hazel and Jolie lean forward. I watch the flames cast funky shadows across their faces, wide-eyed and curious.

I jostle my leg and the plastic edge of my shoelace taps against the leg of my chair.

Quinny tilts her head and fixes me with a no-nonsense look. I still my leg.

Dom continues spinning the story: Elizabeth dies, and John buries her with her jewelry, but falls into disparaging levels of debt from gambling and drinking. The more he talks, the more uncomfortable I get. But, for Quinny's sake, I try to keep it in.

I don't want her to look at me like I'm weird.

"John had to find a way to pay off his debts. So, one night, he crept out to the back where Elizabeth was buried, grabbed a shovel, and began to dig...*chh chh, chh chh...*" He adds shoveling sounds which have me gripping the edge of my seat. I quickly close my eyes and take a deep breath. I feel Alivia rest her hand on my shoulder.

The story continues with John removing the earrings from Elizabeth's body—*chh, chh, chh, chh*—selling them, and beginning to do well for himself. But it doesn't last. He falls again into despair and has to sell her necklace, unburying her again. One last time, he falls into a depression and plans to take her ring.

Chh, chh...chh, chh...

"John slipped the ring from Elizabeth's cold finger and made his way back to the house. But that's when he saw her."

I clench my jaw.

"Elizabeth's *ghost*."

"Um, I have to go to the bathroom," I mutter, standing up abruptly.

"Sit down, Maeve," Quinny snaps. "You're ruining the story."

Jolie grabs my arm and yanks me back down.

"Is everything okay?" Alivia has a crease between her brows.

"She's fine. Dom, continue." Quinny crosses her arms.

She's right—I'm fine, I'm fine.

Dom's voice grows softer as he continues the story. "John spoke to his wife, saying, 'Elizabeth, my love, what are you doing here?' She didn't reply, only stared at him with empty eyes. John felt chills go up and down his spine like spiders." Dom waggles his fingers over the fire. "That's when John noticed that Elizabeth wasn't wearing the jewelry. He asked her, 'Elizabeth, where is your necklace?'"

Hazel and Jolie clutch each others' hands and giggle nervously.

"'All gone, all gone,'" Dom says in a voice that's meant to be Elizabeth's. This continues when John asks where her earrings are. But then, John asks Elizabeth the final question.

I feel fear tangling up inside my stomach, all knots and worry, threatening to burst out at any second as I dig my toes into the ground and ask myself again *why I came to this stupid party.*

But I bite down on my tongue to appease Quinny because there is no way I can let her see me afraid.

"'Elizabeth, where is your ring?' Elizabeth glided slowly over to John and looked into his eyes...'" Dom pauses.

We all hold our breath.

He makes eye contact with me and suddenly jumps up, leaning over the fire and screams in my face, "'YOU HAVE IT!'"

I scream and fall backwards. My heart is pounding, pounding, pounding, pounding. The grass comes up under my fingers in large clumps as I scramble back from the fire, from Dom, and from Quinny's laughing face.

"Girl, you *jumped.*"

"You did too, Quinny." Alivia kneels beside me, but I shove her away. Shame burns hot in my face, pooling from my chest where my heart is still racing. All I can see are outlines of shadowy figures. Ghosts.

"I have to go," I mumble, squinting my eyes so that tears can't seep through. In a blur, I stand up on shaky legs and sprint to the nearest bathroom. I stumble through the laughing teenagers, gossiping and dancing and then muttering about me under their breath.

One of the golden four covered in grass stains and tears? Scandalous.

But all I want to do is hide. People shouldn't see me like this. I'm perfect like the rest of the group, I swear.

I shove people out of the way until I come across a bathroom door. There's a girl standing in front of the mirror, reapplying her mascara.

"Get out." My voice feels numb.

"Geez." She grabs her mascara tube and bumps into me hard as she struts out the room.

I slam the door behind her and lock it. Then, I stare at my reflection, gripping the edges of the sink, and focus. I have to calm down.

I believe I belong here. I believe I'm one of them. And I don't believe in ghosts.

cardboard boxes
May 20

I only take five minutes.

Longer than five minutes will give my friends reason to worry about me. A brief blip in my usual perfect persona should have done that, but we all know that chasing after a panicked friend draws more attention to the situation than if we let it go like it means nothing. Quinny may be a lot of things, but she is meticulous when it comes to cultivating the rules of how to maintain our reputation.

Five minutes.

I practice smiling in the mirror and practice saying the words, "ghosts aren't real" until I can verbalize them without a shaky voice. I fluff my hair and pinch my cheeks, trying to put some color back in my sweaty pallor. I check my phone to ensure that it's only been five minutes —not a second more— and toss open the bathroom door. I feign confidence and try to show people that there's nothing wrong with me.

I don't believe in ghosts.

I find Alivia and Dom sitting by the fire. They both shoot me worried glances, but I smile to show them that everything is fine. Dom looks reassured when he realizes I won't start panicking again.

Alivia, however, does not buy my mask. Maybe that's why Quinny dislikes her—Alivia sees through everything.

I frown at the vacant seats where my friends had been sitting

"Where are they?"

"I think they went to find you." Dom tears open a bag of marshmallows beside his chair and grabs a poker.

"S'more?"

I shake my head. "Okay, I must have missed them coming in."

But if they were right by the bathroom waiting for me, wouldn't I have noticed them? Wouldn't they have waved me down or knocked on the door to check if I was okay? Maybe I did take longer than five minutes.

I feel a hand grab my arm gently when I turn around. Alivia's big blue eyes meet mine. Quietly, so Dom can't hear, she whispers, "Is everything okay? You can talk to me. It's okay to not pretend all the time."

I stare at her. What is she talking about? Does she realize how horrible my life would be if I *didn't* pretend? Pretending is what took me from a sad, bullied kid to the top of the high school social ladder.

I yank my arm back and level her with a look. "I don't know what you're talking about."

She blows out a frustrated breath. "Okay, Maeve. I hope someday you realize that being liked isn't all that matters in the world. You can make perfectly good friends without pretending you're so cool and have it all together."

Her words sting, but I brush them off. She really doesn't know what she's talking about. Without saying another word to her, I march straight back towards the center of the party, scanning the room for my friends. Part of me is frustrated to have gotten angry with Alivia, because she's so sweet and I actually love being around her, even though Quinny only does it so she can put Alivia down.

I spy Quinny's shock of blonde hair from across the room. She's leaning against the kitchen counter, where snacks are lined up in various colored bowls for people to grab from as they walk by. The pit in my stomach is growing larger by the second and I desperately want to know what they're saying, panicked that it's about my incident. I quietly sneak around the back of the kitchen, where their backs are to me, and hide behind the doorway that leads to the main room.

"And it's so dumb, too. She's not even that good. Her jump serves are mediocre at best," Quinny complains.

I press my palms against the wall, feeling the knot in my stomach tighten.

They're not talking about the ghost story incident, but they *are* talking about me, because I'm the only girl on our volleyball team who can jump serve. Coach always said it was one of the best jump serves she had ever seen, but now I'm not so sure.

"And I hate that Coach picks a girl to be captain before we even have tryouts. That's so ridiculous and unfair!" adds Jolie.

My jaw clenches. They never thought that was a dumb tradition before.

"Whatever," Quinny says. "I'm going to talk to Coach and tell her I just don't think Maeve is captain material for the varsity team. I mean, she's kind of fragile. You guys saw how she freaked out over that story tonight. I don't really think it's the best idea to have a wimp as a team captain."

"I agree," says Hazel. "Someone needs to talk to Coach."

I hear footsteps and my heart skips a beat. Quickly, I rush out into the crowd of people before the girls can see me. I'm jostled by multiple people but can't bring myself to move from the eye of the storm. I tell myself that my friends are just jealous, they don't actually mean the things they said. Regardless, a tiny pin slips into my heart.

Quinny saw that opening and she took it, like we've done to everyone else.

But this time it's me.

I drag a hand across my face. I've got to get a hold of myself. I cannot let that one slip-up ruin what I've been cultivating for so many years.

I won't let ghost stories mess up my life again.

I shoot a quick text to Quinny, rambling off some lame excuse about how I ate some bad meat for dinner and I had to throw up, which is why I ran off after the story. I tell her that I'm leaving to go get some rest before school tomorrow.

Could it be true? Does Coach really want to make me the captain of the Varsity team without having to try out? She's known me for practically my entire life and has seen how dedicated I am to the sport. I adore volleyball more than most things, but surely dedication isn't the only thing she's looking for?

But how amazing would that be? It would be even *more* amazing if my friends could just be excited for me instead of being so annoyingly jealous.

I roughly yank my curls up into a frizzy ponytail and make the trek back home. On my way out the door, I bump into Alivia.

"Are you leaving?" she asks, grabbing her bag from the hook near the door.

"Yeah."

"Do you need a ride?"

I hesitate, glancing behind my shoulder. Quinny

hasn't seen me yet, but if I left with Alivia, I'd be in the dog house for sure. But if I walk, it'll take me at least half an hour to get home, if not more. My town might not be a big city, but that doesn't mean I think it's safe to walk down the streets by myself at midnight.

"A ride would be great," I tell Alivia, keeping my words short so she understands that I'm only accepting due to common sense and not because she graciously offered. I'm still mad at her about what she accused me of earlier.

"Sounds great, I'm leaving this lame thing anyway." She throws open the door and we step out into the hot night.

Alivia doesn't try to make conversation as she pulls out of the street. She only asks me for my address, which I give, and then lets music fill the quiet space of her SUV. It's the kind of music I like to listen to when Quinny isn't watching—acoustic, soft, and with a hint of 70s. I smile to myself.

"You like this band?" Alivia notices my expression.

"Only a couple songs," I respond quickly.

Her lips quirk up at the corner. "You don't have to do that, Maeve. I won't tell her, you know. It doesn't matter to me what kind of music you listen to. But I can turn it up if you don't really mind it."

I shoot a glance at her. She's smiling at me, as if she knows I want her to turn it up but she's giving me a way out— I don't have to say I like it, just that I don't mind it. And I believe her—I believe she wouldn't tell anybody because from what I know of Alivia, she's an honest person.

When she says she won't do something, she means it.

She drops me off at my house and I thank her.

"See you tomorrow," she says. "And Maeve?" "Yes?"

"I had a good time hanging out with you. We should do it more often."

She doesn't make me respond. She pulls out of my driveway, leaving me feeling uncertain about where my loyalties lie. All my life I've felt content being part of Quinny's group and no bit of me wants to leave her circle. Even though the scrutiny can be overwhelming at times, I know that I'm admired and awed. I know who I am when I'm with Quinny and there's security in that.

I don't know how to be anything else.

I swing open the front door, immediately hit by the heavy fragrance of lavender and patchouli. Mom and Dad are conversing in the kitchen. I follow their voices where I'm met with something I don't know how to understand.

It's not the feathers spread out on the coffee table.

It's not the essential oils spilling out from various diffusers.

It's not the loud hippie music that my mother is singing to.

It's the cardboard boxes. There are dozens of cardboard boxes, all filled with our things—photographs, clothes, books. There they are, stacked on top of the kitchen table, replacing Mom's lacy table runner. I drop my bag loudly on the floor. It's only then that my parents whirl around, as though I caught them doing something illicit.

"Maeve!" Dad quickly slides the roll of packing tape behind one of the boxes. "We weren't expecting you home until tomorrow! We thought you were sleeping over at Quinny's?"

"What is going on?" I ignore him. "What's with these boxes?"

"Chickadee, how was your day?" Mom opens her arms and wraps me in a hug, I inhale the strong scent of rose and vanilla essential oils.

"It was fine. What's with the boxes, Mom?"

Why does it look like we're about to move?

"We bought a camp," Dad drags a hand through his faded red hair. "We have been figuring out how to tell you for a while now."

"You bought a camp?" I almost laugh. My parents have done a myriad of strange things. I'm not usually surprised by their latest eccentricities or odd ideas. But buying a camp?

"Where is said camp?" I plop down into a chair. The cardboard box in front of me is labeled "Living Room" and I peer into it. Inside, they've packed away all of the books and trinkets from the living room, including framed photos of the days when their strange tendencies didn't bother me.

Mom rests her hand on the back of my chair. "Do you remember the camp you went to when you were about seven? But there's this lovely little camp in the hill country. You've been there! Camp Swallowtail? It was a long time ago, but surely you remember."

Camp Swallowtail.

Instantly, my mind flashes with quick visions, something like ghosts of memories dancing across my visions while kids jeer loudly. I nearly clamp my hands over my ears to get them to stop but remember that it's all in my head.

Ghosts.

I grip the edge of the table. "You're joking right? You didn't actually buy that place. I hated every single thing about it! That summer was miserable!"

Everything about that summer is the bane of my existence. Why would my parents want me to relive the summer when every piece of my life that I had known and been comfortable with up to that point went down the gutter?

I bite my lip. Technically, they don't really know what went down...But I have my reasons for keeping that under lock and key.

"We're moving?" I whisper.

"This has been our dream forever," Dad reaches out to grab my hand.

I yank mine away quickly. My brow furrows. "What about *my* dreams?"

"I know you had plans, but I really think this will be a good experience for you." Mom shoots me a sympathetic smile.

"You never told me about it! How could you just spring this on me?"

Mom and Dad exchange confused glances.

"Maeve," Dad says. "We've been hinting at this surprise all year. Didn't you notice all of the camp gear we bought? We've been trying to tell you."

I hadn't been listening.

I'd known that they were acting strange, but I hadn't allowed myself to really think about the possibility that it was because of a coming change. I hadn't wanted to know, not really.

"You can't just uproot my life like that." I slam my fist on the table. The boxes shake. "I have dreams and plans and things going on here! I have commitments!"

The captain spot on the Varsity team flashes through my mind. Fragments of what this summer was supposed to be dance like memories that haven't even happened yet. Quinny, Hazel, Jolie, and I were going to get summer jobs at the clubhouse, lifeguarding and sharing gossip like sticks of gum. We were going to find dates and spend our Friday nights at the drive-in theater downtown. After the drive-in, we'd grab Pig Sundaes from The Vanilla Pig.

How can I just throw these things away like they mean nothing?

"We leave June 1," Dad says. "The camp is purchased and we have places to live there. You have over a week left here, Maeve."

Disbelieving, I shake my head and rest it in my hands. This cannot be happening.

"How can you do this to me?" My laugh is dry. "Chickadee —"

"Don't call me that." I can't see her, but I can almost feel the way Mom flinches at my icy tone. Serves her right for coming up with this ridiculous plan. But I feel so heavy that I don't know how to fight back. Looking at all the boxes around the room, I know my life is already being packed away.

There's nothing I can do to stop it.

varsity
May 24

The last week of school has passed in a blur.

I managed to keep quiet about the move, although everything inside of me was practically begging to spill the secret. Unfortunately, revealing the secret would let Quinny in on the truth of what my parents really were.

They weren't interior designers like I'd told everyone they were. They weren't a glamorous couple who were always off on business trips, traveling and sampling expensive wines in different countries. Mom doesn't carry Louis Vuitton purses and Dad doesn't wear a Rolex.

My parents are hippies. Not the cool kind, either.

They believe essential oils are the cure-all and chemicals are created by the devil himself. Mom has never dyed her hair and Dad collects feathers instead of baseball cards.

Most importantly, my parents believe in *ghosts*.

I shudder.

"Is everything okay?" Quinny tucks her blonde hair behind her ear. "You've been acting strange ever since the party."

"Just got cold for a second there." I brush it off. My backpack weighs heavily on my shoulder, full of all my study materials for the final exam we took today. Even if I can't control where I'll be by the end of June, I can control how much effort I put into my grades. Studying with my music and green tea the past couple of nights has been my only source of comfort.

"We're thinking about going to the Vanilla Pig for an end of the year dinner as a grade," Quinny informs me. "I think pretty much everyone is coming. You'll be there, right? I can give you a ride if you need."

I shake my head. "I can drive myself, thanks."

Quinny shrugs. "Dinner's at 6:30."

I watch her make a beeline for her car, chatting with a few people she passes by. My heart sinks when I realize that despite Quinny's moments of difficulty, I won't be part of the group we've so carefully cultivated together. Once we move, I'll have to make friends from scratch and try to climb my way up the social totem pole—with only a year to do it.

Senior year at a new place. Pathetic.

Angrily, I move toward the parking lot, clutching my backpack strap tightly. I cannot believe my parents would be so selfish as to take me out of school right before my senior year! Everyone at whatever hick town I end up in will already know each other—I'll be lightyears behind what's cool and what's not. No one wants to be friends with the new girl anyway.

"Everbrill!"

I whirl around, startled out of my thoughts.

Coach jogs up to me, her whistle swinging around her neck even though there hasn't been practice or a game in a week. Her blonde ponytail is pulled as tightly as ever. "Coach?"

"I've been looking for you all day!" she exclaims, patting me roughly on the shoulder. "You're pretty tricky to find."

I laugh weakly. "With finals and everything I've been busy."

"Well, I found ya now and that's what matters. I wanted to have a quick chat with you about next year."

My heart flutters a little bit. *The captain's spot on Varsity.*

"I just wanted to let you know that I've been keeping a close eye on your talent and dedication these past few years, and I think you are the most capable and hardworking player I have ever seen in all my years of coaching. Because of that, I want to make you captain of the Varsity team. What do you say?"

I blink at her. I sort of didn't really believe that Quinny's words were true. This position is so coveted among girls on the team—it seems impossible that it would be offered to me just like *that.*

Coach has done it before, so it's almost like an unspoken tradition. But for the past two years, she hasn't found a girl she thought was right to be the Varsity team captain. And now she wants me.

I pinch the bridge of my nose because suddenly I remember *oh yeah, we're moving.*

There's just no way. No way that this once-in-a-lifetime position would be offered to me, one that I have been dreaming of since freshman year, only to be stripped away the second that it actually becomes possible?

I should tell Coach that I won't be here next semester. I should tell her that this is probably the last time she'll ever see me, as I doubt I'll be able to make it to volleyball camp the last week of June, which *also* means I'll have to miss Quinny's birthday...another thing to worry about later.

But Coach looks so hopeful that I'll say yes.

"The only requirement is that you'll need to be at volleyball camp in June," Coach adds and my stomach sinks because *of course.*

If I tell her I can't make it, she'll find some other eligible girl—probably Quinny. In my head, I hear Quinny's harsh words from last night. I suddenly really don't want her to have this position because it's mine and I deserve it.

Maybe I can find a way to come to volleyball camp. Maybe if my parents see how much this means to me and know that Coach depends on me, they won't

make us move.

Or, if they do make us move, maybe I can convince them to come back here before school begins in August. So, I tell Coach, "I would *love* to be captain! Thank you so much for thinking of me—you have no idea how much I appreciate it! I have been dreaming of this position for years!"

Coach smiles at me. I've made her proud. "Looking forward to seeing you in June! Have a wonderful summer, Everbrill!"

"See you then!" I wave.

I'm such a liar.

I try to push the guilty feeling away as I drive home

to get ready for the party. My fingers find the volume dial when I pull into the driveway. I crank it down until the music is nothing more than a faint murmur of notes. My parents don't like when I listen to "teenager" music too loud. They say teenagers like to blare stupid music so that they can tune out their thoughts and emotions, when really, thoughts and emotions are something we should be in touch with.

I flip down the little mirror on my car visor, pulling out makeup wipes from the console beside me. The chemical smell floats through my car. Quickly and in well-practiced motions, I wipe away the dark mascara coating my lashes and the eyeliner that accents the round, doe-like shape of my eyes. I erase all traces of lip gloss from my lips until my face looks blotchy from the heat. I stopped wearing chemical perfume to school when I realized I couldn't disguise traces of that from my home life as easily.

I've been doing so well trying to avoid my parents since they broke the news to me, but it hasn't been so easy. Mom continues to bring me empty boxes with labels already written in black ink, instructing me on what to put into each box. I've been more than a little bit reluctant to begin boxing my life away, but it seems like I have no choice.

Until now.

Now that Coach has brought this proposal to me, I feel like I might finally have a little bit of hope. For as wacky as Mom and Dad can be, they are firm about finishing commitments that you've begun—volleyball surely counts. If I can convince them of how badly Coach wants me to return—which is accurate—and my need to return in late June for volleyball camp—and Quinny's 18th birthday—then maybe, just maybe, there is a chance of me getting out of that stupid camp. Or better yet, not having to go at all.

Confidently, I march into the house and fling my backpack down by the stairs.

I'm so glad to be done with school.

One more year left until I'm finally out and away from all the complicated pieces of my life. Those days of freedom can't come soon enough.

I find Mom in my room.

"What are you doing in here?"

She jumps and quickly puts her hands on her hips.

"You have hardly packed anything." She gestures around to the deep green walls covered with posters and photos of my friends and me. She glances pointedly at my desk, covered with study materials for the exams I just finished.

"Can't say I'm too keen on boxing up my life." I cross my arms across my chest.

"We're leaving in a week, Maeve."

"It's not like you gave me much warning."

She sighs and sits on the edge of my bed. "How was your last day of school? Do you and your friends have any fun plans this evening?"

I take a deep breath and give in, taking a seat beside her. My bed creaks and the tan comforter shifts underneath us.

"My exams went well—"

"That can be accredited to frankincense and rosemary oils and sunlight," Mom nods with a smile.

I purse my lips. "Yeah. Sure. Definitely not because I worked my butt off studying."

She raises an eyebrow.

"And yes, we do have plans tonight. Everyone is headed over to the Vanilla Pig."

She winces but doesn't say anything. The food isn't gourmet or clean by any means, but it sure tastes like manna from heaven.

"I actually had an interesting interaction with Coach today..." I flex my hands and look at her. "It was kind of a big deal."

"Oh?" She tilts her head. "Tell me about it."

"Well, you know how every year, a senior gets chosen to be captain of the varsity team?"

Her eyes turn sad. "Chickadee—"

"She asked me, Mom!" I say loudly. "Do you know how much of an honor that is? She asked *me*. So basically, all I need to do is show up for volleyball camp in late June, which I was going to anyway because Quinny's birthday is that same week and—"

Mom is shaking her head. I feel my heart begin to sink before she even speaks, but I try to tell my brain that I can make this work, that she has to listen to me, that there's no way that I can move to a summer camp.

Please listen to me.

You don't know how badly I don't want to go back there.

You don't know what happened.

LET ME OUT!

I jerk away from her touch at the sudden memory of a smaller Maeve, one who was naive to the way of the world, trapped in a small, dark room that only seemed to get smaller. In all my life, I had never felt so alone.

Until I wasn't alone anymore.

Mom is saying words that I don't want to hear. Things like, "Chickadee, you know what the plan is

for the summer. I'm sorry, but I don't see how we can make volleyball work."

Things like, "Just explain to your coach and tell her how grateful you are that she thought of you."

Things like, "I'm sorry, but this is what we're doing."

"Please get out of my room."

I don't know when the tears came. But they're hot and they're heavy when I think of all the things to come.

Camp Swallowtail fills me with the strangest kind of dread. Why can't she see that? Why is this happening?

I drop my head into my hands and hear the sound of my door opening. Dad.

"Winnie? Maeve? Is everything alright?"

"We're fine, Dad," I say through my tears. I feel an arm go around me and hold me close. I stiffen but can't bring myself to pull away. "I don't want to talk about it."

While I sniffle, Mom quietly explains the situation to Dad, who hums to himself. I wipe away my tears and blink at him. I can feel my contacts prickling my eyes. I think about wearing my glasses for a second and then remember that I'm going out later—Quinny doesn't really like when I wear my glasses.

"Maeve," Dad says gently.

"Yes?" The word shakes.

Dad rests his hand on Mom's shoulder. "What if we offer you a proposal?"

Mom draws her brows together. "George?"

"If you agree to take on a cabin instead of only assisting us behind the scenes like we originally planned for you, we will pay for you to go to volleyball camp. You won't be able to be captain of the team in the fall, but if you cooperate and have a good attitude, we will fly you back here for Quinny's birthday and the camp."

My eyes widen. "All expenses paid? I won't have to fund my own flight or anything?"

"All expenses paid."

I bite my lip. *Wow.* I'm still bitter about moving in the first place, but the opportunity to at least come back here for that week could mean so much! I might be able to persuade them to somehow let me stay, even if it meant living with a friend for a year. Would that be so outlandish? All I would need is that single week to prove to them that I belong here instead.

I study him and he keeps his gaze locked with mine. "Deal."

We shake hands.

the vanilla pig
May 24

Something doesn't feel right when I pull up to the Vanilla Pig.

I'm later than I told Quinny. Mom and Dad wanted to run through all the expectations of being a counselor before I was able to make my escape. I tried to tell them I had places to be, but they felt it was more important to inform me about the cabin of freshmen girls I'll likely be taking on.

The sun had already set below the horizon by the time I finally evacuated the house, clutching a bag with some drugstore makeup contained within. Which of course meant I had to take even longer once I got to the Vanilla Pig to put it on.

But when I take my first step outside, I'm overwhelmed with this strange feeling. A slight uneasiness in my gut and a chill across my skin, which make no sense. I chose a loose-fitting tank top because it's been so hot recently. I tap my fingers against my thigh uneasily, but ignore the feeling and head toward the restaurant, the cobblestone walkway crunchy underneath my platform sandals.

I toss open the doors and scan the dark eating area for the heads of my friends. I find them almost instantly and put on my best smile.

Quinny has a seat saved for me. "Girl, *finally*! Where have you been? We've been waiting ages!"

"Stuff came up with my parents!" I shout over the noise of chatter, plates, and a performer walking onto the stage, holding a guitar. "How do you think the finals went, Quin?" I glance at Quinny before flagging down a waitress and requesting some water.

Quinny scrunches her nose. "Well, chem could've gone better. I just had a lot on my mind." She throws a look over her shoulder with the barest hint of a pout.

"You're one of the top students," Alivia says cheerfully. "I'm sure you did better than you think! Besides, Mrs. Rhodes loves you."

Quinny sighs loudly. "I don't want to talk about it, Alivia."

"Except that you obviously do," I mutter under my breath, fighting the urge to roll my eyes. Out of all the little things Quinny does that frustrate me, her faux humility probably irks me the most.

Would I ever call her out on it to her face?

Of course not.

"What did you say, Maeve?" She looks at me sharply.

"I said we're happy to listen to you." I turn my attention to the chip basket, skimming it with my eyes to find a perfectly folded chip. "If you need people to listen, that is."

I feel her gaze on me, hot and appraising. Queso has never looked so appetizing.

"Maybe I *will* talk about it."

"Go for it," Jolie encourages her. "Like Maeve said, we're happy to listen."

I found it. The perfect chip. Folded to perfection.

"I just have witnessed a sort of...injustice," Quinny says carefully. "It almost feels like a breach of trust from someone I really, really looked up to."

This queso is just ridiculously heavenly.

"Oh no! Who was it?" Alivia gasps.

"Coach," Quinny says sadly. I glance up just in time to see her shake her head, blonde curls trembling. She brushes one away from her face and narrows her eyes at me. "You wouldn't happen to know why, would you, Maeve?"

Oh my gosh. I stiffen. Is this about the captain's position? Seriously?

Everyone has stopped their own conversations and seem to be peering down to our end of the table. I sink lower into my seat.

But there's no point in lying.

"Coach offered me the captain spot," I mumble.

"But Quinny, it doesn't really matter."

"No, it definitely does matter," she argues. "Because you're not the only one who deserves that spot. Is she even having you try out?"

"It doesn't matter, Quin."

"Oh my gosh, it definitely does."

"Guys, guys!" Alivia spreads her hands out. "Quinny, I think you should just be happy for Maeve! Aren't you guys best friends? Let her have this."

I squeeze my eyes shut. She's just making everything worse.

"Why should I be happy for her? She just acts like she's entitled to everything!"

My eyes pop open. "Me?"

The word shoots out of my mouth before I can pull it back in. I see Hazel and Jolie look at me with shocked expressions. How many times have the three of us discussed Quinny's awful behavior? And how many times have we gone along with it, just to exist in her solar system of popularity?

She tilts her head at me. "If you have something to say, please say it."

I grip the edge of my chair. I should've just stayed home packing boxes with Mom and Dad.

The thought makes me laugh.

Packing boxes. Little does Quinny know I won't even be here to stake my claim on that coveted captain's position. Try as I might to be able to move back here, something inside of me knows that there's not really a chance. It's just something Mom and Dad are saying to make me feel better.

"I won't even be here in the fall!" I throw my hands up in the air. "Is that what you want to hear? That I'm leaving so you can have your stupid captain spot? It doesn't matter that I'll be here for volleyball camp because this is it for me! These are my last few days, and you are absolutely flaming me. So fun, right?"

The table is completely quiet. Even Quinny is at a loss for words.

I don't think I've ever seen that before.

I feel tears threatening to break through, so I give everyone a tight smile, as if that will make anything better.

"You're...moving?" Hazel is the first to speak. She shakes her head at me. "What?"

"Where?" asks Jolie. "Why?"

Alivia rests a hand on my shoulder.

"I'm moving to Texas. To a summer camp." I drag a hand down my face. Those words sound so stupid out loud.

"A camp?" I hear Dom's voice from down the table. "Why the heck would you move to a camp? What are you going to be doing the rest of the year?"

"Guys, I don't know. It's just a dumb thing my parents wanted to do."

Alivia squeezes my shoulder. "That's hard, Maeve. I'm so sorry. We're going to miss you so much."

I glance up at Quinny, waiting to see what she's going to do. But I realize that I have made a colossal mistake.

I realize it the moment that her nostrils flare and she fixes me with a smile—the kind that oozes with sour honey.

Fake.

It's the word she mouths to me. Then she says it for everyone to hear.

"She's a fake."

A conversation about Quinny turned into a conversation about me. How many times have I watched her shred someone to pieces because they took away her spotlight? The pit in my stomach is growing larger and larger and larger and —

"Her parents aren't really interior designers," Quinny announces, keeping her gaze locked on me. "I mean, put the pieces together, people! Maeve always does her makeup when she's not home—"

"Quinny," interrupts Alivia, shaking her head. "Plenty of girls do their makeup when they get to school. It's so they don't have to wake up as early."

"I wasn't finished."

I swear I hear a pin drop. Maybe into the vat of queso I'm begging the universe to let me drown in so that I never have to be in a position like this again.

"Not only that, but she never invites people over. She always reeks of essential oils, and she has panic attacks when people mention ghosts. None of us have ever seen her parents and they aren't on social media. But when you pass by their house, you can see dreamcatchers from every window, and they have a mushroom garden in the back."

"So, what?" asks Dom. "They're like druggies or something?"

"No." Quinny rolls her eyes. "Her parents think they're witches."

A murmur rises over the table and I'm shaking my head so hard that I think my skull might detach from my neck. How is this happening to me? I have spent so long seamlessly cultivating my perfect life—one that did not include my parents in any shape or form. This is exactly what I've been afraid of! Every time people discover who my parents really are, they turn on me. They always assume that I'm the same as my parents.

Weird. Superstitious. Creepy.

We're freaks, we Everbrills. We share blood.

"You've been lying to us," Jolie says quietly. She looks down at the table.

I dig my palms into my eyes. "Jolie, no! No, I didn't mean to lie, I just—"

"But you did lie, Maeve," Quinny snaps. "You lied to everyone. You take and you take. You've been using all of us!"

That accusation from her? Rich. "I have not!"

"Admit it. You used me so you could be popular. And then you stomp all over people."

I gasp incredulously. Shake my head. Laugh. This is not real. This must be some kind of fever dream. She's manipulating me. I know that.

But it's working.

"Quinny, I wasn't using you!" I look at her pleadingly. She knows me. She knows how much I care about her and our friendship.

"Quinny, leave her alone!" snaps Alivia. It's the first time I've ever heard her angry.

"Don't tell me what to do!" Quinny has fire in her eyes when she looks at Alivia. She stands up abruptly and her chair falls to the floor.

The whole restaurant seems to watch.

"Girls!" A robust lady in a green Vanilla Pig uniform saunters over with her hands on her hips. "If there is going to be a shouting match, I'm going to have to ask you to leave."

I'm in complete and utter shock. Quinny is mad at me. I don't know how it happened, but I do know that I have to fix it. I *have* to.

"Quinny, listen, I just didn't want you guys to think poorly of me because of them! They're crazy—trust me, I know that!"

"You are too!" She pops a hand on her hip. "You're a liar."

"Quinny, please!"

"Girls!" The lady, who I assume is the manager, folds her arms across her chest. "I'm not going to ask you again."

"I'm leaving, anyway." Quinny grabs her bag off the shoulder of the chair and throws it over her shoulder.

"Don't leave, Quinny, please let me explain—"

"Hazel, Jolie?" Quinny shoots them pointed looks. They give me apologetic frowns and follow her as she marches out of the Vanilla Pig.

My face is flaming. Everyone in the entire restaurant is staring at me. And now they know that the Everbrills are freaks.

"Maeve," whispers Alivia, "I am so—" I walk out.

til the road begins
June 1

"Who sings this song?"

I startle, dropping the picture frame I'd been holding onto the ground. The glass shatters all over the wood floor and I wince. The fractures cover the photo, depicting a younger me and a younger Quinny, arms thrown around each other, wearing boy band t-shirts and denim shorts.

Sighing, I look over at Mom, turning down my music. "It's just a singer I like. Do you need something?"

She tilts her head at me. "We've hardly seen you this week, Maeve. Where are you?"

She doesn't mean where I am *actually*. I've been here all week, hiding out in my room, only leaving the house to go on walks when the walls feel like they're closing in on me, too tight that I can't breathe. But I don't like to think about that. I don't like to think about tight spaces.

After the eruption at the Vanilla Pig, I have closed myself off from everyone.

I've been avoiding Mom and Dad. Part of me is bitter with them because this is another instance in which, because of their odd ways, I've been isolated and mocked. All of this happens because of them.

Packing up my room, reading, and listening to music have been the only things that can calm me down, along with walking and soaking in the warm summer sun. I try not to think too much about the fact that today is moving day.

The movers took most of our belongings a few days ago, to the place prepared for us in Texas. There's a house on the property of Camp Swallowtail, recently vacated by the previous owners. I remember them a little bit—some old couple that look like the kind of grandparents who love to make cookies. The space is supposedly quite nice, a homey sort of place with real mattresses, not the cheap kind they slap on all the bunk beds in the cabins.

I won't be staying in that building because I'm a counselor. But they did give me a key.

I grab the rest of my things—a duffel bag and one final box filled with things I'll need—and walk out of my room, looking at it one last time.

Our house was purchased almost as soon as my parents put it on the market. It's a beautiful space on a nice piece of land. I'm going to miss it so much.

"I don't want to talk," I tell Mom, when she reaches out for my arm. "I'm going to put my stuff in the car."

"I'll clean up the glass. I'm sorry for startling you, chickadee."

I leave her in my room, walking through the house. It looks naked; I can hardly stand looking at the walls, void of color, void of life, void of any sign of us Everbrills.

Dad is in the driveway with the car. His is the only one left. He and Mom drove hers and mine earlier this week and then flew back home. I wanted to drive my own vehicle, but Mom and Dad thought it would be nice for us to go as a family.

"I can take that for you." Dad reaches toward the bag and the box. I loosen my grip and watch the way he fits them into the back of the car, a perfect game of Tetris. When he sees me watching, he pulls me into a bear hug. He smells like black coffee. Crisp and no non- sense.

I tense.

The slam of a car door has me spinning around. Alivia is parked by our curb, slinging a canvas bag over her shoulder and marching up to me. I pull away from Dad and wrinkle my brow. *What is she doing here?*

"Who's this?" Dad asks me.

"What are you doing here?" I fold my arms across my chest, trying to look unbothered, but hoping she hasn't come to tell me Quinny was right about me.

"I like your glasses," is all she says.

My face reddens. I never wear glasses out. "Thanks," I mumble.

"I just wanted to come say goodbye."

Dad glances between us. "Maeve, I'll be inside." He shuffles his feet a little bit and I feel a pang of guilt. All of the moments when I've tried to hide them from my friends swirl around me and leave a bitter taste in my mouth.

"I'm Alivia." She sticks her hand out to shake his. He glances at me, uncertain, but I nod. At my sign of approval— she already knows about them—he grasps her hand and gives it a firm shake. I bite the inside of my cheek. This feels so weird.

"It's nice to meet one of Maeve's friends. I'm George Everbrill." He looks at me over his shoulder. "I'll leave you girls to talk. I'd invite you in, Alivia, but unfortunately all our stuff is packed up."

"That's okay!" she says cheerfully. "It was lovely to meet you."

"You as well." Dad pats me on the shoulder and heads inside.

I look up at Alivia. My glasses feel heavy on my face. "Why are you here?"

"I already told you. To say goodbye."

I scoff. "Don't you remember the argument at the Vanilla Pig? Why would you want to come say goodbye to me?"

She motions to the porch swing right by the front door.

"Can we sit?"

Begrudgingly, I nod and motion her over. The swing creaks underneath us and Alivia kicks her feet a little bit to start it rocking.

"Quinny treated you horribly," Alivia begins. She tucks a strand of blonde hair behind her ear, showing off multiple dangling earrings cascading down from various piercings. "And I really hated the idea of you leaving Ashdown feeling like everyone here hates you."

"Everyone here *does* hate me. And I can't blame Quinny—I lied to her for years."

"That's still no reason for her to treat *anyone* that way," insists Alivia. "Listen," she holds her hands out when I start to defend Quinny, "I know you guys are best friends or whatever. Frankly, I don't understand why, aside from the fact that I think being cool is really important to you. And that's okay. Different things matter to different people. And I'm not here to shame you for it or anything like that. I just wanted to say I'm sorry."

I snap my mouth shut. "You're sorry? For what?"

"I wish I made more of an effort to be your friend. I wish I stood up more to Quinny."

I laugh. "No, standing up more to Quinny would've been social suicide." But I find myself thinking about what my life would've looked like had I chosen to be friends with Alivia instead. I wouldn't have been so stressed that people would discover that I was the child of freaks. Maybe the bullying at Camp Swallowtail wouldn't have bothered me anymore.

"Are you going to come back later this month?" Alivia asks me. "For volleyball camp?"

I shrug and drag a hand through my curls. "Honestly? I'm not sure. Part of me wants to, I don't know, show off my volleyball skills and stick it to her in a way. But also, I want to show her that I do belong here. I feel like I have to prove myself to her. And her birthday is that week. As frustrated as I am with her, I feel like all our years of friendship haven't been totally wasted. I've had good times with her, despite what a lot of people might think, and I really do want to be there for her birthday."

Alivia nods thoughtfully. "For what it's worth, I think you should come back. Maybe we can pull some strings and keep you here another year?"

My lips quirk up in a smile. "What do you mean 'pull some strings'?"

She skids her feet against the ground, stopping the swing. "All I'm saying is, I don't feel like this is the end of our friendship—"

"We didn't really have one to begin with," I point out.

"Details, details. Maybe if you come back and your parents see how much you loved it, we can convince them to let you stay. With my family. My parents would be happy to have you."

My eyebrows shoot up. "Really? But...why would you do that for me?"

Her blue eyes soften. "Honestly? I think you're so much fun. It made me really sad to watch Quinny walk all over you and see you flounder. I really want to be friends, Maeve. And all of this?" She throws her arms out wide. "Your family shouldn't hold you back from finding good friends. So, come back. And we'll have a wild celebration for Quinny's birthday. It's going to be an absolute blast."

"Maeve!" Mom pokes her head out the open front door. "We're leaving within the hour!"

"Okay!" I shout back. I face Alivia. "I like this plan. I want to stay. You don't know how much I hate that stupid camp."

"Amazing. Then I wish you the best of luck these next few weeks and I'll see you soon. Sound good?"

"Sounds good."

Alivia hops off the swing with a wave and jogs down to her car. I stay on the swing, watching her leave, and am filled with hope at the notion that I've just made a truly good friend. Her plan seems crazy although I'd thought of it myself. Maybe she's right. If I show my parents how much I love it here, despite the issues with Quinny, they have to let me stay. They're why so many things are going wrong in the first place. And now I have a potential place to live! Of course I want them here for my senior year, even though I would've kept them at a distance, but I really think this could work.

Excitement bubbles up within me and I help my parents pack the rest of our things.

When we finally get to Camp Swallowtail, Dad stops the car and leans back in his seat, beaming. "Isn't this place beautiful, Maeve?"

Begrudgingly, I look out the window, keeping my earbuds carefully concealed behind my hair.

The field splayed out in front of me is large and sparse, except for the tall, dead grass that is in desperate need of mowing. Cabins line the sides of the gravel road, with more further down, past a huge building with a tin roof. Dad pops open the trunk, letting hot Texas air flood the vehicle. It smells like nature with a faint whiff of fire pit. Nothing about this place seems "beautiful" like Dad claims it is. All I really notice is the noise.

Young girls and boys mill about—signs of opening day. The entire place seems to be buzzing with life—the ecstatic squeals of friends who apparently haven't seen each other in a year.

Mom and Dad set up Zoom calls with the staff last week. Every time I saw them pull their shared laptop out with mugs of tea resting beside them, I hid. They told me repeatedly that everyone is so excited to meet us. They also assured me that a lot of the staff members are around my age.

"You're just going to love your co-counselor," Mom gushed after one of their calls. "She's just the sweetest girl! Her name is Isla, and she is currently in college. She's been attending this camp for most of her life!"

I cringe now, thinking, hoping Mom won't notice. I've been wondering about Isla ever since Mom mentioned her. If she's been here all her life, maybe she'll remember me. Anxiety stirs in my gut. What if she remembers? What if she knows about what happened?

Mom informed me on our drive that the cell service would be insubstantial. On top of that, staff members are encouraged to unplug and join the campers in a disconnected summer that, in my parents' words, spurs us on toward creativity and discovering ourselves without distractions. I wouldn't consider myself a screen addict by any means, but knowing my friends will be living their lives without me doesn't make me feel fantastic. At the very least, I'd like to know how they're doing, even if they hate me now.

I yank out my earbuds and coil them nicely, leaving them in the car. I grab my backpack and water bottle, swinging the car door open.

"Whoa!" A girl with blonde hair woven in two Dutch braids jumps back before the door slams into her.

"Maeve!" Mom chastises. "You need to watch out before you swing open doors like that. You could seriously hurt somebody!"

"Oh!" Dad closes the trunk. "You must be Isla!"

I quickly glance at the girl, trying to fit the image of her with what my parents have told me. Her skin is covered in freckles, like she spends a lot of time outside. She's wearing a teal shirt with the slogan 'Camp Swallowtail: camp is what you make it!' She's holding three more shirts identical to hers.

I raise an eyebrow. *I'm not wearing that.*

"Yes, hi!" Isla says enthusiastically. She seems like the kind of girl who radiates joy everywhere she goes. "Y'all must be the Everbrills! We've been so excited to meet you!"

"George and Winnie," Dad shakes her hand firmly, smiling.

Mom gazes around at the camp in wonder. I follow her gaze and focus on the structure of the cabins. They are made from wood with decent-sized porches. Each one has a sign in front of the building, with writing I can't read that probably says the name of the cabin. Colorfully painted poles with ropes and balls attached are perched in between cabins, a game I think is called tether ball. Past these, I see a sand volleyball pit and perk up a little. Being able to practice on sand is better than not being able to practice at all.

Isla interrupts my thoughts. "You must be Maeve?"

I meet her gaze. Her eyes are green, like mine. My fingers fidget with my backpack strap. "Yep. That's me."

She's smiling again. "Amazing! We have a cabin of freshman girls! There are six of them, I believe..." She looks down at the clipboard she's holding in her other hand, eyes skimming over the paper. "Yes! Six: Madysen, Charlotte, Kiara, Addie, Emily, and Lena. We're in Misty Monarch." She gestures over toward the opposite side of the camp, past the huge building.

"Misty Monarch?"

"It's a cabin name," she explains. "All of the girls' cabins are named after butterflies—Painted Lady, Golden Glasswing, Caterpillar Corner for the Bitties. The guy cabins are named after moths—Hawkmoth Haven, Diamondback Den. It all fits the theme of the camp."

"What are Bitties?"

"Oh, that's what we call the little campers—kids that are between first and third grade. After that, you're not considered a Bitty anymore."

With a grimace, I nod. Camp lingo was not something I thought I would need to figure out. *Add it to the list of reasons why I won't fit in here.*

"Winnie, George, is it alright if I take Maeve back to the cabin?" Isla hands them two of the three t-shirts. "I want to help her set things up before our girls get here."

Mom nods enthusiastically. "Maeve would love that!"

I roll my eyes when no one is looking but grab my bags and follow Isla.

"Maeve, remember that the movers are bringing the rest of our things later this week!" Dad calls after me. "So, if there's anything you need, we'll make sure to get it as soon as they're here!"

I force a smile and follow Isla toward Misty Monarch. We pass by staff members in identical shirts to hers. They wave cheerfully at Isla and it almost feels like I don't exist. They look so different from the people at my school. Quinny always wanted us to look a certain way. There was pressure to look perfect when I was around her, which could be really difficult when my parents complained about the fabrics that made up my clothes or the chemicals in my makeup. I had to sneak those things behind their backs. But here, everyone is in the same camp t-shirt with athletic shorts, an outfit Quinny would make fun of me for if I wore it outside of volleyball practice. The girls here have their hair thrown back in casual styles—loose ponytails, fraying braids. They look so carefree that it makes me feel self conscious. I tug at my vintage band t-shirt and black cut-offs.

Finally, we reach the cabin. Like the others, it's made of wood and has perfectly square windows and a front porch. The sign on the door says 'Misty Monarch.'

Inside, there are bunk beds stacked across the room, with only a small space for walking. Isla's stuff is already coating the bed by the door. She's taken the bottom bunk and placed a small, plastic bin with drawers beside it. She has an alarm clock perched on top, declaring the time in red. Her bedspread is yellow with little flowers.

"Since we're counselors, we're supposed to share a bunk bed," she says apologetically. "I hope you're okay with the top?"

"I don't care."

She helps me set down my bags but sits back as I pull out my bedding and spread it out across the mattress.

The campgrounds are hardly familiar to me since I was significantly younger the last time I was here, but there's something about the cabins that oozes nostalgia. Especially when I shake out my blanket and glance up.

In front of me is a closet door.

The blanket falls out of my hands and onto the ground.

Isla tilts her head. "Are you okay?" She follows my eyes to the closet. "Oh, that's just for cleaning supplies or if a camper brought a lot of extra stuff that won't fit by their bed. We don't really use those closets much. No ghosts haunting it, I promise."

I glance at her sharply. "Why would you say that?"

Her eyes widen. "It was just a joke. People make jokes about summer camps being haunted. I'm sorry, I didn't know it would bother you."

I pick up my blanket and tuck it around the corners of the flimsy mattress. I want Isla's talking to drown out the swirling memories in the back of my mind. The guilt from snapping at her wedges its way into my chest.

I'm not happy to be here, but I'm also not a mean person.

"What are you studying in college?" I ask her, hoping to make the silence between us less awkward. I need her to drown out the painful memories threatening to sink their teeth into my head.

"Camp management." Uncertainty lingers in her eyes as she fidgets with her braids.

"That's an interesting thing to major in."

Isla crosses her legs and shrugs, like this is something she's used to hearing. "Camp is important to me. It's been a huge part of my entire life." She pauses, then opens her mouth again like she wants to say more but doesn't. I get the feeling that there's some more to the story but decide not to push. I don't know Isla well enough. If there's something she wants to tell me, she will.

Isla holds her wrist up and observes the time printed on her watch. "Girls should be here soon!" She jumps up and tidies her bed while I finish making mine, fluffing the pillow before setting it against the small headboard.

The nervousness I feel surprises me. Back at home, my group never invested much in younger girls. I've never had to wonder if I'm a good role model or not, but something about Isla's joy makes my stomach clench with envy. I have no doubt that our campers will adore her. Why do I feel like I'll need to work to earn their favor?

"Oh, here." Isla tosses me the last teal t-shirt. "Throw this on and meet me on the front porch. The girls and their parents will meet us there and we'll help pull in their trunks. I have the list of names, and we'll let them pick their beds."

"Aren't there any instructions I should know for being a CIT or whatever?" I climb down the bunk bed ladder, shirt in hand. "I didn't really get any instructions."

Isla furrows her brow and unzips an olive green backpack that rests against her plastic dresser. She pulls out a floppy binder full of paper and hands it to me.

"Memorize this quickly. It's got all the rules."

"Memorize it?" I repeat, aghast, flipping through it. She gives me a half-smile, her hand resting on the cabin door

"Most of it is basic stuff. Nothing should be too surprising."

Blowing air through my lips, I flip through while trying to wriggle the t-shirt over my head. Isla smooths her clothes and plops down on the front porch steps, eagerly awaiting our campers. Through the window, I see her tapping her fingers excitedly on the porch. I turn away, my stomach clenching.

My eyes dart to the closet, feeling almost unsafe now that I'm in the cabin alone. Before my imagination gets the better of me, I toss my other shirt onto my bed and follow Isla to the front porch, holding the counselor rulebook tightly in my hand.

The sound of voices and walking makes Isla turn her head eagerly.

I swallow the lump in my throat, ready to meet the girls I'll be leading for the summer.

Before long, our cabin is swarmed with parents and young girls, bustling with chatter and laughter as the girls hug their old friends and catch up on their year away from camp. I hold the clipboard with the girls' names tightly, glancing down and trying to match faces with names.

Madysen is the girl with highlighted blonde hair, who holds herself in a way that exudes confidence. The girls around her, Charlie and Lena, don't seem quite as confident. Charlie has prominent ears and Lena has wispy bangs that curl in front of her face.

Emily clutches a book to her chest and has dark eyes rimmed with even darker liner.

Kiara screams carefree. She has tumbling, wild curls and multiple piercings lining her ears. Her parents bring in her bags, introduce themselves to Isla and me, then leave after saying they love Kiara. They don't hover. Kiara seems to like it that way. She seems like a sweet girl, but not desperate for the approval of others. I like her spunk and wish I was more like she was when I was a freshman. I think Alivia would love her.

The last girl is Addie. Her parents linger the longest, casting uncertain glances towards the other girls. Addie is quiet—she doesn't talk to the other girls at all. Her red hair hangs like a curtain in front of her face, shielding herself away from the others. I tilt my head, con templating her. It's not like she doesn't want to be here, exactly—her eyes are wide with curiosity. She just seems nervous, based on the way she fidgets.

There's something interesting about her.

brother bane
June 1

Much of the first night goes by like a blur. Everyone plays all camp games underneath a domed pavilion, and I mostly try to stay out of everyone's way. I avoid contact with my parents and do what Isla tells me to. I don't talk much to the girls because I don't want to be here, but I'm also weirdly worried about what they'll think of me.

There's so many people here, which normally doesn't bother me, but everyone here is a stranger to me. I feel like I'm floating aimlessly in a sea full of fish who all know the right way to swim. If I ever thought that being in the center of everything back at school was overwhelming, I have no words for how I feel right now. It's lonely but chaotic.

Before bed, I changed into a t-shirt and athletic shorts, hoping to fit in.

I'm lying on my top bunk, staring at the dark ceiling of Misty Monarch, when Isla hisses my name.

"Maeve!"

My heart skips a beat, and I roll over on my side to peer down at her. The bunk creaks and I feel the wooden board holding the bed together through the flimsy mattress.

Isla is leaning out of her bunk, hair pulled back into a ponytail. "Hey, are you coming?"

I scrunch my eyebrows. "Coming to what?"

"Counselor Late Night! We have it once a week and meet up in Lightwing Lounge."

"I really don't understand anything you just said."

She glances over to the bunks full of sleeping Misty Monarch girls. "Counselors get a break once a week to go hang out, eat snacks, occasionally check phones in Lightwing Lounge, which is close to the heart of camp, by the dining area. Tonight is the first Late Night and everyone will be there. I'm about to go and I wanted to check if you were coming."

One of the girls snores loudly.

"We're just allowed to leave them?" I ask dubiously.

That doesn't seem right? What if something happens and they need one of us? I wonder if my counselor was at Late Night when the girls began to harass me, back when I was a camper here.

"They'll be fine, I promise," Isla dutifully replies. "Late Night only lasts about an hour, maybe a little more, and other staff members know to keep an eye out for things on Late Nights."

This could be your chance to show everyone that you're cool and get a head start before they cast opinions on you based on your parents.

This could be your chance to make friends.

But do I want to make friends? If I make friends, won't that show my parents that they were right in bringing me here? Unless I can find friends that can help get me out of here.

I slide off from the top bunk, grabbing my glasses, and slip on a pair of socks and my Converse, before following Isla out the door. It creaks when we close it.

The pathway is dusty, covered in rocks and dirt, with tall, yellow lamps flickering as they line our path. Bugs flit around the lights in a crazed sort of way, dancing around us as we pass by and then soaring up into the endless night. I follow them with my eyes, as much as I can see, and am amazed when I find myself watched by a sea of stars, like nothing I've ever seen before. The moon is full and bright with what must be thousands of little diamonds, glittering in the sky.

For the first time in a while, I feel myself soften.

Isla makes idle conversation as we walk but stops to stare at the sky when she notices my awestruck expression.

"There's nothing like this anywhere, huh?" She smiles, sticking her hands in the pockets of her shorts.

"It's beautiful," I admit.

Lightwing Lounge is bustling with noise and excitement. Light pours through the windows and shoes are left in piles by the woven doormat. It's a small stone building with a name plate carved into a slab of wood. Attached to the building are two little rooms, which Isla tells me are bathrooms.

As Isla reaches for the door, I'm suddenly overwhelmed by the idea that everyone here will be conversing and having a good time, while I might be the freak standing in the corner by myself. Being seen as socially awkward is definitely not something I need if I'm trying to prove to others that I'm not like my parents.

I grab Isla's arm before I know what I'm doing. She looks at me, bemused.

"I just..." I don't have the words. All these people are older than me by at least a year—I'm basically a junior counselor just because my parents needed something to do with me. I cannot be seen as the weird kid who somehow jumped up the hierarchy. "Don't leave me in there, okay? Can you introduce me to people at least?"

Isla tilts her head, eyes softening. "Maeve, I wouldn't ditch you in there. And you don't have to be nervous—I get that it's intimidating with all these people you've never met, but a lot of them are really nice. I think you're going to love them and this place if you let yourself. C'mon." She smiles and pulls me into Lightwing Lounge.

I scan the room, trying to assess what I've gotten myself into. There are benches with cubbies built into the wall and a huge whiteboard covering the wall opposite. A rocking chair and a couple of loveseats are covered with strange green cushions. A fridge sits in one corner, with a big black trash can already overflowing with food trash. There looks to be about sixteen people—eight girls and eight guys. They mingle and fill the room with laughter and gasps, music playing softly from a speaker perched on the wooden coffee table in the center of the room.

Isla pulls me over to one of the little circles of people. A girl with short brown hair and glasses glances up first and smiles when she sees the two of us. She's wearing an oversized t-shirt with a band that I like on the front. I perk up when I see it.

She throws her arms around Isla. "Haven't seen *you* in ages! Or at least that's what it feels like!"

Isla laughs. "It's been a while. I wanted to introduce you guys to my co-counselor this year!" She pulls back from the hug and pats my shoulder. "This is Maeve Everbrill. Maeve, these are a few of my friends."

She introduces the girl with glasses as Josie, who is co-counselors with Mia, a girl with beautifully long hair. They have 4th, 5th, and 6th grade girls—just old enough to not be considered Bitties. These girls stay in Starry Skipper.

One of the girls from the oldest female cabin, Ginny, is also standing in our group. She's chewing gum and has a nose ring. Her co isn't really close to her and hangs out with a different group of counselors, but her name is Julia. Their cabin is called Golden Glasswing.

Next are a couple of guys. The Bitty boy counselors are from Hawkmoth Haven, two really nice guys named Hendrix and Alex. They already seem to have many stories about the hyperactivity of the children they'll be managing all summer.

Finally, I meet Quinton and Walker from Diamondback Den, which houses the middle school boys. I cannot imagine what they must be going through.

Everyone seems friendly enough. I find the tension leaving my shoulder. I've never had trouble making friends. It's keeping them that gets tricky. Once they find out too much about you—like that your parents are superstitious goons—they always, always leave.

I sit down with the people in our group, and they bust open a bag of chips and some cookies. Alex is handing sweet tart ropes out to each of us while Hendrix digs around in the fridge for some sodas.

"You moved from Arkansas?" Ginny confirms. She reaches out to tug one of my curls. "I bet the weather there was incredible for your hair. You have amazing curls."

I find myself smiling, knowing how difficult the curly journey is.

"Did you live in a small town?" asks Mia. "I've always wanted to live in a small town, but unfortunately working here in the summers is likely the best I'll ever get."

I nod. "It was pretty small! There were cute parts of it, like a restaurant where people can go for open mic nights, but everyone knows everyone. Or at least knows of them."

"Do you sing?" Isla tears off the end of her sweet tart rope with her fingers and pops it into her mouth.

Laughter bubbles up from my mouth. "No way, but I do love listening to music."

"Mia sings." Ginny elbows her.

"Guys," Mia complains, looking down at her feet.

"She only pretends to be embarrassed." Quinton smiles, dimples poking little indentions into his cheeks. "But she knows how good of a singer she is."

"What do you like to do for fun?" Mia ignores him.

"I read a lot. I play volleyball."

Alex jumps up when I say "volleyball". The chip bag flies into the air, throwing chips everywhere. "Dude!" he exclaims. "You have to join our sand volleyball specialty and help me teach it! I hardly know a thing about volleyball, but somehow, I got stuck teaching it!"

"Dude," Josie mocks him. She gestures to the chips all over the floor. "You made a mess *and* wasted snacks."

Everyone laughs, and I'm surprised to find myself joining in, falling into the rhythm of these new people.

"You guys look like you're having fun."

I turn around and meet the gaze of a tall guy with dark hair, clutching an energy drink in his hand. He looks at me and doesn't smile. Isla tenses up beside me. The laughter within our group dies down quickly.

"Who are you?" I ask the boy, feeling confident.

"Archer." He doesn't ask for my name, but I give it to him anyway.

"I'm Maeve Everbrill." I stick my hand out.

He looks at it and frowns. "So, you're *their* kid."

I match his frown. "Who's kid?"

"The new camp directors' kid."

I bite my lip but nod. *So what?*

"We're just not excited to have them here. That's all."

I glance at Isla, and she looks away and takes a breath. "Why? What does them being here have to do with anything that concerns you?"

"They're our employers," he says like I'm stupid. "They're changing the way camp is supposed to be. We don't really like that, do we, guys?"

A few people nod. I wince when I see people from my group look away in silent agreement. My stomach clenches.

I never really thought about what the people at camp would think of my parents moving here. Of course they wouldn't like the change, especially when they'd been used to things for so long. I can't blame them, but that doesn't mean I don't feel bad about it.

"Well." Archer glances at the people behind him, other counselors I haven't yet met. "We were about to tell a scary story, per camp tradition. So, if you guys could settle down, that would be great."

One of the girls in his group shuts off the light, enveloping the whole room in darkness. Then, there's a click and a flicker. Archer appears, holding a lighter up to his face, casting eerie shadows across his skin.

I clench my fists. *Scary story?* I lean over to Isla. "Hey, I think I'll probably head back to the cabin. I'm kind of tired."

She puts a hand on my arm. "Aw, I wish you would stay! Archer is kind of a jerk, but this part is so much fun."

"This story is about Brother Bane, a ghost that haunts the grounds of Camp Swallowtail, searching for his lost sister." Archer pauses and my brain takes me back to the party I attended with Quinny, only a few weeks ago. How do I end up in these uncomfortable positions?

"His sister was lost in 1996, many moons ago. Her body was never found. So, when her brother died a madman's death, his spirit stayed here, wandering the grounds, crying out for his sister who would never be found."

If I stand up now and leave, everyone will look at me like I'm weird. But does it even matter if they all hate my parents?

Or should I go ahead and stay, suffering the panic attack that's sure to follow, and let them talk badly about me anyway?

No, better I keep my dignity in the little way that I can and put a stop to this now.

I stand up and all heads swivel toward me. Archer's expression says he dares me to walk away. Maybe he already knows what my parents say about ghosts.

"Carry on with your cute little story," I tell him. "I'm leaving."

"You're not afraid of ghosts, are you?" His voice is cold. "I'd go ahead and get pretty comfortable with them since you're staying here, if I was you."

"Well, you aren't me," I snap. "And I think ghost stories are stupid."

"Wait, Maeve, I'll come with you!" Isla grabs her stuff and begins to follow me out the door, but I stop her. I really appreciate her willingness, since everyone else is looking at me like I'm a balloon about to pop, but I would feel bad about taking her away from things that mean a lot to her just because I'm sensitive.

"No, you should stay," I insist.

"Yeah, Isla, it's not your fault Maeve believed the scary bedtime stories her parents used to tell her," Archer chimes in.

Isla shoots him a scathing look. "Shut up."

I ignore him. My skin is prickling with the way the light still flickers off Archer's face and I *have* to get out of here. "Isla, please stay. Please."

She hesitates. "Okay."

I stumble out of there before anyone else can say anything. And although there was no point in staying, I feel the words they're all thinking about me.

The second I feel the night air on my skin, I lean back against the wall of Lightwing Lounge and take a deep breath to calm my racing heart. I brace my palms against the cold brick and sink down until I'm crouched in the dirt, resting my head against the brick and closing my eyes as I inhale deeply.

Just breathe, Maeve.

"Is everything okay?"

My eyes rip open and I'm staring into the face of a good looking guy about my age. He has shaggy brown hair with big, striking hazel eyes. He's wearing beat up Vans sneakers and a hat on his head.

"I'm...fine," I mumble. I wipe my hands on my legs and stand up, straightening my clothes. "Yeah, I'm fine. Sorry, I just..." My voice trails off as I hook my thumb back to the doorway and then shake my head. I'm not going to explain myself to this stranger. "Yeah, I was just on my way back to my cabin."

He studies me. Shoves his hands into his pockets. "Okay, just thought I would check."

I clear my throat. "Are you...headed in there?"

He snorts a little. "Me? Definitely not. I'm not sure I would be well received."

That puts me at ease. "Oh? Me neither, it seems."

"You look like you'd fit in just fine." He gestures to my shorts, t-shirt, and bare feet.

"I've always been good at dressing the part."

We meet each other's gaze.

"What's your name? Are you a counselor?" I ask.

He takes off his hat and drags a hand through his hair. "No, I'm more of...general staff. Kind of like a floater—I just go wherever I'm needed. My name is Hayes."

"I'm Maeve."

"I know who you are."

"Let me guess," I sigh. "You hate my parents too?" I lean back against the wall and cross my arms over my chest.

He studies me. "I try not to hate anybody. It's taken me a long time to let go of a lot of the bitterness I've helped against people."

"A long time, huh? What are you, eighteen?" "

Eighteen," he agrees. "I just feel like I've been here forever."

"Then I get how my parents changing things could be hard. But if you could convince those guys in there to maybe cut me some slack? I had nothing to do with any of this and honestly, I want to leave just as badly as they want my family gone."

Hayes puts his hat back on his head. "I don't really interact with them if I can help it. But if they seek me out first, I'll put in a good word for you."

I smile a little. "Thank you. I would really appreciate that."

He smiles back, hesitantly. "See you around, Maeve."

I watch him go.

misty monarch
June 2

There are towels everywhere.

It grosses me out a little bit to see all the girls in our cabin leaving their towels all over the bathhouse floor or draped over stall doors, but I get that cleanliness isn't always the biggest concern at camp.

The bathroom is filled with noise as the girls in Misty Monarch chatter away about their lives back at home, anticipations for the summer, and which cute guys returned.

Isla ran back to the cabin to grab sunscreen, so I'm in the bathroom with all the girls in our cabin. They all are busy changing into their swimsuits in the stalls, while I study my reflection in the mirror. I mess with the straps of my dark green suit until the top fits snugly. Then I toss my brown t-shirt over my head and smooth it down.

"Wow, I still can't believe we're here!" Kiara practically sings.

A few of the other girls giggle excitedly.

Lena chimes in, "Me neither!"

"Maeve?" calls Emily.

"Yes?" I grab a brown paper towel from the dispenser and set to work cleaning off my mascara so that it doesn't run in the pool.

"How many summers is this for you?"

"Technically my first." I wipe away the black smudges under my eye, noticing my jaw clench at the question.

"Why technically?" Madysen wonders aloud. She tosses open her stall door to reveal a dark purple, one-shoulder swimsuit.

I crumple up the paper towel and toss it into the trash. "Well, I came once when I was seven. But I had a bad experience, so I left early."

Plain and simple.

Madysen props a hand on her hip. "What kind of bad experience?"

"Let's call it homesickness." I shoot her a pointed glance that says we're done talking about it.

She raises an eyebrow and shakes her head. "I've never been homesick. Has anyone here been homesick before?"

"Only when I was really little," Charlie says. She grabs her towel and emerges from her stall, golden brown hair tied back into a loose braid. She self consciously pats the sides of her hair and checks to make sure her ears aren't sticking out. I haven't known her for very long, but I can already tell she's very self conscious about her prominent ears. I want to tell her that they're cute.

Kiara and Addie are the next to come out. Kiara bounds over to the mirror and shakes out her wild hair, smiling at her reflection in the mirror. Addie, however, is much more shy. She wraps her towel around herself and stays quiet.

"Don't you want a makeup wipe?" Madysen asks Emily, who is the next to leave the stall. Her eyes are still rimmed with dark eyeliner.

Emily looks at Madysen, deadpan. "Why would I?"

"Is your makeup waterproof?"

"No."

I crack a smile at Emily. I like her—she's funny, but in a blunt sort of way.

Lena is the last to come out, fidgeting with a clasp in the back of her swimsuit that doesn't seem to be cooperating. She turns around in the mirror and tries to hold back her hair with one hand, while securing the clasp with the other, but to no avail.

"Here," I hand my towel and backpack to Addie. "Would you mind holding this?"

Addie nods silently.

"Can I help you with that?" I ask Lena.

She looks relieved. "Yes, please. Thank you. I don't know why I'm struggling with it so much."

"Maybe your swimsuit doesn't fit anymore," Madysen suggests, glancing at her nails casually. "Maybe you gained weight last year"

I narrow my eyes at her. "Don't say dumb stuff like that. Her suit fits her fine."

I hear an annoyed huff from her direction when I turn back to secure Lena's clasp.

As the girls walk together out of the bathroom and down toward the pool, I find myself thinking about what just went down, wondering why I felt the need to stand up to Madysen like that. I barely know her.

Madysen reminds me of Quinny, I think with surprise.

People like Alivia wouldn't stand to see a fledgling Quinny picking on younger girls if she could help it.

Isla meets us at the pool gate and punches in the code. "I assume you all know how to swim? No life jackets?"

"We aren't *Bitties*," Madysen says scathingly.

"I'm required to ask." Isla holds up her hands.

The area around the pool is swarming with campers and counselors and lifeguards. The Bitties are starting off doing their swim test and a few begin to cry that they can't swim, which is heartbreaking to watch. I hear one of the lifeguards blow their whistle and I scan all the people in bright red suits to see if Hayes is one of them. He said he goes wherever he's needed. Lifeguarding seems like a pretty essential job.

But I don't see him.

"Who are you looking for?" Kiara asks me.

I shake my head. "Just taking in all the chaos."

I'm mostly just watching everything happening and talking to Isla by the time it's Misty Monarch's turn to dive into the water. Isla perches on the edge and impatiently waves me over.

"We have to do it too?" I reach up to pat my curls in alarm.

"You can borrow that kid's swim cap if you want. I'm sure it would look fabulous on you," snipes Madysen, gesturing to a little boy with a bright blue swim cap and goggles.

I scoff.

Addie claps her hand over her mouth to stifle a giggle, much to my surprise. My mouth curls up into a little smile.

Isla slingshots a hair tie over to me. "Hustle."

Dejected, I toss my hair up into an ugly, tight bun and then slip into the water beside the rest of my cabin. They all cheer—except for Madysen—when I get in, which makes me smile again. Isla lightly punches me in the shoulder with an amused expression on her face.

"Okay, are you guys ready?" shouts the lifeguard.

I glance up to check for Hayes one more time but find something far more horrifying instead.

Directly across from me at the other end of the pool, standing on the cobblestone, is a little girl. But she isn't just like any other little girl and she's certainly not one of the dripping wet Bitties, huddled in a princess towel. This girl is barefoot and wears a flowing cream nightgown, with little bows and embroidery along the collar. She has two dark braids, each looped with a small pink bow to tie off the ends. She tilts her head at me in an unnatural way and her image wavers a little bit when the splashing around me begins.

The sky darkens and the wind blows harshly, whipping little tendrils of hair across my face. But the girl's nightgown and hair don't stir at all. The air seems to grow cold, so cold that I start to shiver and grip the ledge of the pool.

When she sees my reaction, she smiles a dark smile and her mouth begins to open wide, like a snake, gaping and horrible.

My eyes stretch as wide as they can possibly go and I bite down on my fist to keep from screaming out, but *no one else seems to see her*.

From that horrible mouth, she speaks. But it's not a voice I can hear with my ears—more something that I feel etched into my bones, my very core, like a memory or something deeper.

"Welcome to Camp Swallowtail, Maeve Everbrill. We're so glad you're here."

And then she's gone.

I blink and reach out to Isla, but she's already halfway across the pool.

The lifeguard pokes me in the back with his foot. "Hey, you really need to get going. You're supposed to stick with your girls."

Everyone else around the pool is just chattering away like nothing happened.

Maybe nothing happened?

Unsettled, I dog paddle across the pool for two reasons.

First, because I don't want to get my hair wet. But second, I'm afraid if I stick my head under water, that ghost girl is going to shove it under, and I won't come back up.

I don't believe in ghosts, I remind myself. I just didn't get enough sleep last night or I'm dehydrated. That's all it is. I'm sure of it.

Misty Monarch all passes so we get green wristbands shackled around our wrists. I fidget with mine, not used to wearing things on my wrists. Coach never allowed it in practice or games.

I can't stop glancing over to the edge of the pool, wondering what it was that I just saw. Wondering where that little girl went.

Am I going crazy?

I do my best to push it away and interact with the rest of my cabin, hoping that it will keep me distracted and ease the chills running across my spine.

We follow Isla out to the dining area and claim our table. The girls continue their conversations, and I listen in, trying to chime in whenever I feel like I have something fitting to say. Isla seems to always have the right words, and I envy her a little because of it. Eventually, I give up and scoot down to talk to Addie, who sits alone at the end of the table.

"Hey, is everything okay?"

She blinks at me. "Everything's okay. Your bun is falling out."

"Oh!" I reach up and sure enough, my hair is slipping out of the knot I created. I shake it loose and slide the hair tie down the table to Isla. "Thanks. That would've been an embarrassing hairstyle to walk around camp with."

Addie smiles a little.

"Let's go around the circle and say our names," Isla suggests. "I can go first. My name is Isla, and this is my eleventh summer at Camp Swallowtail. A fun fact about me...I really enjoy crime podcasts!" She looks around, pleased.

"My name is Kiara, and this is my third summer," Kiara offers, twisting a wet curl around her finger. "Um, I have a pet turtle back at home named Rosemary."

"Aw," Isla chimes in.

Madysen goes next. "My name is Madysen, and this is my sixth summer. I'm on the cheer team at school."

Charlie pipes up next. "I'll go. My name is Charlie, and this is my second summer. Um. I have a twin sister named Sienna."

"My name is Emily, and this is my fifth summer," Emily says. "I'm a big bookworm."

"What are you reading now?" I ask.

She holds up a beat-up copy of *Twilight,* grabbed from her backpack. "I'm really into vampires right now."

I say, "Amen!"

"My name is Lena. This is my fourth summer. I think." Lena counts on her fingers, then looks satisfied. "Okay, yes. Anyway, I sell clothes online with my mom."

Isla looks pointedly at the last member of our group.

"My name...is Addic." Addie's voice is soft, gentle. "This is my first year."

"I can't really hear you," says Madysen.

"This is my first year," she repeats. "And I'm a writer."

"That's really interesting, Addie," Isla encourages. "Thank you for sharing."

I realize that it's my turn. "I'm Maeve. This is my first year —"

"Are your parents the new directors?" Madysen interrupts.

Slowly, I nod. "Yeah...they are."

"Is it weird? Having your parents move and decide to own a camp?" Madysen continues.

"Let's listen to Maeve's fun fact," Isla tells her.

"I play volleyball," I finish lamely.

We don't get much more time to talk because soon, my parents are standing in the center of the outdoor dining area, announcing that it's time to eat.

"Good evening, campers!" Mom says cheerfully.

"We have a delicious dinner prepared for you all before we go discuss rules, changes, and expectations for the summer!"

"Tonight's dinner," Dad continues, "is a vegetarian meatball sub on a sprouted ancient grain bun!"

"We have zucchini and carrot-veggie salad on the side and a date-sweetened chocolate cake slice for dessert," Mom finishes brightly.

I drag a hand down my face.

All the previously excited chatter has completely died off and with it, my frail, tentative feelings of maybe this won't be as bad as I thought.

When no one reacts positively—not even most of the counselors seem to know what to say—Mom shoots me a panicked look. I want to ask her what she was expecting. But there she is, asking me to lead Misty Monarch through the doors and convince everybody that vegetarian meatballs are actually really good. Her eyes are big and pleading; her eyes are green like mine.

Instead, I sit there. I look away. Guilt tugs at my stomach the second I do. Maybe everyone last night was right about my parents ruining this place.

How can they expect me to be on board with this when they go ahead and pull something like this? What seven-year-old is going to be excited about vegetarian meatballs?

"Come on, guys!" Isla shoots up and ushers our cabin forward. "Meatball subs are always delicious! Let's go, girls!"

I lean my elbows against the table and rub my eyes.

"Maeve?" Addie looks at me expectantly.

I force a smile. "Not hungry. Go with Isla, okay?"

She shrugs but follows Isla to the Great Hall. Mom beams at Isla as Misty Monarch walks by, looking like she could hug each and every one of them. I'm acutely aware of the horrible example I'm setting for the girls already but distract myself by flipping through the counselor handbook again. When I hear the other cabins start to shuffle forward, I feel a sinking in my stomach.

Dad walks over to me as soon as everyone is gone. "Maeve," he says. "This wasn't the agreement."

"People don't like what you're doing to this place," I tell him. "You and Mom need to loosen up. Vegetarian meatball subs, Dad? Really? Most of these kids are in middle school."

"We thought that parents should be able to rest at ease knowing we're feeding their children beneficial, nutritious food instead of the stuff they usually get at camps. What's wrong with that?"

I drag a hand through my hair. My swim band snags on a curl.

"It's too much, okay? Just tone it down a bit. Seriously, I'm trying to help you."

He frowns at me. "I didn't see you trying to help a second ago when your co-counselor was the only one who saved your mother from embarrassment."

"You guys did that to yourselves when you mentioned date-sweetened dessert."

"I don't understand." He takes a seat beside me.

"You *love* your mother's cooking."

"Yeah, maybe *I* do, but that doesn't mean everyone else will. Just do normal stuff for once...please."

He flinches like I've hit him, face red with anger or hurt. I feel the wound in my own heart and wish I could take the words back. "Dad, I—"

"No, I understand. Your mother and I aren't going to change the way we do things just so people will think we're cool or likable, but it's good to know what you really think of us. Excuse me." He stands up before I can say anything else.

I pound the wooden table with my fist and then rest my head against it. As people begin to take their seats, I hear them muttering things about my family, about my parents.

About me.

ghost stories
June 2

The flames of the Big Fire reach up into the night, like hands groping for the stars, reaching up into the unfathomable darkness. I watch the crackle and the dance, mesmerized by the movement. My parents were always wary of fire because Mom said it brought bad luck and arguments. But sitting here now, I can't help but think that all their superstitions were ridiculous. Fire is dangerous, but it's also beautiful. It smells like the end of something.

Most of the campers and counselors—except for the Bitties who are giggling amongst themselves—are swaying as a group, singing a pop song that came out this year. The stars above are the audience as the camp sings shamelessly, like they're all old friends. Isla beams at them, encouraging our girls to join in. Kiara looks on, amused, humming under her breath and nodding her head. Addie stares at the fire, fidgeting with the ends of her hair. I think about what Dad said to me earlier at the table. Maybe I don't want to be here. But Addie clearly doesn't either. Maybe I can help her.

Scooting over to her, I lean down and whisper, "So, you like to write?"

Slowly, she nods, turning her head back toward the fire.

"That's really cool! I enjoy reading, which isn't the same as writing, but I can still appreciate talented writers," I babble, a little nervous but just wanting to say *something*. "What kind of things do you write? Do your friends back at home read your work?"

"I'm used to being on the outside." Addie fidgets. "I'm not very good at making friends."

"It can be hard," I agree. "But I'm sure you'll meet plenty of friends here."

We sit quietly, but I feel accomplished, like I've broken some ground with this girl. I'm surprised by this emotion because I didn't know I would care.

My parents walk in front of the Big Fire, waving their arms to encourage everyone to settle down. The singing dwindles into the night and there's shuffling on the benches as campers and counselors rush to take their seats.

"Welcome to Camp Swallowtail!" Dad says cheerfully, gazing out across the bleachers in the night. "We're so glad to have you. My name is George Everbrill and this is my beautiful wife, Winnie." He smiles at Mom, who gives a dainty little wave. "We bought the camp this year from the previous owners, Bo and Abigail. Winnie and I have always wanted to own a summer camp." He pauses and I see him smile nervously.

What does he have to be nervous about? *More meatball subs?*

"Thank you for letting us be a part of your summer." Mom takes Dad's hand. "It means so much to us."

"Before we begin the summer," Dad continues, "we have a few guidelines we should go over. Winnie and I didn't want to change too much because we understand that most of you have grown up here, but there are some things we felt were a bit...outdated."

A cough from behind startles me. I glance over my shoulder and find Hayes, cocking one eyebrow as he gazes at Mom and Dad. He's leaning against the bleachers, barefoot in the dirt. When he catches me looking, I whirl back around quickly. His gaze prickles the back of my neck.

My parents go over basic rules: no girls in boys' cabins, no boys in girls' cabins. Make sure you drink enough water. Stick with a buddy at all times. Be respectful, be on time, and have fun!

"Camp is what you make it!" They say in unison.

I roll my eyes. *Super corny.*

I'm going to lose my mind if I hear that catchphrase one more time.

The two of them sit down back on their bench and the campers dissolve back into chatter. But before the singing can begin again, Archer stands up and hushes everyone dramatically. I get an uneasy feeling in my stomach.

"Does anyone know what happened here in 1996?" he asks, dragging his gaze across the campers and counselors, tilting his head in an eerie way, a slow smile sweeping across his face.

Isla rolls her eyes, shaking her head at me like here we go again.

My stomach clenches. *I won't run off, I won't run off, I won't.* There's no messing around this time. I heard whispers about me last night when I left. I have to make myself stay. There are too many people here who would see.

Campers begin to whisper among each other. Addie glances at me uncertainly and I force a smile. Behind me, I hear Hayes sigh. He and Isla seem to be unimpressed with these stories. I like that about them.

"There was a camper in 1996. Sat in the same seats that we all do now. Slept in these cabins, walked these trails, spent her summers here. Many know the story of the ghost of Brother Bane, who was her older brother, searching the grounds for his lost sister. Her name was Cora Hart."

Dad stands up abruptly, his silhouette outlined by the flickering firelight.

"One night, Cora died in an accident," Archer continues. "No one really knows what happened."

"Archer, that's enough," Dad snaps. I watch him, confused. Dad isn't usually one to shy away from ghost stories since he actually believes in ghosts. Mom's face looks pale, but that could just be the lighting.

"Some say she was murdered. Some say it was an accident just waiting to happen" Archer smirks. "But all we know is that she haunts Camp Swallowtail still."

One of the Bitty girls in Caterpillar Corner begins to cry. Her counselor consoles her.

My heart starts to race.

Maeve's parents are witches! Lock her in the closet! We don't want to catch her crazy, too!

LET ME OUT!

I feel a cold presence beside me. It chills the air with a haunting whisper that sounds like my name but hardly sounds like a voice at all.

I turn and see it.

I scream.

The memory is back. I'm back in the closet for a second. I can't move.

Go away, go away. I can't run. People will stare. I can't run.

"So, if you hear whispering in the woods at night, or feel fingers running up and down your spine, or a burst of cold air, that's probably Cora." Archer stares at Dad.

"That's enough." Dad's mouth is in a firm line. "There's no need to tell stupid stories to scare the younger campers. That is completely irresponsible of you as their counselor."

"George," Mom whispers.

"But, sir," Archer's co-counselor, Jacob, complains. "We always tell that story at Big Fire. It's a Camp Swallowtail tradition. The younger camps learn to roll with it. It's like an initiation."

"It's a stupid tradition." Isla rolls her eyes.

No one seems to agree with her. Hayes stays quiet.

"Is that story true?" Addie pipes up.

I stare at her, shocked. The last thing I expected from this standoffish girl was a question in the middle of a confrontation from my father.

Archer seems surprised too, but he smiles at her. "You'll have to ask Cora."

Chills race up my spine. I clench my arms around my stomach, so no one sees me shivering. I think of the girl I saw at the pool.

That's the final straw for Dad. "Archer. Come see me after Big Fire. Everyone else, go back to your cabin. It's time for bed."

Mutters about how boring my parents are shuffle throughout the crowd as campers and counselors amble back to their cabins. I hear Madysen grumble about how they're no fun. My cheeks burn.

First the food, now this. Why can't they be cool? Why can't they just be okay with ghost stories like a normal summer camp? Why do they need to tear down the traditions of this place that was thriving on its own without them? I'm second guessing my decision to follow them here every time they speak. Normally, they're all in on ghost stories because they actually believe in ghosts. Why did they have to wig out like me?

They can't even be cool camp directors.

Isla and I guide Misty Monarch back to the cabin. Isla flicks the overhead light on and after we all shower and brush our teeth in the old bath house, we gather on the floor of the cabin for a time of debrief.

After, everyone climbs into their bunk beds. Isla waits until she hears everyone situated, then, she turns out the lights. Within seconds, the darkness sinks into the room, lurking in every corner, mocking me from the direction of the closet.

I think back to the story Asher was telling at Big Fire. Mom and Dad were so angry with him. Why? They used to tell me ghost stories all the time when I was little, so there's no way they were really that concerned for the Bitties, unless they didn't want to deal with the parents who might complain about the things their children were hearing from camp. I understand not wanting to encourage creepy stories, but Mom and Dad moved us to a camp. I mean, what were they expecting?

Asher told the story like it was real. But Isla didn't believe him. She would know, wouldn't she? She has to have been here longer than anyone else. Mom and Dad might believe in ghosts, but that doesn't mean I have to.

When my mind takes me back to the locked closet the summer I was seven, I feel a presence behind me, lurking. I want to tell myself I was just being hysterical—no one likes being locked in small spaces they can't escape from, especially if they are claustrophobic. Just because I panicked doesn't mean there was a ghost inside there with me.

Something knocks against the window, and I nearly scream. I roll over in my bed and feel a little bit of relief when I see a tree branch tapping against the glass absentmindedly.

It's not a ghost. It's a tree.

Maybe...Dad was right. Does one bad experience warrant such hatred toward this place? Maybe I could do some good here. I listen to the sounds of the girls' breathing slowly, signs that they're falling asleep when I'm still wide awake.

I shift, trying to find a comfortable position on this horrible mattress. Sleep eludes me for a while longer, while my mind spirals and spirals, still shocked that I'm actually here. If this were a normal world, I'd be sleeping over with Quinny, Jolie, and Hazel, planning our day at the pool and the mall. Things changed so quickly. I feel like I've hardly had any time to process everything.

Crickets sing outside my window. The last time I was here, I was so young, so naive. I barely knew anything. I wasn't ashamed of my parents. I was a completely different girl back then. I wonder if I would even recognize her.

I wonder if she would recognize me.

I bite my lip and can't stop wondering what my friends are up to right now, back at home. My phone is safely locked away in my parents' little house. I wonder if there's any way I can sneak in and peek at it—my mind is pounding with all the things my friends might be doing without me.

As I slide down my bunk and tiptoe towards the door, grabbing my glasses and borrowing Isla's slides, I tell myself that I shouldn't care what those girls are up to. They cut me off from their world and I was on my way out anyway. They aren't part of me anymore. But my brain is sick with a sudden fear of missing out and a need to know exactly what kind of life I would be living right now, had I gotten to choose.

I wince when the door creaks, but soon I'm jogging down the pathway, feeling a strange sense of deja vu, probably from last night's walk to Lightwing Lounge. So many haunts have appeared since then.

I navigate the way to Mom and Dad's bunk by the walkway lights and the moon. Using the key they gave me a couple of days ago, I unlock the front door and creep down the hallway to the bucket that contains my phone. Thankfully, my parents have left it charging. I remove it from the outlet quietly and take a seat in the office, on a green footrest, trying my best not to wake them.

My phone is filled with notifications from all the things I haven't checked or answered in two days. I scroll through the texts and head straight to Instagram, my feed overwhelmed by photos of Quinny, Hazel, and Jolie. The three of them are at the movies, sleeping over, going to parties, at the pool—doing a whole manner of things in the span of a couple days. I wonder if they feel my absence, because I sure do. In every photo, I feel like there's an empty space where I should be. The pain rips a chasm through my chest, and I draw my knees up to my chest, scrolling and scrolling, pouring salt into the wound.

Seeing these photos makes me feel like I never existed.

Texts from Alivia begin to find their way through the spotty reception. I click on them and my phone takes me to a new text conversation. She asks me what I think of Camp Swallowtail and if I've made any friends. She checks up on me and asks for photos. She wants to know if there are any cute guys.

I haven't received any texts from Quinny, Hazel, or Jolie.

Fresh tears trickle down my nose as I type out answers to Alivia.
I'm surprised how easy it is to tell her things, after spending so many years feeling like I had to filter everything I said. I tell her about the girls in my cabin, about Isla, about Archer. I tell her about Hayes.

My fingers hover over the keyboard, twiddling a little bit as I debate telling her about the little girl I saw at the pool. I bite down on my lip.

I think I'll just keep that for me.

the breakfast club
June 3

When Misty Monarch steps into the pavilion for breakfast the next morning, all the counselors are gathered around one of the tables, muttering nervously, casting cautious glances over their shoulders.

Isla looks at me and I shrug, equally confused.

"Girls," I say. "Stay here. Isla and I will be right back." I don't really expect them to listen to me because I don't feel like I should be a counselor. I'm surprised when they all take a seat at our designated picnic table, yawning and talking quietly among themselves, clearly not morning people.

"You don't know what's going on?" I glance at Isla.

She scrunches her nose as we walk. "No. Maybe there's a schedule change?" She rifles through her backpack and pulls out a folded piece of paper. The schedule is printed in black ink.

"Hey, what's going on?" I look at Josie.

She bites her lip and glances at one of the guys, Jacob, Archer's co-counselor. "Well..."

Jacob scowls at me, curling his lip in disgust. I feel my cheeks flush even though he hasn't even said anything. It's clear what he thinks about me and it's such a violent feeling that I want to puke or run away.

"Archer's *gone*," he spits. "Because somebody's daddy can't handle a scary story."

"What?" I gasp. "He sent Archer home? For that?" I shake my head, furrowing my brow. Why would Dad do that? Why would he fire a boy on the first night for telling a scary story at the campfire? Everyone knows that ghost stories are part of camp. Why did they think buying a camp was a good idea if they couldn't handle the lore surrounding it, especially since they actually believe in ghosts? They warned me about ghosts my whole life, but I never really believed them.

Until—

I shake my head. *No, it doesn't matter.* What does matter is that Dad fired Archer for no good reason at all. And now everyone hates me for it.

"Look, I'm sorry," I say, "but that has nothing to do with me. My dad's kind of crazy sometimes."

Jacob rolls his eyes, exchanging a smirk with some of the other counselors. "You really think that I'd believe you? You flipped out after hearing a ghost story during Late Night—you're probably as crazy as your parents. They've been here for three days and are already ruining this place. Most of us have been here way longer than you, Mauve."

"It's Maeve." I narrow my eyes. Although Jacob's words are a knife in my chest, I know his type. Quinny often played dirty like this to get what she wanted.

"Jacob, seriously?" Isla shakes her head with incredulity. "You're going to treat Maeve poorly just because her dad made one bad decision?"

Why did my parents make me come? What is there to gain in buying this stupid place anyway? I close my eyes, wishing I could just go back home. What would my parents do if I contacted Alivia and asked if there was any way she could come and get me?

You'd lose the chance to go to volleyball camp. There's no way you can ever get the money to pay for it on your own. You promised *them.*

"No one asked for them to take over the camp," Jacob mutters. It's clear he thinks I'm a waste of time. I wait to see if any other counselors are going to speak up against him, tell him to leave me alone, but no one does. I swallow the lump in my throat but try to look unbothered by this.

I don't want to care what they think of me, because I didn't ask to be here. This was never my plan. I don't need to prove myself to Jacob.

But even as I think this, there's something in the back of my mind, nagging me. It's one thing if there's something about me that makes people form negative opinions and dislike me. If I earned a bad reputation, that would be fair.

But that's never what happens.

I can't believe Dad would send Archer home.

"Let's go back to the girls." Isla tugs on my arm. I briefly wonder why she doesn't just join in with the crowd. As much as I hate to admit it, if I were in her shoes, I would. I wouldn't want to stand out, not if it meant I'd be unaccepted by the crowd.

I let Isla pull me back to our table, my mind flooding with angry thoughts about Jacob, Quinny, my parents, and this horrible camp. The girls pause from their conversations and watch as Isla and I sit down. I try to focus on certain things, like the jagged feeling of the bench underneath my hands and the cool, invisible morning breeze.

"What was that about?" Emily looks back and forth between Isla and me.

I look away, making it clear I won't be the one answering her.

"Archer had to go home," Isla says delicately. "He just had some things going on, that's all. But don't worry—he's okay! Jacob was just bummed because he and Archer have been friends for years."

Moodily, I look around the pavilion. The counselors all dispersed back to their cabins' tables after Isla and I left. I catch a few glancing at me, either annoyed or curious.

"Can I see the schedule?" I point to Isla's bag.

Isla passed me the paper. "I can try and get you one printed in the office later today if you'd like."

I nod and scan over the sheet. After breakfast, everyone goes to Reflect, which, if I'm remembering correctly, is when either the directors or some counselors give a lesson about life, share their experience at camp, or say something else that's supposed to be life changing. Following that is Rec. I perk up a little bit when I see that today's activity is sand volleyball. Although sand volleyball usually ends up a chaotic free-for-all, it's better than nothing. Any chance to participate in volleyball is a win for me.

Mom and Dad come from the Great Hall, wearing camp shirts and bright smiles, clearly more ready for the day than anyone else. I feel bitter seeing their sunny faces—it seems unfair that they can be happy about everything while ruining my life. I wonder if they'll send home anyone else who so much as mentions a ghost.

"What's for breakfast today? Whole grain toast and sprouts?" Jacob calls out.

Mom waves her hand at him, thinking he's joking.

Dad watches Jacob warily. I wonder if he realizes that Jacob was Archer's co-counselor.

We're soon dismissed for breakfast—which is breakfast tacos with corn tortillas, relatively normal food, actually—and the girls all munch contentedly. Relieved, I gobble mine down. I'm starving after skipping last night's meal.

It's not long before the heat of the day begins to kick in, making my curls cling to my neck with sweat. Wincing, I yank my hands through the tangles, wishing I thought to braid it after my shower last night.

My parents weave in and out of tables, making small talk with the counselors who try to give them bright smiles, but their eyes betray them. The second my parents turn their back, I see them throw irritated looks at their co, as if they can't believe how ridiculous these new directors are.

"Winnie! George! Good morning!" Isla says cheerfully, spotting my parents ambling up to our table before I do. "How did you enjoy your second night at Swallowtail?"

"It's very nice, thank you for asking." Mom folds her hands. I pretend to be busy with my food.

"Maeve?' Dad sighs heavily, waiting for me to give him my attention. I look up at him, pretending like I didn't see them before.

"Oh, Dad! Good morning." It's so petty.

"How are things going for you?"

"Swell," I say, biting my tongue so that I don't ask why they sent Archer home in front of my entire cabin. Something tells me that stirring up drama wasn't what they had in mind when they asked me to engage with the girls.

He nods, satisfied, and scans over everyone's plates. "So, the tacos were a hit?"

"Very good," Kiara says, her mouth full. "I, personally, am a big fan of corn tortillas."

"I'm so glad to hear that!" Mom places her hands on Kiara's shoulders. "You're Kiara, aren't you?" When Kiara nods, Mom continues, "I had a lovely chat with your parents yesterday. They seem like wonderful people."

"My dad has his own business," Madysen offers, not to be out done. She leans back confidently when everyone looks at her. "And my mom has a clothing line on Instagram."

Mom smiles politely, pulling her wispy hair over her shoulder. She's very good at this, I'll give her that. "That's very nice. They must really enjoy what they do."

"The money's nice, too."

This place is full of a bunch of mini Quinnys. I can't catch a break.

Mom and Dad eventually begin to make their way into the Great Hall, the main meeting area connected to the dining pavilion.

"Isla, I'll be right back." I hand her the schedule.

She nods. "No worries. We'll meet you in the Great Hall, okay?"

I take my dishes to the bus tub and let them sink under the soapy water along with the growing stack of utensils.

"Wait!" I follow Mom and Dad at a brisk pace.

They turn, eyebrows raised.

I hesitate for a moment. Often, I find that I create this idea of my parents in my mind, painting them out to be crueler than they really are, sometimes pretending that they don't love me, even though I know it's not true. Moments like these reinforce the reality that my parents do care about me—they just are different from other parents. It makes me contemplate demanding to know what happened with Archer.

But then I remember the look on Jacob's face when he accused me of being a freak just like my parents.

"Why did you send Archer home?" I demand. "Do you realize how angry everyone is? They're all talking about you guys being unfair and sensitive. Doesn't that bother you?"

Dad shakes his head, looking at me like I can't possibly understand this situation. Mom swallows deeply, casting a nervous look at Dad, fiddling with the necklaces adorning her neck.

"I don't understand," I shake my head at Dad. "Usually, you guys are okay with stuff like ghost stories."

"No," Dad corrects me sternly. "We don't appreciate ghost stories. Ghosts are real, Maeve, you know that your mother and I believe that. But stories turn the ghosts into something grotesque, something they weren't. It isn't any different than starting rumors."

I laugh loudly. There's no way he's serious. "So, you fired Archer because he hurt the ghost's feelings?"

"Maeve," Mom chastises. "This isn't something to joke about."

"No, of course not." I roll my eyes. Don't they understand how crazy they sound? I start to tell them that ghost stories are part of camp, but shut my mouth, the tight expression on Dad's face silently tells me that I don't understand, that nothing I say will change their minds.

"Forget it." I leave the two of them standing there and try to find my cabin through the swirl and ruckus of campers cleaning up after breakfast.

I guess I never realized that my parents never told ghost stories the way people do at sleepovers or at a campfire. Their stories were always told in gentle tones, reverent, solemn. There were no dramatic hand gestures or deep voices or mocking screams. Dad never once held a flashlight under his face to cast ghostly shadows across his skin or against the wall.

Once upon a time, I was little and loved all their interesting hobbies and conversations. I thought my parents were the most fascinating people on earth. I was barefoot everywhere—reveled in the feeling of mud squishing beneath my toes. I collected feathers and mushrooms with Dad, paying close attention to the patterns and details. When I could finally identify and classify them on my own, he was so proud of me.

There used to be laughter and dancing and stirring up concoctions to soothe sore throats.

I can see that moment where everything went wrong, and ghosts became something more than the stories my parents taught me.

camp evil
June 5

"Addie tripped me!" screams Madysen.

The rec director, a tall guy named Trent, blows his whistle and jogs over to where Madysen sits on the grassy field, clutching her knee. He glances up at Addie, who is shaking her head vehemently, Dutch braids swinging wildly. "I didn't trip her, I swear."

"I believe you," he sighs. He pulls Madysen up. "You're fine. Everyone, back to your positions!" He blows his whistle again.

I squint through my sunglasses and glance at Isla. "She's sure going to be a handful this summer, huh?"

Isla gives me a wry smile. "It's always fun to get one like her in your group. Annoying, sure, but it certainly makes things interesting."

I scrunch my nose. "I guess. But I don't think she should be picking on Addie."

Isla bends down and grabs a baseball cap clipped to her backpack. She loops her ponytail through the back and gives it a good tug down her forehead. "Obviously not—we should do what we can to discourage behavior like that. But we aren't teachers, Maeve." She glances at me. "We're counselors. Any big issues just go straight to your parents."

I frown and turn my gaze to my shoes.

Since being here, they've developed a layer of dirt and sweat. It's kind of disgusting but also, I'm a little bit proud to have shoes that fit in with everyone else now. The only thing they're missing are colorful beads or tie-dyed laces.

"Hey! She pushed me again!" cries Madysen, pointing an accusatory finger at Addie.

"That's not true!" Addie clenches her fists.

I bristle. "People like her just like to pick on the weak ones, don't they?"

Isla shoots a look at me. "Seems like there's trauma there? But yes, you're right."

I bite my lip. We've been here for four days, and Isla has been trying to wiggle information about my life out of me in the name of friendship. But I've been determined not to create deep connections with anybody, so I am happy to leave when the time comes for me to join my team at Volleyball Camp.

"Hey," Isla says. "I didn't mean to make you uncomfortable."

"It's no big deal." I shrug.

"Hey!" Trent blows his whistle. "All players freeze!"

Isla and I jerk our heads toward the field, where all the campers freeze. One boy clutches the kickball. All their gazes are locked onto Madysen, laying on the ground, clutching her ankle and moaning in pain.

"It wasn't me!" cries Addie, folding her arms across her chest. "I didn't even touch her!"

Trent is kneeling in the grass beside Madysen, who's whipped up a whole barrage of tears and rolls side to side, gripping her ankle.

"Maeve, go grab the nurse," Isla sighs. "I'll stay here with the girls."

"This is ridiculous."

"Nurse." She hooks her thumb toward the nurse's office.

I follow her thumb towards a path leading me through a grove of trees and cabins. The cabins look relatively similar, with small front porches and cabin signs. Each cabin has a tin roof and plenty of windows. Every now and then, I pass a cabin with a back porch and stairs. Usually, these are the ones with railings covered with pool towels and swim trunks.

These must be guy cabins. I smirk, crunching dry leaves and sticks underneath my feet, wishing again that I brought better shoes for camping. No one wears expensive shoes here —there's no reason to, which I'm quickly learning.

The trees are tall around me, leaves clinging to them, barely alive in the summer heat. Everything here feels so dry, but I appreciate the dry heat instead of the humidity I was so used to back home.

I finally see the nurse's office across the path but stop short when something painted on a cabin wall catches my eye. I turn around, squinting at the wall of one of the cabins— Hawkmoth Haven, which I think houses the youngest group of boys, Bitties. It belongs to Alex and Hendrix.

On the wall, painted in an ugly, jarring shade of deep red, are the words "**WELCOME TO CAMP EVERBRILL**", except some of the letters in "Everbrill" are crossed out in bloody x's, so it really reads, "**CAMP EVIL.**"

A shiver crawls up and down my spine and I feel the hair on the back of my neck prick up. A sudden burst of cold air causes goosebumps to trail across my skin and I feel like somebody's watching me. Whirling around wildly, I find no one. The world is silent around me. I don't hear anything.

What if it's that little girl from the pool? I clench and unclench my fingers. How could she have written this? If she really was a ghost, how could she come into contact with things? But I remind myself that it doesn't matter. I don't care about the physics of ghosts because *I don't believe in them*. Still, my brain conjures up an image of that ghostly thing, writing these words on the wall of the cabin, shooting a numb sort of look over her shoulder. At me.

I don't believe in ghosts! I tear my hands through my curls. A *person* wrote this.

But who? I think of Jacob and his hideous sneer when he told me I was a freak like my parents. Of course he would do something like this. He wouldn't write it on his own cabin because that seems too obvious. I'm almost relieved that it was him.

"What a jerk," I mumble, backing away from the cabin. "He's just trying to scare me."

But it's more than that. He didn't know I would see this, but obviously other boys would, especially the little boys in this cabin. That is so cruel. He must've painted it on the door to scare campers into thinking my parents are horrible people or that the supposed ghost of Cora is unhappy that my parents refuse to let her story be told. Whatever his goal, there is no doubt he's still furious about what happened with Archer.

What if the story was true? What if there is a ghost here?

I close my eyes tightly, as if that will make the thought go away. I don't want to remember that day, when I was seven. I don't want it to become real. Because if it becomes real, then everything my parents have said could be true...

"Fancy finding you here."

"Oh my gosh." I clutch my middle, startled out of my skin. Hayes stands behind me, smiling a little bit.

"I didn't mean to scare you."

"I'm just on edge," I admit, lowering my arms. I glance up at the vandalism on the cabin wall. "Do you know who did this?"

He frowns. "No. I was wondering that myself when you walked up."

"You've just been standing there the whole time?"

He shrugs. "Stuff like this is always bound to happen when new management is involved. People are trying to riot. They do stuff like this to scare you."

"It's working," I say quietly.

Something flickers in his expression. Sympathy? Worry? "Why are you over here anyway?"

"I...was getting the nurse." I blink, remembering my task. "One of my campers sprained an ankle. Well, not really, but..." my voice trails off. I feel silly, babbling like this. I squint at Hayes. "What are *you* doing here?"

"One of my many jobs is to clean the cabins. I check the AC filters every Wednesday to make sure things are still in order. I exterminate scorpions and spider infestations. All that fun stuff." He sticks his hands in his pockets.

"I better get back to finding the nurse," I say. "I'll see you around?"

He nods. "I'll get started cleaning up this mess." He gestures to the graffiti.

By the time I make it back to the rec field, my paranoia of being watched is finally dwindling. The whole way back, I kept glancing over my shoulder, as if I were walking down the streets of a large city instead of a summer camp in the middle of Nowhere, Texas.

The Misty Monarch girls are all sitting in a patch of grass, guzzling water like crazy.

There are no such things as ghosts.

Only bad people.

"You okay?" Isla whispers to me, keeping her eyes on the girls.

"Do ghost stories ever progress from something more than...stories?" I finally decide to take the bait.

She wrinkles her nose, confused. "What do you mean?"

"Like, do people ever play pranks to make the camp seem like it's haunted?"

"Why do you ask?" she says slowly. "Did you see something?"

I hesitate. Should I tell her? What would she say? What if she says I'm crazy like my parents? What if she asks if Jacob was getting to me?

Realizing that I care what Isla thinks about me is such a heavy feeling—I don't want to care. I don't want to be attached.

"The stories are just stories."

I think about telling her what I saw on Hawkmoth Haven's wall. But I don't.

I think about telling her about Hayes. But I don't.

If Isla doesn't believe in ghosts after coming to this camp year after year, then I won't either.

neon
June 7

Camp Swallowtail lives for Fridays.

There was so much I had forgotten in my years away, but it's all coming back to me, surrounded by strobe lights and loud music. Food—normal food—sits on long, plastic tables covered with tablecloths. Tonight's theme is Neon Pool Party, so everyone has gathered around the pool, decked out in glow-in-the- dark paint that is giving my parents anxiety. But the counselors talked them into keeping the theme night tradition—music, food, and paint included.

The girls in my cabin sit by the edge of the pool, painting their arms and legs with neon pink, green, and yellow paint. Counselors from another girl cabin make the rounds, passing out glow sticks. I sit back and observe, watching Isla laugh with the girls, with other counselors. I watch the campers chomp down on the hot dogs and funnel cakes, like they haven't eaten anything in their lives. It's as if my parents have starved them.

When Quinton climbs into the lifeguard tower, everyone dives into the pool. The water glows and warps with the neon colors and glowing bodies. It's almost disorienting—the combination of the loud music, the strange colorful blur of the water, and the addicting sweet smell of the funnel cakes. I feel like I'm in some kind of alternate reality.

"This happens every Friday?" I yell to Isla over the music.

She nods enthusiastically. "Yeah! Didn't you check the schedule?"

I had, but I didn't know theme nights were so...exciting. "Is it the same one every single week or do they change them up?"

"They change them up. I don't know if your parents ended up picking any themes, but if they give counselors control, it'll probably end up being rodeo, Hollywood, superhero...stuff like that! But Fright Night...I don't like scary stuff, but that's when things really get good."

"Fright Night?" That's one I don't remember.

"Isla, come on!" Kiara waves her into the pool.

I'm surprised to feel a twinge of envy when Isla leaves. The girls don't care about me, but that's because I've shown them that I don't really care about them. It's no one's fault but my own that they prefer Isla over me. No one can love this place as much as she does. I just wonder why she's so dedicated to it. Her love of Camp Swallowtail is almost infectious.

My parents mill around, keeping an eye on the campers while making small talk with the counselors. Things have cooled down about them now that the camp is a little more used to their quirks and obsession with health. People don't like them, but they tolerate them.

For now.

I've considered mentioning the message on the cabin wall to them, but decided against it, not seeing what it would help. I don't need more attention on me for any reason, and my parents aren't known for being subtle.

"Someone is lacking in glow sticks and paint."

The voice startles me so badly, I nearly topple into the pool. Hayes stands behind me, an amused expression painted across his face.

"Sorry, I didn't see you." I say, catching my breath.

"I noticed."

"Lost in thought, I guess." I shrug. "Did you need something?"

Hayes smiles a little, motioning to the glow sticks in the plastic tub beside me. "I saw your cabin partying it up in the pool. Didn't seem to me like you should be missing out."

I take a glow stick from the edge of the pool and snap it, watching the light drift across the plastic, creating a faint purple glow that almost looks white. I clamp it around my wrist, admiring it for a moment. "Want one?"

He shakes his head but keeps staring at everyone in the pool.

"Don't you swim?" I raise an eyebrow.

"I'm not here to party. I'm just here to make sure no one does anything stupid."

"Is that your official job title?"

"I'm more of a floater." He sits down, folding his legs up so they don't touch the water. Hesitant, I sit down beside him. I don't know why I do it. Something about him interests me.

"Did you ever get tired of coming back?" I wonder if I met him when I was here as a camper, ten years ago.

He laughs dryly. "This place used to feel like a home to me. It's changed a lot. Sometimes I hate it. But I just feel like I can't...leave, like it's impossible. I have a lot of history here." His jaw tightens.

I think if I were to have met Hayes in my first year, he would've been welcoming. He seems serious, but also like the kind of person you could always talk to if you needed it. I think I would've liked to be friends with him, in another life.

But that's not what I'm here to do.

"I better go find my cabin," I say, right as he says, "Have you ever been here before?"

I freeze. If he knew about my episode, he would know I'm crazy like my parents. He would probably see me the same way Jacob does. Which shouldn't bother me, but I find myself wanting Hayes to like me, even if we aren't meant to be friends.

"Once," I say, leaving it at that. Then, I dive into the pool before he can say anything to me. Just in case.

The water soaks through my suit, chilling my skin. It feels pleasant after sitting in the heat for so long. I almost don't want to come up for air. Maybe staying here would solve all my problems. This way, I don't have to face my parents, or pretend for Isla, or wait for Volleyball Camp. I don't have to put myself through the pain this place is sure to cause me.

When I finally do bring my head up, my cabin surrounds me.

"You came in?" Addie is tentative.

"I came in," I say.

Isla passes me a beachball and motions to a giant volleyball net.

"I know it's not real volleyball, but let's get a game started." She offers me a smile, wet hair plastered to her head.

I point to the other side of the net. "You go over there. Pick your team."

She beams this time, excited to do something together as a cabin. To bond. I almost want to give her a sad smile. That's *definitely* not what this is.

I set the ball over, but harder than I should've with a beachball. It goes flying across the pool and Emily and Lena gawk at me. My heart soars with a sudden, light feeling.

Yes. I've missed this.

"We get it. You play volleyball." Madysen rolls her eyes.

For some reason, I die laughing. There's this giddiness inside of me, playing volleyball with my cabin mates, in the dark, in a pool, with Hayes watching from the side.

I don't want to be here.

But at the same time, I'm almost enjoying this.

It's just one game, I remind myself. *It's not like I'm going to be inviting any of these people to my wedding or anything. We aren't friends.*

We're just cabin mates.

As we play, more people join. We split them evenly between Isla's team and my own, getting a good ratio of guys and girls. I'm surprised any counselors would want to be on my team after what went down at breakfast on Wednesday. But it looks like theme nights bring everyone together.

"You killed that spike!" Hendrix raises his hand up for a high five. I return it, smiling.

Addie sticks to the edge but cheers me on every few minutes. I can tell she wants to join in but is nervous. While the other team decides who is going to serve, I paddle over to her.

"Do you want to join?"

She shakes her head quickly, water droplets flying from her red hair. "No, no. I don't think I would be very good. Not as good as you, for sure. Thanks, though."

I hold out my hand. "Don't be nervous. It's only a game."

Maybe this will help her.

Cautiously, uncertainly, she offers me her hand and follows me as I pull her along through the water. We paddle over to my team's side, and I position her beside me. She looks up at everyone with wide eyes, fear splashed across her face like water droplets.

"All you need to do is hit the ball," I raise one hand and swat it through the air, hitting a phantom ball. "It doesn't have to be crazy or powerful or impressive. It just has to go over the net."

"What if it doesn't?" She bites her lip.

I shrug. "Then we get the next one." When that doesn't reassure her, I put a hand on her wet shoulder. "Look, if you miss, it's not a big deal. We're all just playing for fun. There's no prize involved or anything. Just...have fun. Don't think about it too much. Eye on the ball," I repeat the phrase Coach always drilled into our heads. "Eye on the ball."

Addie sucks in a deep breath and gives me one determined nod. "I can do that."

"Good." I fist bump her and swim over a little ways to give her some space.

I meet Isla's gaze from the other side of the net and she gives me an approving smile. A flutter of warmth courses through me along with a flicker of surprise. I sneak a glance at Addie, who is mouthing the words, *"Eye on the ball, eye on the ball."*

Am I becoming a *counselor?*

I shake myself and prepare for the ball to fly over the net.

My parents shut off the music and the lights at around eleven, ushering everyone off to their cabins for the night. People protest, but I can tell that a lot of the campers, mostly Bitties, are exhausted. They yawn and rub their tired eyes as they climb out of the pool and bundle their shivering little bodies in towels.

The glow stick around my wrist flickers, like a lightning bug. I climb out of the water with the rest of Misty Monarch, who haven't reached the point of exhaustion yet. The girls are still bubbly, recounting their best volleyball hits or the bitterness they hold from the counselors who spiked on them.

"At least Hendrix was cute," argues Madysen with a sniff. "None of the cute ones spiked on me. I wish Jacob spiked on me."

In the dark, Isla makes a face at me, and I clamp a hand over my mouth. Unfortunately, my laugh comes out of my nose in a snort. Madysen whips her head around, wet braids swirling in the air, coming to rest down her back.

"What is so funny?" She narrows her eyes at me.

"Jacob?" I can't help but say. Isla snickers beside me.

"What?" Madysen crosses her arms defensively. "He's a ten."

"Oh *no,*" Isla groans. "He's a ten but he's Jacob." She links arms with me.

"Then he's so not a ten." I wink at Madysen.

Kiara and Addie look like they're also trying to stifle laughs, but Emily, Lena, and Charlie look wide-eyed at Madysen, as if she were a viper about to strike.

The thing is, I'm not scared of Madysen. After years of kissing up to someone just like her, I know how to maneuver —I know how to dodge the viper. By the no nonsense look on Isla's face, I know she's thinking the same thing. I wonder if she ever found herself tied up with her own Quinny, her own Madysen.

Isla is so easy to be around, and maybe that's why. She doesn't put up with the stuff I got tired of. Not that I want to be best friends or anything. But maybe friends is doable. Maybe friends is even okay.

I want to go to Volleyball Camp. But since I'm already stuck here for the next few weeks, maybe it's okay to just go with it. And then everything will go back to normal at the end and that will be okay.

Madysen spins on her heel and marches away, deciding she's too dignified to give us a response. Kiara sticks her tongue out at the back of Madysen and then links arms with a startled Addie, trailing after Lena, Emily, and Charlie.

"Maeve?" I turn at the sound of Mom's voice.

"Go ahead." I nod at Isla. "I'll be right there."

She gives me a thumbs up and chases after Kiara and Addie.

I turn back to my mom. She's wearing a lilac swimsuit with a flowy off-white see-through swim cover up skirt. She's barefoot, but water droplets cling to her purple toenails and dainty toe rings. Her blonde hair is tied in a thick braid, draped elegantly across her shoulder. As much as they drive me mad, I can't deny that my mother is one of the most beautiful women I have ever seen.

"How're you doing, chickadee?" She smiles affectionately.

I see Jacob and some of the other counselors out of the corner of my eye. "Mom," I quietly protest looking away.

Her smile falls, but only for a moment. "I just wanted to check up on you. Dad and I haven't had the chance to talk with you in a few days. How did you feel about your first week? It looks like you and your cabin are getting along great!"

Something bubbles in my stomach. Things *were* going great. But the fact that this seems to please my parents irritates me. Does that make me petty? Probably.

"Don't get your hopes up," I say sourly. "I'm still leaving for Volleyball Camp at the end of the month."

Mom folds her hands in front of her. "Oh, I know. Your dad and I intend to hold up our end of the bargain, so long as you do."

I steal a quick glance at her, watch her smile that is kind but a reminder that I need to keep my promise to them. It doesn't matter how much they push me or question me. I must behave.

"I am," I say flatly, looking her dead in the eyes. "No worries."

I walk away, ignoring Jacob's snickering and whispers to the other counselors.

I wish I had just walked with the Misty Monarch girls, finishing the night together, instead of allowing Mom to dig her claws into my head. These doubts and questions wouldn't be swimming around in my mind.

Plus, it's hard to find my way back in the dark. No one is here to shine a flashlight on the path or reassure my overactive imagination that I'm okay. The trees tower over me as I struggle to find the path that leads back to Misty Monarch. I know it's toward the back of the girls' grove of cabins. But I don't know how to get there.

Why didn't I ask Isla for her flashlight?

I take a step forward and crunch some dead leaves. Pause. Take another step.

A clatter fills the air. Something is shaking something. The sound is soon replaced by a ghostly whirring. Almost like spray paint, but that makes no sense. Spray paint?

Camp Evil. Hawkmoth Haven. That's on the other side of camp. Is someone writing messages on the girls' cabins? Why? What cabin? What happens if they catch me?

Heart speeding up, I trek as quietly as I can through the grove, searching desperately for any sign of life that doesn't have to do with ghosts or Jacob or anyone else who likes to spread rumors that my family is haunting this camp. But...it can't be Jacob. He hadn't left the pool yet when I made my escape.

LET ME OUT!

It's the ghost. It's real.

I sprint in what I hope is the direction of the cabin, not caring anymore how loud my steps are. I just want to get as far away from this as I can. It feels like the wind is watching me, the trees are reaching for me.

Like the whole campground is mocking me.

be
June 7

"Night sprint?" Isla lays on the front porch of Misty Monarch.

I double over, taking a moment to catch my breath.

"You thought you saw something, didn't you?" She sits up, folds her legs crisscross, tilting her head attentively. "You wouldn't be the first."

"I...wouldn't?"

"No. I think we've all seen things here, when it's dark." She squints. "Or at least, we thought we saw something."

"I thought you didn't believe in ghosts."

"I don't." She pats the empty space next to her. "But I believe in the power of imagination. It can do crazy things to you if you aren't careful."

I sink to the solid ground beside her. The wooden porch feels solid, stable under me. I splay my fingers across it, grateful for its sturdiness. "What are you doing out here?"

The lights are off in the cabin. The only faint glow comes from the stars and moon, clear to see now that I'm no longer surrounded by trees.

"Sometimes I like to sit out and reflect. I try every night. It's easier here, though. Nature is just so beautiful, and it seems peaceful here. At home, everything is loud. Everything is a distraction. I don't have to worry about phones, social media, or keeping up with people when I'm here. I can just...*be.*" Isla gestures up to the sky. I follow the motion with my eyes, tracing lines between the hundreds of stars that dapple the sky, depths I can't understand or truly appreciate the way I feel they're meant to be appreciated.

When I was with Quinny, we never talked about reflecting. We didn't look at the stars. We thought *we* were the stars—everyone looked at us.

"Why do you love this place so much?" I twist my hair around my finger until the tip turns purple. "I don't understand. Out of everywhere you could be in the world as a college girl, you chose here. Why?" There's a quality to her that I envy. She's so carefree but so in love with the idea of life, like a little kid who finds magic in every situation.

I don't expect her to tell me, not really.

But Isla stretches back out, resting her head against the porch and her feet on the steps. She cradles her head in her hands, elbows out at the sides. The sigh that puffs through her lips seems heavy, carrying a million sorrows. I watch her as she decides what to say.

Eventually, it looks like she settles on the truth.

"I've been coming to this camp for my whole life," she says softly. "I met him here."

"Him?"

Her eyes flutter close. "Josiah. My fiancé."

My breath hitches. *What?*

"We met when we were ten. It was his first summer and my fourth. He was shy. I wasn't. We were the complete definition of opposites attract. We wrote letters to each other throughout the year and were inseparable at camp. People never thought we would last—they said we would grow apart as we got older, as our lives revolved less around camp and more around important things like high school and grades and friends."

"They were wrong," I whisper. I picture Isla growing up with this boy, imagining her falling in love with her feet in the river, stretched out under a blanket of endless, all seeing stars.

"They were," she agrees. "Our bond grew stronger. We fell in love." A single tear slips down her cheek, tracing down slowly. "Josiah proposed to me when we were eighteen."

Eighteen? I almost ask, my eyebrows shooting up, but I bite my tongue. I can't imagine anyone asking me to be their wife in a year. That seems so alien. I've never loved someone enough to want to be their wife. I've never had a serious boyfriend.

"Josiah loved this place like no one else," Isla continues, gentle, soft. Her eyes gloss over, lost in memories. "He came for me, but also because it just felt like home to him. This is where he felt free."

"What happened to him?" My voice shakes. I search for a sign of anything on Isla's face, but all I see is pain. Pain doesn't clear up anything except that he's gone.

"He died in a car accident. The other driver was drunk." Her whole body shudders.

"Isla...I'm so sorry." I reach out but don't know how to comfort her. I assumed he had broken up with her or cheated on her. It was quite another thing to lose the love of your life in this way. There, and then gone. Young love snuffed out like a flame.

"It's given me the opportunity to choose how I see life." Isla traces patterns in the wood. Ants and spiders scamper away from her fingers. "When something this extreme happens to a person, I believe they have three choices. There are always three choices.

"One, they can stay stuck forever. They can stay where they are—in their pain—and refuse to move forward. I knew this approach was never an option for me, although it seemed like that's what people expected from me. I'm a young woman who just lost her best friend and lover. People expected that from me. It's a valid way to live—it's justified. But I knew I couldn't do it.

"Two, they can pretend it never happened. This requires numbing your feelings and thoughts until the pain can't hurt you anymore. A lot of people expected this from me, too. But all I could think about when I considered these two options was what Josiah would tell me. He would say to grieve, to feel things—which kicks out option two. But he would also tell me to live my life, make new friends, find new loves. And while I'm not sure I'll ever love a man the way I loved Josiah, I know that living is what he would want me to do."

"So, you chose option three." I tilt my head.

Isla nods. "Option three is feeling the pain but learning how to move on. Not *forget*," she emphasizes, "just grow. It's okay to hurt, but at some point, you have to move forward with your life. For me, it meant finding something Josiah was passionate about and pursuing that with my life."

"That's why you're here," I realize aloud. "You want to serve here because this place meant the most to him."

"He loved this place so much." Isla looks around fondly, gesturing to the stars, the cabin, the whole place. "And so, I decided that I was going to dedicate my life to camp. It's the reason why I'm studying camp management in college. I don't know exactly what I'll do—if I'm meant to open my own camp or lead this one someday—but I do know that this is where I want to be. I want to show people how incredible summer camp can be. It's become my dream, too."

I frown. So many people seem to think Camp Swallowtail is the closest thing to magic that the world can get. People are fascinated by it, even though it's just a stretch of dry land decorated with wooden cabins. It's just a *place*. Nothing here *seems* that special.

"I don't think it is a secret to anyone that I didn't want to be here," I admit, "but I'm struggling to figure out what's so magical about this place. It's just a summer camp."

Isla shakes her head emphatically. "I can't speak for all camps, but there is something special about this one. Coming here as a child every summer is one of the most magical experiences in the world."

I scoff under my breath, imagining younger me, crying myself to sleep in my bunk bed.

"You have a slice of independence because you're away from your parents. You stay up late. You play games. It's like a giant sleepover. And then you keep going back and see the same people every summer and it feels like you pick back up where you left off." She looks distant, but happy, lost in a sea of memories that I've never experienced. "And then you get older. You have rough years, and you come here and can just be—"

"Free," I finish for her. "You can be free."

"You know the feeling?"

"No." I shake my head honestly. "But I wish I did."

"You should've come to camp. You would have loved growing up here."

I think it's interesting that she says, "growing up here". This isn't where kids spend most of their year, but it sounds like it's where they're most impacted. This is where the growth takes place. I can't imagine having a sanctuary where I could escape my problems in a way that really allowed me to be free. I wouldn't have to pretend. People would just understand, and I could be like Isla.

I could learn how to *be*.

But...be what? Be *myself*? Be *open*? Be frank with the fact that I pretend, exactly like how Alivia accused me of?

I don't tell her that I did come here once. I don't tell her no one taught me how to be free. Instead of freedom, I learned what it meant to wear chains for the first time in my life.

"Why were you so against coming?" Isla furrows her brow.

I didn't want to come, that's true, it's something I already confessed—but I also don't want Isla to think I'm a child who pouts unless she gets her way. A lie flashes across my brain, but I close my mouth before it slips out. She was honest with me about Josiah. I can be honest about this.

"I had a good thing going back home." I pause. Was it a good thing? Was I really happy at home? I know for a fact I certainly wasn't free. All of my actions and words were carefully chosen and crafted, anticipating the reaction I would get from Quinny and the others. I wore masks so that no one could see. Even though that's what I wanted at the time, I can't call that free.

"Why? What was the good thing that made you want to stay?"

"I guess a *"good thing"* might be untrue," I admit begrudgingly. "I had friends. I was comfortable where I was because most of the time, I felt secure. And I miss it."

Coming here was Mom and Dad's idea, not mine. I can't let them get into my head and make me believe that coming here is what I needed. I'm just...making the best of my bad situation. That's all.

Isla stands up and dusts off her legs. Moonlight glows dimly off her skin.

"Well, Maeve," she says. "Then I'll just give you some advice. I know it's cheesy and whatever, maybe even the last thing you want to hear, but maybe you're here for a reason.

Those girls in there need you—all of them," she insists when I open my mouth to say Madysen's name.

We smile at each other.

"But seriously," Isla continues. "They need you and I think that you need this place. I know you're leaving for your volleyball week in July," she adds. "But camp is what you make it."

I roll my eyes but fight a smile.

"That's just a fact." Isla smiles back. "If you are intent on being miserable here, you will spend your summer miserable. I'm beginning to see you open up to the idea of being here. But while you're here, just be *here*. Go all in. Make friends. Don't just tolerate it to get back at your parents."

"You don't understand them," I laugh humorlessly. "They aren't your parents."

She shrugs. "No one has a perfect family."

"No one has one quite like mine either," I mutter.

Isla rests a hand on the doorknob. "Just think about what I'm telling you, okay? Just think about being here even if it's just for the experience. Worst case scenario, you learn a thing or two from being here. Best case, you love it."

I look away, back at the stars. Could I really love it here?

"I'm going to bed. Are you staying out here?" Isla asks.

"I'll be in soon," I tell her.

She nods and slips in quietly.

I sit and stare at the stars, wondering why I'm really here. What would it look like for me to dive deeper into this experience and pretend to be another Maeve?

Or would I be the *real* Maeve? Who even is that girl? Isla seems to think you can find yourself here. Hayes told me this place felt like home. The two of them just seem to think that being here allows you to be free.

Is freedom something I can attain with a family like mine?

I go to bite my thumbnail in frustration and my eye snags on my green swim band. This is supposed to be a token that says I belong.

I stare up at the stars the way Isla had been. They are breathtaking, especially now that I'm out here alone with my thoughts. I've never seen a sky quite like this. It's so endless and sprawling that my mind can't really keep up with everything my eyes are witnessing. Millions of stars dance and twinkle across the sky, a mix of deep blue and black and purple. The moon is full, sharing light with the stars.

I think of the ghost stories, the bullying, and people like Jacob. I wonder how those negative, bad things can exist in a place so beautiful. What would my friends from home think?

There's a mailbox in the Great Hall, I remember. What would Quinny do if I wrote her a letter, telling her about this place? I don't know what she would think.

But I do know someone who would appreciate it.

I think back to Alivia's texts and the way she wanted to know what was going on—the interest she had. She reminds me a lot of Isla.

I grab my notebook from my bag, sit out on the porch, and write.

the river
June 8

Tall, long grass itches my skin as we make the hike down to the river. Madysen grumbles the whole way there and Kiara does cartwheels, her tumbling curls flying in the air every time she goes upside down.

I've thought a lot about what Isla and I talked about last night. There are so many things about this place that wouldn't be hard to appreciate if I let myself. Thinking back, I've already seen glimpses of things I have enjoyed, moments where I've caught myself smiling. I want to hate how easy it was for my parents. I'm still not ready to *move* here. I still have a captain spot waiting for me, calling my name.

Every few days, the schedule changes things up a bit. Everyone prefers the pool, with its crystal blue water and clean floor over the river. The second Isla told the girls we were going to make the trek, everyone deflated, except Addie, who'd never been there before.

I remember the feeling now, walking through the grass. I sympathize with them.

"Is the slide open this year?" Lena asks Isla, flicking tall grass away from her bare legs. She shrieks when a cricket angrily soars up at her face and swats it away.

Isla nods reluctantly. "It's supposed to be."

"The slide?" I frown.

"You'll see." Isla waves a hand. Today her blonde hair is atop her head in a sloppy bun that shows off the wraps and beads in her hair.

The river flows nonchalantly, the sound faint like white noise. The other girls' cabins are perched on the hot metal bleachers leaning against a tall oak tree that must be at least a couple hundred years old. Sun peers through the leaves and beats onto the girls, causing them to wipe beads of sweat off their foreheads and noses.

Some girls work on braiding hair or making the friendship bracelets everyone inherently seems to know how to make. Some girls are playing some crazy version of Uno, and some just talk. No one is in the water yet.

"What's up?" Isla looks around, her question directed at Josie.

Josie shrugs, glancing at me like she's wondering if I remember her from that breakfast with Jacob.

I do. I wave.

She blushes and faces Isla again. "No one wants to get in. Ginny even offered to be a lifeguard instead of Zoe." She motions to a counselor wearing reflective aviators and another one with the lifeguard whistle around her neck, swinging it back and forth like a tire swing.

Josie's co, Mia, joins us. "What's the tea?"

"Nothing yet," says Zoe, her expression impossible to read behind her sunglasses, but I feel like she's looking at me. "New girl? Any guys? Any drama?"

I smirk a little, debating between telling her I want to get to know Hayes or keeping my mouth shut. Both have their perks. On the one hand, confessing my fledgling crush would allow me to get to know these girls better. But I know better than anyone the risks possible when giving girls an in on your emotions.

It *never* ends well.

So I shrug. "Maybe. Maybe not. Got an answer to that question yourself?"

I know how to play this game.

Zoe's lips quirk up. "I like you. You're tricky. I'm dating Hendrix, just so you know."

"Noted," I tell her, "Although I hardly know who he is."

After a few minutes of making small talk and exchanging a few laughs, Josie warms up to me. Soon, the other girl counselors join us—Julia, Heather, Hannah, and Aislinn. I notice that Hannah and Aislinn, counselors of Caterpillar Corner, the Bitty girls' cabin, glance back at the little girls every few seconds, aware that they oversee about ten first through third graders.

We talk about funny things girls in our cabins did—Isla quietly mentions a few of Madysen's best and worst remarks —and it's really fun to just laugh with these girls.

I look over at the Misty Monarch girls, who are debating the pros and cons of getting into the murky river. Addie looks like she's on the verge of dipping her toe in.

"Your parents are George and Winnie?" This is from Aislinn, who seems like a really sweet girl. She reminds me of Hazel. She has these big brown eyes framed by long lashes and a dimple that flashes in her chin when she talks.

"Yes." I wait for her to say something sarcastic, but she doesn't—she just smiles.

"They seem like really nice people." Her voice is sincere; not a sweetness that oozes with false honey. She really means what she says.

"Hey," Josie offers quietly. "I'm sorry about what Jacob said to you. I just wanted you to know that yeah, your parents changing things up was a little..."

"Unexpected and annoying?" I venture, giving her a half-smile to show her that I understand.

Josie stammers but laughs a little when she sees that I'm chill. "Just unexpected," she decides, going with one of my word choices. "I mean, most of us have been here our whole lives. You can understand how strange it would feel to have things suddenly changed up on us."

"They aren't *bad* changes," Aislinn assures me.

"Speak for yourself," mumbles Hannah, pretending to shoot a glance at the Bitties.

Isla rolls her eyes at me and mouths *ignore her.*

"I just wanted to say that you shouldn't let Jacob get to you." Josie shoots Hannah a look, even though she isn't watching. "He just likes to be difficult. He's the big man at camp." She rolls her eyes.

"Has anyone gone on the slide yet?" Isla's voice turns sharp. I guess that she means the counselors because they all shake their heads, looking confused about the tone of her voice. I follow her eyes, leading up to a tall metal system that holds a yellow and blue water slide. It's a tall slide and leads straight into the river.

And Lena is standing on top of it, dark bangs blowing around her face.

"I'm gonna be the first one in the river all summer!" She claps her hands and does a little dance on top of the platform. Charlie runs toward the stairs leading up to it, squealing with excitement.

Ginny, the girl with the lifeguard whistle, walks swiftly to the lifeguard chair, a wooden thing with red and white paint decorating the side. She opens the umbrella that stands overhead, covering her pale skin from the persistent sun.

Isla wrings her hands together and bites her lip. As Lena sits down and looks ready to push off into the water, Isla suddenly screams, *"LENA, STOP!"*

Lena freezes right before she pushes off. She scoots back just a few inches and looks at Isla, wide eyes and a trembling lip. "What's wrong? What did I do?"

Isla doesn't answer, instead runs over to the slide with Josie and Zoe right behind her. Curious, I follow, wondering what on earth Isla could be so freaked out about. It looks fine to me.

Thick ties lay loose by the edge of the slide, letting the edge blow up with the wind just a little bit, waving ominously. Isla reaches for them with shaking hands. Josie's mouth forms an "o" of horror, and she puts a hand over her mouth like she might be sick.

"Off the slide," Zoe, the girl with aviators, commands. "Now."

There's a chorus of "awws" from the girls, who I realize had all lined up behind Lena. Lena scoots back and holds her arms around her middle, hunching her shoulders disappointedly. I notice tears in her eyes. She looks jarred, shaken.

I look around, confused. "What's going on?"

Josie's knuckles are white from squeezing her hands too tight. Her teeth are digging into her bottom lip so hard it looks painful.

"Josie?"

"Don't ask me," she says. "We should leave. This is a sign."

"What? What sign?" But she walks away, shaking her head.

"Get off the slide!" Zoe roars again, flipping her sunglasses on top of her head, causing the short strands of her hair to stand up at weird angles.

Quickly, the girls scamper down the stairs and huddle together. Some of them are crying, afraid of Zoe's anger. I can't blame them. I'm a little stunned.

"What's the big deal?" I hiss to Isla. "Just tie the slide. Problem solved."

"No, Maeve," she says, firmer than I've ever heard. "You don't get it. We need to get the girls back to the Great Hall. It's almost lunch, anyway. Go get them together."

Feeling like a kid taking orders, I slink over to the girls from our cabin. "Misty Monarch! Head back to the Great Hall."

Obediently, the girls begin to grab their things and hurry back through the tall, sharp grass. I pause before going after them. I want to wait for Isla. I want to know what happened. But she looks at me, waves me on toward the girls, and stays behind with some of the other counselors.

I don't get to know. Of course I don't. I don't belong here.

A ripple of hurt courses through me. I thought Isla and I were friends. Why wouldn't she tell me something like this? Especially if it were important. Are they hiding something from me?

"What was that about?" Kiara throws her towel around her neck.

"I have no idea," I answer her honestly. I glance back at the counselors remaining—one from each cabin, whispering in hushed tones so as not to be overheard. They motion urgently to the slide. "I'm just as lost as you are. But I intend to find out."

We had gender split swim time today, so while we were at the river, the boys lucked out and got to have the pool. They're already at the flagpole in their cabin lines whenever we make it to the top of the hill with the Great Hall and patio.

My parents stand by the flagpole, on top of the little platform that raises them above the rest of us so they can be seen.

"You're late," Dad observes.

"Sorry, George, we ran into a few small issues down by the river, it won't happen again," Josie is quick to assure him, herding the girls from her cabin, Starry Skipper, into their row so that we can begin Shout Off, a roll call to ensure everyone is present before meals.

Mom scans over the girls' cabins, her eyes widening a little when she sees that we're all missing one of our counselors. She tries to exchange a look with me, but I tear my glance away, focusing on the American flag flying over their heads in the faint wind.

Dad draws attention back to the purpose of Flagpole and instructs us to place our hands over our hearts as we recite the pledge of allegiance while the flag is lowered and folded. Dad said learning how to respect the land you live in—even if you don't agree with the way things are done—is an important part of going to camp.

When the pledge has been recited and the flag lowered, Dad calls out each cabin's name and we listen to whatever motto or chant or catchphrase they've decided to choose for Shout Off. The girls in my cabin lamely pump their fists and say, "Let's eat."

I can hardly focus on anything. My mind is too centered around what could've freaked out Isla so bad. Obviously, I've seen her upset, like when she told me about Josiah, but she seemed *scared*. Like this was a huge deal. The only thing I can think of that makes sense is that campers being injured on the slide could be some kind of lawsuit. But for some reason that hypothesis just doesn't sit right with me.

It's more than that. It has to be.

Misty Monarch is dismissed for dinner—field green salad with gluten free flatbread, one of the better menu items—and we stroll into the Great Hall. The girls are all chattering with each other, but Addie sticks beside me. Seeing the way she's fiddling with her green swim band, I decide to push the thoughts of the slide out of my mind for a few minutes.

"How're you doing? How has your first week been?" I ask. "It's crazy to think that tomorrow is Sunday and we'll be on to week two."

She shifts from foot to foot. "It was good. I'm still figuring out how things work here. It's so pretty. Someone should write a book about this place."

That's right, I forgot that she loves stories.

"Does it help you think through things?"

Addie nods once. "It helps me clear my head. But sometimes—it's kind of funny—my brain will kind of muddle my imagination with what's actually there."

I put my hand over my heart in consolidation, thinking of my fear on the way back to Misty Monarch the other night. "I can relate with an overactive imagination."

Addie looks at me eagerly. "You can? Thank goodness! I was sure I was going crazy! It's so hard to say that because I feel like people will say I'm weird. But I guess they already do. Which is mostly okay with me." She shrugs, but it stings me a little, wondering what the girls in our cabin might've said to her.

"People here?" I try nonchalantly.

Addie shoots an unappreciative glance at Madysen. "You could say that."

"I won't say anything to her," I promise quickly, remembering how annoying it was when I'd confide in someone older than me and they would confront the person which only made things worse. "I just want to be aware. But what kind of things is she saying to you, Addie?"

"It's stupid stuff," she rushes to tell me. "Really, it's no big deal."

"I won't say anything."

Her pause tells me that she's weighing how much she trusts me. Finally, she gives in.

"Okay...but I'm not doing this to snitch. So, it's whatever, okay?"

I nod.

"You know that movie *The Sixth Sense*?"

"'I see dead people,'" I quote in a pretend-scary voice, waving my hands out in front of me.

"Yeah, that one," she laughs at my impression. "Well, Madysen calls me Cole."

"That's the kid who sees the ghosts, right?" My stomach sinks.

"Yeah. She says I'm freaky like him."

"Why...why would she say that?" I shake my head, scowling. "That's so mean. Where did she get that idea?"

Addie looks away from me quickly, Fidgets again. "I don't know, Maeve. I just talk to myself sometimes, I guess. Doesn't matter."

She's shutting down. She's lying to me.

She mentioned an overactive imagination and sometimes confusing reality with fiction. But then she mentioned the ghost kid from that old movie. Is there something that she's trying to tell me?

An image of a younger, shorter-haired Maeve burns in my memory, trapped in the closet in the cabin at age seven, screaming because she saw something in the dark. Something that shouldn't have existed. Something that traces eerie long fingers down her spine every time the memory surfaces from the pit she's tried to bury it in.

There was something in there with me. And Addie is seeing it, too.

friendship bracelets
June 10

Imagine my joy when I discovered that Isla and I have the same music taste.

She brought a speaker with her to camp and was given her phone to play music whenever our cabin has some time to just hang out and chill. The girls all eagerly sprint towards the Junction, which is actually just a big, open-walled structure complete with a rock wall and sand volleyball pit. There are a few corn hole sets alongside the edges of the wooden floor, the beanbags resting against them.

Isla pulls a transparent plastic box from her backpack. Inside are dozens and dozens of plastic white floss holders, embraced by colorful string. She rummages through her bag again for scissors and a satin pouch full of beads.

"Wow, that's the whole enchilada," I observe.

Addie laughs lightly beside me. She shyly reaches out to examine the bag of beads.

"I have letters and a few other little random ones." Isla begins unraveling red string from a floss holder. "Hopefully I have multiple of each letter, but I apologize in advance if I don't."

Addie fishes around and pulls out an "A".

The other girls crowd around. Madysen pulls out her own box of threads. "You guys can use these too," she says.

"Thanks, Madysen!" Isla exclaims. "That's so nice of you."

She rolls her eyes. "Whatever."

Kiara reaches for orange and blue thread. I watch her take the scissors and cut out two arms' length of thread. She ties a knot after looping the strings and then slides it onto the handle of her water bottle.

I look at all of their wrists, decorated with countless bracelets. Even Addie, who is new here, has managed to watch and learn the proper way to make a summer camp approved friendship bracelet. Hers look a little messier than some of the other girls, but she still seems to enjoy making them. Everyone has their own little collection of colors, of memories, of friendship. All woven into a little thread band wrapped around their wrists.

Aside from the swim band, my wrists are depressingly bare.

Emily notices and blinks at me with those dark lined eyes. "Maeve, do you know how to make a bracelet?" She pushes the scissors toward me.

Lena tucks her bangs behind her ear and passes me the thread box. "Go ahead and pick as many colors as you want. We'll show you how."

"Oh, sure. Thanks, guys." I blink, feeling my eyes begin to tear up for some reason. Maybe it's because these girls who are younger than me want to help me fit in, just because they see that I'm uncomfortable and want to be part of the group. I pick up three shades of green and a light, latte shade of brown. I hold them up and then Charlie tells me to unwind the string two arm lengths.

So, I do.

They walk me through the process of cutting them. Addie helps me make the knot and loop it around my water bottle handle. And then, they all chip in to show me how to make a chevron, one of the most basic patterns, but one of the coolest.

The first couple of rows are lumpy and lopsided. Addie reminds me that I need to tie each knot twice instead of just once, otherwise the bracelet won't be steady. Even Madysen chimes in to tell me, gratuitously, when I'm not doing them right.

We all talk and listen to the music while we make bracelets for what feels like hours.

At first, I find myself listening more than talking because I'm trying to focus on getting the bracelet right. But the longer I do it, the more comfortable I get.

"I think after college, I want to travel the world," Kiara tells us. She looks up from her bracelet and thinks for a second. One of her hands reaches up to fiddle with her beaded chokers. "There's too much to see for me to ever want to settle down and just live in one place. Where's the fun in that?"

"There's stability and a steady income in that," Madysen retorts. She grabs a hair tie from her wrist and pulls back her bright blonde hair.

"Everyone is entitled to their own dreams." Isla shoots a glance at Madysen. "Just because what Kiara wants is different than what you want doesn't make it bad."

"What do you want to do, Maeve?" Charlie props her feet up on one of the vertical beams holding up the roof of the Junction. Her toes are painted baby blue.

I hesitate and tilt my head. "Honestly? I haven't given too much thought to it. I know what kind of things I definitely *don't* want to do."

"Would you play volleyball professionally?" Lena asks.

"Maybe for fun in college, but I don't think it's a profession for me."

Isla glances over at the volleyball net. "We can go start a game if you'd like."

I shake my head and smile. "No. I'm happy here for now."

I ask Charlie what she wants to do in college, and she tells me she's interested in interior design. As she talks, I find my mind wandering to volleyball camp, which is coming up in a couple of weeks. I glance over at the volleyball net, blowing gently in the wind. If I am going to return to camp, I need practice outside of just pool volleyball and showing campers how to serve. I wonder if I'll be able to sneak out some nights and work on my jump serves on my own. I need to be in tiptop shape if I'm going to convince my parents that volleyball is so important I must stay with Alivia next year.

We work on our bracelets all through dinner and Meeting, which is when Mom and Dad give us a talk on attributes of a good person. By the end, my bracelet looks decent and I'm proud of myself.

"Our characteristic today is consistency." Mom is perched on a little wooden stool, clutching a microphone and wearing a long orange dress. Her feet are bare, dangling and barely skimming the ground of the stage. Dad has his own stool, sitting beside her.

"Consistency is crucial to being a good human being and making relationships in the real world. If you aren't consistent, how will people know they can trust you? How will they even know who you are?"

A strange feeling tugs at my stomach. I scrutinize my bracelet and undo a couple of knots. Lena rests a hand on my arm. "Is everything okay? You're kind of shredding the string."

I glance down and see a ripped piece of string resting between my fingers.

"Everything is fine." I give her a smile but am thinking about consistency as an admirable attribute for the rest of the evening.

My brain is spiraling and wondering so much that I find myself slipping on sneakers and grabbing a flannel and my glasses and sneaking out the Misty Monarch cabin door at midnight, way after all the girls and Isla had gone to sleep.

There's a ball closet in the Junction, closed with a broken lock. I yank on the door a little bit and rummage around for a volleyball. The night air is cold on my skin, and I pull my flannel tighter, clutching the volleyball under one arm. I shuffle over to the volleyball pit, lit by dangling fairy lights plugged into an outlet from the Junction. They move delicately in the wind.

I take a deep breath and slide off my shoes and socks. The sand shifts under my toes and I close my eyes for a moment. I feel so open and seen underneath this sky full of stars, like there's nothing between me and the elements.

I drop the ball into the sand and pick it back up again. My eyes go to the net and for a second, everything else falls away. I don't think about the drama with my parents or the girls back at home. I don't think about the things here that scare me.

I toss the ball into the air, like a spiraling moon, and feel my feet lift off the ground as I form what feels like a perfect jump serve. The ball soars over the net in a gorgeous arc when my hand meets it. Sand flicks up in the air after the ball hits the ground. My chest feels light.

That was a perfect serve.

If I can continue to practice and do more serves like these, the captain spot will be mine. Mom and Dad *have* to let me come back.

I smile a little and dive through the sand to grab the volleyball, eager to set up again.

When I turn around, my heart stops.

"Need someone to practice with?"

"Hayes!" I gasp. "Oh, you startled me."

He smiles and walks forward, straightening the hat he's wearing. It looks like a vintage Texas Rangers cap. He stops when he's right in front of me—he's so tall I have to look up at him. I notice that he doesn't give off much warmth—maybe he's chilly, too since he's not wearing any long sleeves.

"I just couldn't sleep." He shrugs. "Needed to take a walk and I saw that crazy serve of yours. It was really impressive."

I look down at my feet and bury my toes in the sand. "I didn't know you played," he supplies.

"Yeah, a bit. Back at home. I'm...practicing so that I'll be good when I go back to volleyball camp..." My voice trails off. It feels stupid to tell him. I wish I was still by myself.

"You can tell me." He tries to meet my eyes.

"I just want to go home." I cross my arms across my middle, the ball dropping to the sand. Hayes kicks it toward me.

"Can I help you practice?"

I squint at him. "You want to help me practice?"

His smile is gentle. "Yeah. I do."

I keep a careful watch on him as he jogs to the other side of the net. A little voice in my head wonders why he would want to come and help me, a girl he barely knows? Briefly, I recall that I saw him at Hawkmoth Haven when I stumbled across the "Camp Evil" graffiti, which makes me wonder if he's like a spy for Jacob. Maybe Jacob sent Hayes to befriend me so that in the end, he could somehow expose my parents for how crazy they truly are.

I banish the thought almost immediately. It's probably very stupid to trust someone so quickly into a relationship—if you can call it that—with them, but something about Hayes feels familiar. Like he already knows me in a way most people have never been able to. While that puts me a little bit at ease in his presence, I'm not entirely sure how I feel about it.

I expect to have to instruct him on the volleyball motions, but he serves the ball over the net and I quickly jump into position, hitting it back over. We volley for a couple of rounds until I spike it over the net and he misses the dive.

Energy courses through me. I feel absolutely alive.

Hayes dusts off his clothes, sand raining to the ground. "That was a wicked serve." He slides the ball over to me under the net. "You definitely put me in my place!"

I laugh at his use of the word *wicked*. Definitely a throwback. I toss the ball up into the air and catch it, throwing him a smug grin. The material coating the ball is cold to the touch.

"You thirsty for more?" I raise up on my calves.

He briefly pinches the ridge of his nose between his eyes but resumes a casual smile soon after. "Bring it on, Everbrill."

We carry on well into the night, stars overhead cheering us on.

I'm about to set the ball over the net after a particularly good hit on his part, when he stumbles and rubs his forehead.

The ball falls to the ground. I race to the net, fisting the material in my hands. "Hey, is everything alright?"

"Yeah," he mumbles. He waves a hand at me. "I just get these migraines sometimes. It's really not a big deal. I think I just need to get some rest."

I duck underneath the net and hold my hand out. Hayes glances at it quickly and then smirks, going for the ball and spiking it over the net one last time.

"Hey!" I plant my hands on my hips. "You're a disgusting liar."

He holds his hands up in innocence. "I do really have a migraine. I just couldn't resist."

I grab the ball and hug it against my stomach. "Thanks for practicing with me. Maybe we could do it again sometime?"

I don't really expect him to say yes.

"Sure. I'd like that a lot."

My eyes widen.

"Maybe eventually you'll get as good as me."

I roll my eyes. "Goodnight, Hayes."

He leaves me with a smile. "Goodnight, Maeve."

graveyard girls
June 12

Isla smears black liner under my eyes—borrowed from Emily—and lines my lips in blood red lipstick.

"How did you get my parents to agree to this?" I shake my head at my reflection in the bathroom mirror. The overhead lights flicker and moths dart back and forth, as if they're preparing for tonight before it's even begun.

"Fright Night is tradition," Isla waves her hand. "There was no way they could say no. And you know I'm not one for ghost stories, but Fright Night is a blast."

"Right, but the rumors about the ghost?" I meet her gaze in the mirror. Her makeup is done similarly, except she's painted open wounds across the left side of her face.

The girls in our cabin are already down at the Great Hall, the new ones anticipating a peaceful movie night, while the old ones smirk and keep quiet. I vaguely recall Fright Night from my time as a camper, but for the record, every night I spent here terrified me.

I avert my eyes from Isla's when I think of Addie. I didn't tell anyone what she said at the river yesterday. She didn't bring it up again, instead pretending as if it never happened and letting Madysen's comments bounce off her as if they meant nothing. But I watched her cautiously, waiting for her to start walking around like she was possessed or muttering to herself under her breath, eyes shifting back and forth manically.

None of that happened. She was just Addie.

I'd thought about telling Isla, but held my tongue when she refused to tell me what was going on with the slide. It felt weird to confide in her about something when she didn't feel like she had that same liberty with me.

She bends down and rummages through her duffel bag before tossing me a black dress with long, trailing sleeves and gauzy, gray fabric making up the skirt. It is bone chilling, but beautiful. I try to picture Hayes' face when he sees me in it, but quickly tuck away that thought with a rush of embarrassment, chiding myself mentally for being such a child. He's participated in so many Fright Nights that it surely takes more than one creepily gorgeous dress to impress him. *Why do I even care about that?*

I roll my eyes at myself. One night of volleyball doesn't seem like enough to be having thoughts over if he finds me pretty or not. This is ridiculous. I need to get my head back into the game.

"Are you sure about this?" I ask hesitantly, pawing at the fabric. "This seems kind of over the top. What am I even supposed to do?"

"You scare campers." Isla lays a dark veil delicately atop my head. She's teased my curls, purposefully creating the frizz I normally try to avoid. It almost resembles a lion's mane, but gets the job done, making me look crazed and wild. My eyes are slightly bloodshot, but if I'm being honest, it's from nearly sleepless nights, not because I was desperate to fit the part Isla wanted me to play.

She and I are the graveyard girls, rumored to come out on Fright Night alone, finding souls to drag back to their residence. I didn't want to participate. This was too much, too creepy, too weird. But Isla insisted that I don't miss out on camp traditions. I can't understand why any place would terrify campers intentionally this way. It seems sick.

Of all the things my parents called quits for, this somehow couldn't be one of them?

"How did this start?" I turn away from my reflection. Tossing the dress over my shoulder, I slip into a stall to change. My athletic shorts pool around my anklets and I throw my oversized volleyball t-shirt over the stall door. I frown at the dress before resigning myself to my fate, slipping it on. It feels light and airy against my skin, as if it weighs nothing at all. Almost like it was made for me.

"Like I said, I'm not big on ghost stories," Isla calls from the other side of the door as I zip up the back of the dress. "But I guess since you're participating, you should know."

I fold up my clothes in my arms, listening.

"Rumor has it that the old camp directors had a fondness for all things eerie and spooky. When Camp Swallowtail opened in 1996, they wanted some event to occur annually that would bring their ideas and ghost stories to life. So they created different stories that were passed down from camper to camper."

They sound like my kind of people.

The stall door creaks when I swing it open, stepping back out, clad in the black dress and veil, my clothes bundled in my arms. Isla grins wickedly at me in the mirror.

"The graveyard girls were two of the first ghosts created." She gestures to her matching black dress. "They haunt the graveyard outside camp, trying to bring any lost souls there so that they won't be lonely."

Chills race up and down my back and I shudder, hugging my own clothes closer to my chest, catching a glimpse of how horrifying I look in the mirror.

I look like death, if death were personified as a woman who looks both hauntingly beautiful and demented. I shudder, scrunch my nose up at the veil, and smash it down on my head.

"There's the Scarecrow," Isla continues, counting off her fingers. "Played by a guy counselor, usually. He stands in the fields by the exit gate, warding off kids who try to sneak out. That's the only *useful* ghost."

Isla lifts another veil out of her duffel bag and places it on top of her blonde, matted hair. The dark fabric falls in front of her face, hiding her eyes.

"Next is the Lavender Lady. Story goes that she was eighteen and chased butterflies across town. Swallowtails are poisonous and this place used to be full of them." Isla shakes her head. "She died from their poison, but continues to haunt the ground, looking for them. That story is kind of dumb, but her costume is really pretty."

"Are we talking about the Fright Night stories?" Josie ambles into the bathroom with her co, Mia.

"I'm playing the Lavender Lady." Mia jostles a mass of purple fabric in her arms, decorated with butterflies with wilted wings.

"I'm playing the Missing Mistress." Josie unfolds a long dress with holes and patches covering the fabric. "She was killed by the betrothed of the man she loved. They were going to be married here before the camp opened, but now she's buried in the graveyard."

My heart is pounding. I know these stories aren't true, but I feel like these ghostly women are reaching their hands out toward me, pulling me deeper into the mysteries of this place.

"They're just stories," Mia assures me. "None of it is real. Fright Night is just for fun. I know it seems kind of intense but just give it a chance. Odds are, you'll probably enjoy it."

"Don't the campers get upset that we freak them out?" I glance at my face again in the mirror. The dress hugs my curves, and the veil makes me look like some kind of evil bride from *Dracula*. I can't imagine Addie being okay with something like this, especially after the comment about *The Sixth Sense* from Madysen.

Isla touches up her lipstick. "They're scared initially, but they get over it. It's part of the fun. We explain it afterward and then they get excited to do it once they become counselors. It's a rite of passage."

"Does anyone play the ghost of the girl who died in 1996? Or Brother Bane?"

Josie bites her lip. "No...We don't have someone play them."

"It's supposedly 'cursed'." Isla does quotations, holding her makeup brush in one hand. Isla rolls her eyes and moves to the fake wounds on her cheeks.

"It is, though," Mia adds quietly. "In the past, every time someone played Cora, bad things happened."

"Like what?" I think of CAMP EVIL written on the cabin wall.

"It's just a story," Isla reminds everyone. "And if we don't hurry, we're going to be late. We have to hide in our spots and prepare before the campers are released."

"Released?" I follow Isla out of the bathroom as Mia and Josie duck behind the stalls to change into their costumes.

"It's kind of like one big scavenger hunt," Isla explains, the gravel crunching underneath her feet.

The moon has already begun to show in the night sky. I squint up at it.

"The campers are given clues to follow, which leads them to the spots all the counselors are hiding. The campers have to be quiet and sneaky, otherwise we pop out and scare them.

Some characters are supposed to trail them anyway, like the Wanderer, who I anticipate will be played by one of the older guys' counselors. The Wanderer is a man who got lost hiking at Camp Swallowtail and died here. He wanders the grounds, looking for a way out. When he sees someone, he follows them, in hopes of taking their place and leaving them trapped here, for all eternity." She says the last part extra dramatically, wiggling her fingers ominously.

I force a laugh. "A lot of people die here according to these stories."

"Makes for a scarier Fright Night."

People do a lot here for the sake of tradition. Asher spoke up about the ghost story from 1996, even when Dad tried to shut him down. Counselors whisper amongst each other when things change. Isla is willing to participate in something she would usually find dumb as long as it is a part of Camp Swallowtail.

Another thing that I've been noticing is that maybe there really is something ghostly about this place. No one has mentioned the graffiti on the Hawkmoth Haven wall, to my knowledge. Is that the sort of thing that just happens around here?

Isla and I meet up with the other counselors behind the Great Hall, where campers won't see us. I hardly recognize anyone in their costumes, but plenty of people compliment mine. I feel like I'm at a Halloween party, where all the bullies in your class are nice just because they can't tell who you are. That thought alone calms my nerves.

Mom and Dad are dressed up, which only partly surprises me as much as the fact that they let Fright Night continue. As reverent as they are for ghosts, they sure know how to go all out with this kind of thing.

Mom is wearing a ghostly white ball gown with rubies and onyx decorating the waistline. The bodice almost resembles a skull. Her gloves are blood red and tipped with more onyx pieces. Her blonde hair is woven back into a braid, threaded with more red and black stones. The kohl around her eyes makes the green pop.

Dad wears a tattered tux, complete with fake blood and claw marks, like a groom who got attacked by a werewolf on the way to his own wedding. Looking at their costumes together, I realize that they are intended to be a bride and groom.

Parents must have some kind of sixth sense, because they walk over and address me specifically, even though Isla is dressed exactly alike, and our features are covered by heavy black veils.

"Maeve," Dad says, smiling. "So happy to see you participating in Fright Night."

"Yeah." I let myself lean into the hug he offers. "To be honest, I'm really surprised you guys were okay with this."

"We don't like irreverence to ghosts," Mom says seriously. "But these stories aren't true, so it's all harmless fun!"

I want to ask if they think *most* ghost stories are true then, but decide not to when I see Hayes slip in quietly. He's so much like a ghost himself that no one notices as he walks by. My eyes follow him to the back of the crowd.

"We have to go and make the announcement that campers are allowed to be given their clues soon," Dad tells me. "I really hope you enjoy what we have planned for tonight, Maeve."

I nod distractedly. Hayes doesn't look dressed up, but nobody else seems to notice. It's possible that he doesn't like to participate in this kind of thing.

Dad and Mom leave and Isla glides over to Ginny. Quietly, I follow Hayes through the crowd, maneuvering around people and trying not to step on fabric trains

He sits down on a tree stump in a secluded spot, keeping to himself. He's so quiet, which strikes me as odd. Every time I've interacted with him, he's been joyful and full of light. Which seems like a strange thing for me to think about, considering that I hardly even know him.

I bite the inside of my cheek. *What am I doing here?*

"Hey there," I say, pushing back my veil so he can see my face.

He glances up, looking over me. I feel my cheeks flush. "A graveyard girl?"

I nod. "Yeah. Isla and I are. I'm not really sure about this whole thing."

"It's tradition." He raises a fist in the air, but his heart isn't in it.

"I noticed. Mind if I sit?"

He scoots over, giving me extra space so that we won't touch. I perch on the stump and listen to the counselors chatting excitedly with each other.

"You aren't participating?" I motion to his lack of costume. He appears to be bothered, judging from the way his brow is furrowed and his mouth forms a permanent frown.

"No. This tradition is stupid. Camp shouldn't be doing it at all. But it's everyone's *favorite* activity." His voice drips with sarcasm, frustration.

I frown, watching him curiously. A cheer erupts from the group of people in front of us as more members join the fray. "Is there always this much excitement?"

He glance at my hands, which are folded across my lap. "Every year. But it feels wrong. It's like they invite in more than just the ghost stories."

I tilt my head. "What do you mean by that?"

"Did they tell you that no one plays Cora during Fright Night?"

I nod. *Why is he acting so strange?*

"Did they tell you why?"

I shake my slowly, keeping my eyes on him. "Only that things...happened."

"Right." He rolls his eyes. "Things 'happened'. Of course that's all they said."

"I don't...What are you saying?"

"There's something about Fright Night that never sits well with me, Maeve." His eyes lock with mine and I feel my stomach clench. "Never has. Even when I was little and all the other campers were enjoying it, I always thought that the whole thing was so *wrong*. Weird things would happen and it would just be blamed on Fright Night. But when people started to play Cora a few years ago, they couldn't just explain away the happenings.

"Kids went missing for hours. When they were found, they would sob to the counselors about the horrible things they'd seen until the camp directors let them talk to their parents. Obviously, the parents didn't believe anything here was haunted. Why would it be? Fright Night isn't real; it's all make-believe. Parents just assumed the kids were having some sort of homesick meltdown. But when Cora's character came around, everything changed. Everything felt more real." His expression grows dark. "So, they decided that no one would play Cora. It's better that way. For everyone."

My skin is prickly with goosebumps. I fiddle with the edges of my veil, trying to find some little tedious tasks that will still my racing heart. I don't like the way he said "everyone" as if there was some larger entity at play.

"Do you believe she really died here?" My voice comes out timid. I'm surprised Hayes is acting so serious about this—it doesn't seem like an emotion he usually wears.

It scares me a little bit.

He tightly grips the tree stump, and I watch his knuckles turn white under the soft glow of the moon. "You better get back to the group."

I bite my bottom lip. All I do is seem to ask all the wrong questions. My head is asking me to push, but Hayes' face is telling me not to. His lips are pursed and his eyes flit back and forth between the rest of the counselors and me. Is it just my imagination, or do I spy a flash of something like regret in those hazel depths?

Quietly, I rise and follow the path back to Isla and my parents, reeling over everything Hayes said.

Everyone here seems to know something that I don't. The longing of wanting to be included, to *know*, overwhelms me. I don't feel like I can make these connections I'd just warmed up to making if everyone refuses to let me in on the secret side of Camp Swallowtail. Frustration runs hot throughout my body.

Isla greets me by pulling down my veil. "Get into character, Maeve! We're about to start."

There's so much I want to tell her at this moment. It bubbles up inside of me. I want to tell her what Hayes said and what Addie told me about seeing things. I want to tell her that I saw a ghost here when I was seven. I want to tell her as much as I can possibly fit into these next few minutes. Something in the air tells me things are about to change. That something's coming. And I can't tell if it's my overactive imagination or intuition or what. All I know is that Hayes had to be right.

Fright Night is more than a game.

The second I open my mouth to tell Isla, my parents usher everyone around and I know I've lost my chance. For tonight, I have to put my fears to the side and be a graveyard girl, haunting the camp with her twin sister in their identical black veils.

"Okay, counselors!" Dad raises his arms to get everyone to quiet down. He stands on a chair, towering over everyone. Discreetly, I glance back at the stump where I had just been, but Hayes is gone.

Where did he go?

"We are about to begin this summer's Fright Night. You've all been assigned your characters and costumes. Any missing pieces of costumes can be found in the skit closet inside the Great Hall but let Winnie or I know. We don't want any campers to see you in costume before Fright Night begins."

Mom holds up a stack of little envelopes. "Here we have your locations. This is where you will be hiding and protecting the clues that the campers are trying to find. Inside, we've also given you a short story about your character. If you don't know the story behind them or have forgotten little details, this information will help you stay in character, making it more fun for everyone." She passes out the envelopes to each counselor.

"While Winnie does that," Dad continues, "I'll inform you of the rules. Yes, tonight is meant to be spooky and scary. But there is no need to traumatize campers. We want them to enjoy tonight, not go home because they feel like they're going to be murdered."

A few of the guys jokingly groan in annoyance.

Dad rolls his eyes. "If you are partnered with someone, like the graveyard girls," he motions to Isla and me, "stay with your partner. There is no need to wander off."

"Also," Mom chimes in, passing out the final envelope. "Don't puppy-guard the clues. Yes, it's okay to scare the campers, but you also need to let them complete the game. If they are traipsing like elephants through your area, stop them. But if it's clear they are trying to be quiet and sneaky, just let them go."

The excited chatter begins to rise again, like a living, breathing thing, but Dad claps his hands and gets a wild look in his eyes. "Who's ready for Fright Night?"

Not me.

something in the dark
June 12

Isla and I sit in the graveyard behind camp.

The world is quiet around us—almost *too* quiet. I feel like prey, being stalked by a monster that feeds off sound, but it's all in my head. Isla looks unbothered, but I remind myself that it's because this isn't her first Fright Night rodeo. I'm like those poor new campers, thinking this all feels far too real.

Every creak of wood or crunch of leaves has me bolting upright. Dressed in this costume, I should be the scariest thing in this graveyard. So why do I feel like that's not true?

"Hey." I look at Isla. "There's something about Addie that I think I should tell you."

Isla pulls up her veil, looking taken aback. Little blonde strands of hair curl around her face. "Is everything okay? Did she talk to you about something?"

I nod, adjusting my veil away from my face. "It's about something Madysen said to her."

"Oh wonderful."

"Addie says she talks to herself sometimes? I haven't really noticed it, but I was wondering if you had?"

Isla glances up as if she's trying to remember something. "Yes, actually...I've noticed that a couple of times, but I never thought anything of it."

"Well, Madysen is telling the other girls that Addie is seeing ghosts." The words are out before I can change my mind.

They hit home a little too closely.

There's a rustle of leaves when Isla kicks her foot across them in annoyance.

"That's ridiculous. Thanks for telling me. I'll handle that. Did she say anything else?"

"She's calling her Cole from the old movie—"

"The Sixth Sense," Isla finishes, shaking her head, a frustrated look painted across her face. "That's so mean. I will be having a conversation with her, for sure."

When I open my mouth, Isla adds, "Don't worry. I'll be sure to keep you and Addie out of it. I know that the worst thing is when you confide in someone, and they confront the bully, only to make the situation so much worse than it was before."

The tension in my shoulders eases. "Thanks, Isla. I wasn't sure what to do."

There's a snap of a twig and I jump.

"It's just a game, Maeve," Isla says quietly. "Let yourself relax."

I appreciate the words of comfort she's attempting to offer me. But they don't do anything when the sound of crashing footsteps reaches my ears. My skin prickles with goosebumps and a cabin of middle school boys comes into view, loud and reckless. They freeze when they see Isla and me, clad in black gowns and thick veils, standing by headstones like we etched them ourselves. I feel Isla's excitement beside me, ready to play the part of a melancholy graveyard girl. She tilts her head stiffly toward the boys, their eyes widening with genuine fear.

Flaring up inside me is the feeling that *this isn't right*, like Hayes mentioned.

"Guys, freeze!" hisses one of the boys. I recognize him from Quinton and Walker's cabin, Diamondback Den. The boys tread lightly on the sticks and dead leaves, approaching us quietly in hopes of getting the clue.

The clue is written in Dad's heavy scrawl on a folded piece of paper which resides in my sweaty palm. There are nine identical slips—one for each cabin.

"Who goes there?" drawls Isla, in a whispered, high voice. She reaches out her hand like it's caught on a puppet string. Watching her performance is bone chilling—she truly looks like a jerky marionette. "What do you want from us?"

Isla tilts her head ever so slightly toward me, encouraging me to play along. Before the boys respond, I mimic her body language and try to channel the sound of a ghost in my voice.

"Have you come to offer your souls?" my voice cracks on the last word, but it doesn't take away from the scary effect. I flex my fingers like claws for good measure.

The boys huddle closer to each other which is almost enough to make me smile. But then I feel sick for enjoying this, even a little.

"Don't let them fool you!" spits one of the boys. He straightens up and puffs out his chest a bit, trying to appear unflustered. "They do this every year. These are counselors, not *ghosts*."

I can almost see Isla smirking behind her veil. She walks with such grace that it's almost like she's floating, stopping only when she's five inches away from the boy. He cowers underneath her stare.

"Hey, it's Winnie and George's daughter," says one of the boys, squinting at me.

My fingers still. My palms begin to sweat.

"Are you as much of a killjoy as your parents?" demands another boy, one with a deep voice. "Our counselor says that Camp Swallowtail has never had a family as terrible as you. He told us there are rumors about your parents."

"Probably rumors about you too," sniffs the first boy. "Quinton says you're kind of freaky. Dude," he elbows one of his friends.

"What if she's, like, possessed or something since her parents *actually* believe in ghosts?" another one asks.

I stiffen, ignoring Isla's surprised gasp beside me.

Quinton said that?

All of a sudden, the boy reaches out and snatches the envelope of clues from my hand. The boys of Diamondback Den sprint off, back to the camp. The other boys in Diamondback Den follow, cackling like lunatics, so proud that they outsmarted two ghosts.

I throw my veil to the ground. "I'm going after them." My blood boils.

Isla throws her veil back and looks at me incredulously. "Maeve, no! Yes, they were jerks, but it's not worth it."

"I'm so sick and tired of everyone acting like they're better than me!" My hands ball into fists.

Isla reaches out, but I shake her off. "Maeve, seriously, crazy things can happen on Fright Night, please don't go."

I ignore her and bolt after the boys.

Wind whips through the trees, casting shadows that reach out to grab me. I pant, trying to catch my breath, but fear grips my senses tightly, close-fisted. Darkness creeps along my vision and I'm lost in the forest, alone.

I don't know these woods. I don't know how to get out.

Maybe Isla was right. Maybe I shouldn't have run off. But the anger in the moment was so hot and so righteous. I can't believe Quinton would go behind my back and trash talk me *to his campers!*

I spin around. Cold air coats my skin and sinks sharp teeth into my bones. Unnatural cold, unsolicited cold, for a Texas night in June. It's like January, bitter and harsh and horrible.

I shouldn't have run. I don't know these woods.

I don't know how to get out.

"Isla!" I scream, panic seeping in. My heart is racing with my pulse, running circles around my paralyzed legs. *"Isla!"*

I whirl around in a circle, but the only thing I can see are trees and headstones and trees and headstones and trees and headstones. Overhead, clouds slowly dance in front of the moon, covering my last pinprick of light until I'm drowning in darkness and the only thing I can see is a memory.

Little Maeve stands in front of me, curly hair wild, big green eyes stretched wide with fear as she opens her mouth wordlessly and points at something in front of her. Something no one else can see.

Little Maeve falls to her knees and squeezes her eyes shut, clamping her hands down on her ears and screaming soundless screams.

No one can hear her. She's lost. She's alone. She's surrounded by ghosts.

I'm lost. But all of a sudden, I feel like I'm not alone. There's something *here*. In the woods. It's with me. And it's *not* human.

Ghosts.

I spin around in a circle again, trying to find them. They're here. I feel them.

"Hello again, Maeve Everbrill. I'm so glad you came to my side of the forest..."

I scream, gripping the fabric of my dress and whirl around.

Standing there, staring at me with large, unblinking eyes, is the girl I saw at the pool one of the first days I was at Camp Swallowtail. The air is frigid and I shudder, but the girl stands there in her flowy nightgown and twin braids. Her head is tilted to one side and her horrid mouth is gaping open, like a snake that's ready to snatch me up and gobble me whole.

"Wh—what do you want with m—me?" I whisper, backing away slowly.

Her expression doesn't change, but she does raise one hand. *"I thought you might like to meet some of my friends."*

The air gets even colder. I'm surrounded by this faint, strange humming that fills up the space and makes my brain foggy. I can hardly remember where I am, why I'm there, or even *who* I am.

Dancing in front of me are two girls dressed in black veils. They spin and sway, twirling each other around me. One of them reaches out a frail hand toward me and I see that her skin is tainted with black.

I scramble away, falling to the floor, only to be jumped by another ghost—the Lavender Lady. She cries purple tears that burn down her face like acid. And then there's the Scarecrow and the Weeping Woman and all the other ghosts, around me, dancing, enjoying themselves while frightening me. I tear up the grass below me with my fingers, desperately needing to clutch onto *something*.

"This is my friend, Maeve," the little ghost girl gestures to me. All of the other ghosts jerk their heads to look at me, stopping the dance.

My heart pounds.

Slowly, all of the ghosts approach me slowly. There's no more sound save for the howling wind ripping through the trees, ripping through my skin, ripping through my bones.

Ripping through me.

The closer they come the more panicked I become. *How can I get out of this?*

My brain flashes to the name of the girl I'd been calling for help. *Isla!* Yes—that's right! My co-counselor! *Surely she's nearby. She has to be.*

"ISLA!" My voice tears at my throat.

Suddenly, all the ghosts loom over me and I sink into the ground until I'm flat on my back, shaking shaking shaking shaking...

All of their eyes become empty, soulless, dark, and they eat away at me until I feel absolutely hopeless. My lips feel like numb, foolish things as I try to form Isla's name again with them, but they can't do it. All that I can emit are short little sobs as tears pour down my face, blurring the ghosts in front of me.

They don't go away. They twitch and reach toward me with distorted, mangled fingers with long nails that could probably tear out my heart.

Finally, another scream rips its way from my mouth, and I close my eyes, accepting the fact that this is where I die.

But when I open them again, only one ghost is left.

"Who are you?" I whisper to the little girl, slowly picking myself up off the ground. My hands are clammy, and my knees knock together a little bit.

"You know me," she says. She takes a step forward.

I whirl around wildly, looking for any sign of the other ghosts.

The little girl laughs. *"They aren't real."*

I grip the fabric of my black dress. "What do you mean they aren't real? They were right here a second ago! I *saw* them!" My voice goes shrilly.

I feel like I'm going crazy. *I don't believe in ghosts.*

The little girl's eyes light up with a sick kind of glee.

"One of my favorite things about ghosts is that we're able to use powers that are mostly closely tied with the emotions we harbor in death." She holds out both of her hands, palms up. She raises her left. *"Bitterness, anger, call it what you want."*

I swallow.

She holds up the right palm and takes a step closer, until she's right in front of me. *"Do you know what the strongest emotion I've harbored is?"*

I shake my head. I can't bring myself to speak.

Her dark hole of a mouth seems to grow darker. She pauses for a second and suddenly, a cloud of dark butterflies emerges from her mouth. I scramble back again and swat them away.

"Madness," she whispers gleefully. *"I'm able to create illusions, hallucinations, if you will, that make you see the things I want you to see."*

"No," I choke. "That's...that's impossible."

The girl smiles. *"You don't know who I am, do you?"*

She doesn't wait for an answer. Instead, she reaches out one finger to catch a butterfly. Its delicate wings tremble as she brings it close to her face. My brain can't make sense of how she's touching it if it's not actually real.

"Swallowtail butterflies are some of the most deadly known to mankind." She tilts her head. *"And they aren't particularly native to this area. Don't you think it's strange that Bo and Abigail would name their camp after something so dangerous?"*

"Maeve?" Isla's voice pierces through the forest, sending me a shudder of relief. The girl shoots a sharp glance over her shoulder and narrows her eyes at me.

"Isla, I'm over here!" I croak.

"She won't find you," hisses the girl.

"Maeve?" I hear another voice, a familiar one. *"Mom?"* I scream.

At the sound of that word, the girl's eyes stretch wide and with a shriek she vanishes, leaving me alone, cold, and terrified.

When Mom and Dad find me, I can't even speak.

I numbly watch them exchange glances. Mom says, "Let's go make some tea."

fog on the mirror
June 12

Smoke from the tea curls up into the air and I trace the amorphous shape with my eyes, wrapping my fingers around the steaming mug and breathing in the blanket of warmth. It's such a stark contrast from the biting cold I felt only a little while ago, but it coats my skin in the feeling of summer —warm and welcoming.

Safe.

Mom and Dad haven't said much to me, a thing for which I'm grateful. My mouth still fumbles around words, though my heart aches to open up and tell them that I think something is wrong with this place. But deep down, there's a darker secret, something that feels like a little monster, trying to worm its way out of me, with claws that tear into my insides.

The table is made of smooth wood that I focus on, trying to center my thoughts instead of allowing them to fly free like wild swallowtail butterflies.

"We need to talk." Dad rests a hand on my arm. "I know you're scared, but you have to tell us what happened."

"What you saw," Mom corrects, shooting me a meaningful glance.

I jerk my head up and narrow my eyes. "What are you saying?"

They exchange glances. I gulp down a mouthful of tea and burn my tongue.

The stinging on my tongue reminds me of what's real.

"There's something going on here that's bigger than us," Mom says gently. "And your dad and I don't fully understand it. But we want you to know that we're here for you if anything happens or if you ever need to talk. We love you, Maeve."

My expression softens and my gaze falls to my green tea. It reminds me so much of my childhood.

While some kids get Gatorade when they're sick, my mom always made me green tea. I've loved it forever and it feels like home.

The thing is, despite everything I've thought about them, I know that they love me. Even with all of the oddities, that has never been something that's in question. They've shown me in ways that might be a little more unorthodox, but I never worried that to them I was a mistake or something they didn't really want.

Maybe it's the fear still lodged inside of my heart or the way my eyes are growing heavy with exhaustion, but for a moment, my mind clears of all the reasons why I've ever disliked my parents. I blink and see them as normal people, pursuing interests and trying to raise me in a way they genuinely think is for my good.

I blink and they're just my parents.

I drop the tea to the table, liquid sloshing over the edge, and run into their arms, clutching them tight and trying to show them that I do care about them. I'm trying to show them that I need them right now.

When I pull away, they look at me with expressions I can't exactly discern.

"I should go and get back to Misty Monarch," I say. I take one more sip of scorching tea. "Thank you, guys."

"Your cabin should be asleep by now," Dad says.

My eyebrows shoot up. "What time is it?"

"Midnight." Dad cringes. "You were zoned out for quite a while."

I bite the inside of my cheek, thinking back to everything that happened, and nod. I want to do my best to block all of that from my memory. I'm grateful Mom and Dad didn't make me talk about it once I was so clearly uncomfortable.

"You'll be okay walking by yourself?" Mom's eyebrows draw together.

I nod seriously, even though goosebumps prickle my arms at the idea of a certain little girl following me all the way to the bathroom and then my cabin with dead eyes.

They watch me leave and the night instantly feels cooler, but not the same way the air felt frigid during Fright Night. I glance up at the sky and suddenly see all of the Camp Swallowtail stars.

"Beautiful," I whisper.

I glance up at them occasionally as I trek to the bathroom, wincing a little when I see lights on and hear voices pouring from the open door. I hope no counselors will ask me about what happened. Isla's no gossip, but news like that only takes minutes to fly through a place like this. Hesitantly, I take a step inside and then make a beeline for the rack that holds all my shower supplies.

A speaker plays some sort of alternative band and one of the counselors sings over the sound of running water. I scan the shower curtains for a stall that looks empty and set up my shower supplies, draping my fluffy green towel over the hook on the wall.

I turn the shower handle and let the water warm up while I strip, so far not hearing any talk about the horrible goings-on of Fright Night. I test the water and grab my shampoo, conditioner, body wash, and razor and let the warm water wash away all of the bad memories from my skin.

I'm drying off, wrapped in my fluffy towel when I hear Isla's voice, a little breathless, as though she just ran to the bathroom.

"Josie, have you seen Maeve?" she asks.

Josie's voice calls out from the shower next to mine. "No! Is she okay after what happened?"

I stand there, dripping wet and wrapped in my towel. I'm practically holding my breath.

What will Isla say about me?

There's a shuffle and I clutch my towel tighter around me when I watch Isla's feet stand walk past my curtain. She pauses by the wall and then slinks down to the floor. I can see her fold her legs up to her chest and her beat up Birkenstocks and painted toenails.

"I'm really worried about her," Isla admits. "I feel so horrible just letting her run off. Who knows what sort of thing she saw in the woods? Not to mention the fact that stories like this always get out and people are bound to make fun of her for it, the way they always make fun of her parents."

"You can't blame us for the parents, Isla," argues a voice I recognize to be Hannah. "They are certifiably insane."

There's the shutting off of water beside me. Josie.

"Stop saying stuff like that, Han," she retorts. "Winnie and George have been nothing but kind to all of us. The same goes for Maeve."

A startled little sound escapes my lips. No one seems to notice.

"I just want this to be a good experience for her," Isla sighs. "And so many things keep going wrong. I'm doing my best to try and be positive, help her look on the bright side and see what a great opportunity this place can be, but..."

"Things keep coming up," finishes Josie. She throws open her curtain and I watch her sit down beside Isla. "We should do something that would cheer her up or make her feel like she belongs," suggests another girl. I think it's Aislinn. "What if we invite her to do something with us on our off weekend?"

The last shower shuts off. I hear Mia, Josie's co. "I think that's a great idea."

"It could be so much fun," adds Zoe.

"I think that's a great idea, guys!" Isla's voice lifts.

She stands up with Josie not far behind. "We'll definitely have to talk about it and I'll float it by Maeve when I see her."

Her voice grows worried at the end, but then Josie says, "I'm sure she's just with George and Winnie. She'll be okay."

As they all walk out of the bathroom together, I think to myself *I'll be okay*.

I gather up all of my things, then slip on my sleep shorts and an oversized t-shirt. I scrunch up my wet curls and run my fingers through them, coated with product. It's a little unnerving to be in this bathroom by myself, but I feel warm and safe when I think about the reassuring words the girls were saying about me.

It's such a weird experience to hear people talking about you. When it's negative, it feels like receiving a punch to the gut. I blink and remember how it felt when I overheard Quinny telling Hazel and Jolie that I didn't deserve the captain spot.

I blink again and wonder about the difference of being talked about in a complimentary and compassionate sense.

I pop out my contacts and slide my glasses up my nose. I weave the wet strands of my hair back into a braid, hoping it'll result in nice curls when morning comes.

"You'll be okay," I tell the girl in the mirror, wiping away the foggy surface. "It might not seem like it after tonight, but you will be."

You'll be okay.

combative contentment
June 20

If I thought ghosts were bad, someone should have warned me about Panel.

I'm drumming my fingers anxiously on the picnic table outside, underneath the overcast sky, while Isla reads me the expectations and possible questions I'll be asked. My brain feels like it's running a mile a minute, which, after a whole week of pushing aside all my difficult thoughts, is like trudging through sand.

"Maeve." Isla slaps my fingers. "Are you even listening?"

My parents have chosen an unbelievable topic for me to cover: contentment. Which feels like playing dirty, especially considering some of the questions Isla's been floating by me. Standing up in front of campers and giving advice on how to be content, which is the very opposite of what I've spent my life being, wasn't exactly on my bingo card for this summer.

Sighing, Isla checks her watch. "It starts in ten minutes and we need to get the girls from arts and crafts. Do you want to stay here and look over the sheet one more time?"

Hesitantly, I nod and take the paper from her. As she leaves, I scan over the words and try to absorb every bit of them so that I can be prepared for anything the campers have to ask me.

How do you be content when you struggle with jealousy?

What things do you tell yourself when you are feeling discontent?

If only I knew.

I glance up when Hayes slides across from me and squints down at the paper. The bill of his hat casts a shadow on the table.

"Summer school?" he asks.

I smirk. "Rude of you to think I need summer school. I'm an A plus student."

He raises his eyebrows. "Didn't peg you for an egghead. Color me surprised."

That makes me snort. "I'm far from an egghead."

"I thought you were an athlete."

"Who says you can't be athletic and smart?"

"Every high school movie ever."

"Have you never seen *High School Musical*?" I demand. "The whole idea is that you can break through high school stereotypes and be more than one thing."

He gives me a weird look.

My eyes go big. "You haven't heard of *High School Musical*? What rock are you living under?"

Hayes looks away. "One that exists at Camp Swallowtail."

He must be like Isla and under the impression that life is worthless outside of camp. I might be working to still feel completely comfortable here, but that doesn't mean I think this place is heaven on earth.

"Maeve!" Mom pokes her head out of the Great Hall, attached to the dining area. "It's almost time for Panel. Where's Isla?"

"She's getting the girls. She left me the sheet to look over. I'll be in in a second."

She nods at me and slips back into the building. I let my gaze follow her through the glass doors, where I see most of the cabins already sitting.

"Coming in?" I jerk my head toward the door.

Hayes shakes his head. "I have some maintenance stuff to get done."

"That's too bad." I smile at him. "Could've seen me give adolescents advice on a topic I know absolutely nothing about."

He grins at me. "Contentment? Honestly, just spit out some nonsense that sounds clever and talk a lot about self-reflection. It'll get the job done."

"Thanks for the tip." I stand up and smooth out my dark green shorts. "See you later?"

He nods with a small smile. "Best of luck. You'll kill it."

"Let's hope!" I pump my fist in the air and let his smile fill my stomach with warmth. I turn away but when I get to the door of the Great Hall, I peek over my shoulder and see him still sitting on the bench, watching me. Our eyes meet and I feel my cheeks flush.

Do I like him?

No way I'm falling for a *camp* guy.

I shake myself a little bit and step into the Great Hall, buzzing with noise. Most of the counselors have already taken their seats on the stage, in chairs all lined up in a row. There are two open ones left; one for Isla and one for me. Quickly, I walk through the crowd of campers sitting on the floor in front of the stage, backpacks and water bottles strewn about and take a seat beside Josie.

"Where's Isla?" she whispers to me, twisting a short strand of brown hair around her fingertip.

"Just ran to get the girls. There she is!" I point towards the door where Isla is racing in, with the Misty Monarch girls in tow.

Breathless, she takes her place beside me. "That was a disaster."

"What's wrong?" I whisper.

"Madysen was having a cow about not having enough time to do her hair before seeing some guy from Atlas Arbor."

"Gross."

"Amen, sister."

A hush falls over the campers when Mom and Dad walk on the stage. Dad holds a microphone in his hand and taps the top, shooting a quick look to the sound guy in the back.

"Welcome to Panel!" Dad says. "We're so glad all of you are here to participate in this Camp Swallowtail tradition, counselors and campers alike."

"Not like we had a choice," mumbles Jacob, sitting a few chairs down.

Dad shoots him a pointed look. Jacob shuts up. Mom reaches for the microphone. "We invite you all to find the freedom to ask these counselors anything pertaining to the specific topics that have been chosen for each one of them. We will have a session of time dedicated to each of these topics. Starting us off will be Aislinn from Caterpillar Corner. Aislinn will be talking to us about joy."

I lean over a look at Aislinn as she takes the mic from Mom. Her smile is radiant, and I think she is the perfect person they could've chosen to give advice on how to be joyful. For a little while, no one raises their hand to ask questions, which brings a few minutes of awkward silence. Eventually, the silence gets too stifling and Aislinn breaks the ice a little bit.

"I know how intimidating it can be to ask questions," she says honestly. "I felt the same way when I was a camper. But I want you to know that there's no such thing as a stupid question. Ask us anything and we truly will do our best to answer. I'm sure I speak for all of us up here when I say we've made a lot of mistakes and want to give you advice so you can avoid those things as you grow up."

I'm surprised when I find myself nodding along with the other counselors.

Her words of encouragement do the trick. Soon, campers of all ages are raising their hands and asking questions about how to be joyful and positive when things are hard at school. One girl asks how to find joy after she lost someone close to her.

Isla grips the edge of her seat tightly and focuses on the little girl with sad eyes.

Josiah, I think to myself. Tentatively, I rest my hand on hers. She looks at me, startled, but her face softens, and she flips her hand over to squeeze mine appreciatively.

I find myself enjoying Panel much more than I thought I would. I listen to the campers ask the counselors things about anxiety, dating, friendship, and honesty, taking mental notes and reflecting on all the ways I could let these things impact my own life. Each counselor seems so animated when they talk about the topics my parents assigned them, as if these are things they are truly passionate about.

Maybe there are. Maybe my parents somehow knew all the right topics to hand out. As if it was exactly what each of us needed.

Mom and Dad stand off to the side, smiling at us all.

How did they manage to get to know each of us so well?

Isla talks about pursuing dreams. "Camp is my dream," she tells the kids, smiling a nostalgic smile with a gleam in her eyes. "I've known for quite some time that working at a camp is the best fit for me, even though it won't give me the lifestyle that a lot of other people my age are working towards. And if business is your dream, go for it. But I would encourage you all to pursue the things that make you shine and make you smile instead of the things the world pushes you to do. Don't just sit in an office because it makes you rich.

Find the thing you love and go for it." She pauses. "Yes, there is an element of responsibility that comes with taking care of yourself and maybe someday, a family, but I believe that you will be more satisfied with a job you love instead of one you hate."

People applaud.

And then it's my turn.

I take the microphone, trying not to let anyone see how shaky my hand is. There are some moments of silence and my stomach clenches. What if no one asks me anything? What if I'm the only counselor who doesn't have any advice to give?

I know Hayes said it's okay to make up answers. But an icky feeling inside of me makes me feel like I should try and dig something real out of myself.

I look at my shoes—a pair of Birkenstocks. Shoes I wouldn't have worn around Quinny because they aren't part of the style she carefully cultivated for us. But I always liked them. I always found them to be so comfortable.

But maybe contentment is something I'm learning. And even though I might not have it all together, surely there are some elements of wisdom I can offer to these campers.

So, I force my gaze up and find a comfortable smile. Something must click because Addie shoots her hand up.

"How can you learn to be content with who you are and what life has given you?" Her lip trembles a little and I feel her question sink its teeth into my heart.

I glance at Isla and she gives me an encouraging smile.

Taking a deep breath, I lock eyes with Addie. The rest of the room almost fades away as I construct an outline of coherent thoughts to speak about.

I don't know why this matters so much to me, but it does.

I want to get this right.

"Contentment is easier said than done," I begin. My voice shakes a little. I clear my throat. "And I think it's one of those things people continue working on for a long, long time. I know I don't quite have it figured out yet, but I am learning."

Addie tilts her head.

I glance down at my shoes again and smile. "Contentment is like being able to wear your favorite pair of shoes because they're comfortable, not because they're cool or popular. It's being happy with the things you do have and not always about chasing what's next. I think you have to," I pause, searching for the word, "surround yourself with people that aren't always chasing. People who can just...*be.*"

Isla squeezes my free hand discreetly.

"Yeah," I finish, feeling slightly lame but also like my answer was a good one. "I think part of being content with the elements that you can't change is learning how to exist peacefully with them instead of always being combative." My eyes stray to my parents when I say those last words. They're holding each other and smiling at me, words written clearly across their faces.

We're so proud of you.

I take a deep breath, feeling a little bit like a hypocrite, and pass the mic on to someone else. Addie is smiling at me, and I know that she understands what I mean.

If what I said impacted one person, that's enough.

lavender latte
June 21

When Isla invited me to join the other girl counselors for a night out in the town, I told her I had to rummage through the boxes in my parents' lodge to find my party clothes. I have to admit, I wasn't thrilled about the idea of stuffing myself into some close-fitting outfit after spending weeks in sandals, shorts, and oversized t- shirts. I had no idea what the other girls would be wearing, but to my relief, Isla shook her head with a laugh.

"No, don't worry about it!" she exclaims. "Just wear whatever you feel comfortable in."

I raise an eyebrow. "I don't have to dress up?"

"Not if you don't want to."

"Well...what are *you* going to wear?"

She taps her finger on her chin and then rummages through her little plastic dresser. She pulls out a pair of denim shorts and a Yellowstone sweatshirt. "Probably these with my Birks. I'll throw on some more makeup and braid my hair or something."

"So, I can really wear whatever I want?"

A crease forms between her brows. "You're not used to this sort of thing, are you?"

I shake my head.

She smiles. "Seriously, there's no hidden agenda here. Wear whatever makes you happy. Don't stress about it—we wanted this to be a fun time for you. Whatever shoes make you happy, right?"

I grin. "Birkenstocks it is."

"Good pick."

The other staff members take over watching the girl campers tonight as they bring all their bedding into the Great Hall for an all-girls' camp sleepover. Isla and I ensure that everyone is settled before we head out for the night with the rest of the female counselors.

"Take photos!" Kiara tells me.

"Kiss boys!" teases Charlie.

"Or don't," grumbles Madysen. "As if Maeve could get any guys anyway."

"Hey, Isla?" I ask. "We said we weren't bringing back snacks for Madysen, right?"

Isla raises her eyebrow at Madysen. "We only bring back treats for good girls."

"Do I look like a pet to you? I don't care about 'treats' because I'm not six."

"I care about treats!" laughs Lena. "Bring me back some Sour Patch Kids!"

"I want chips!" adds Addie.

Madysen rolls her eyes.

Giggling, Isla and I scamper off to the girls' bathroom to get ready for our night out. She is singing a pop song, and I join in, feeling light and giddy. Most of the other girl counselors are already in the bathroom, playing a girl power playlist over the speaker. They sing and dance in front of the mirrors, getting ready and complimenting each other.

I can't help but compare the atmosphere to what it was like getting ready for events back at home, when we needed to curl our hair a specific way. It was less fun and way more work.

Before long, I'm clad in denim shorts and an oversized, striped button down shirt with short sleeves. I've let my curls go wild and am wearing my glasses, my hair pulled back by a thick green wrapped headband. I smile at myself in the mirror.

Is this what it's like to feel free?

"Maeve, hurry!" shouts Isla, waving like a lunatic. "We're pulling out soon!"

I smile at my reflection one more time and then sprint after her, grabbing my water bottle and backpack. Isla holds open the door to a blue Jeep, parked on the gravel road outside of the girls' bathroom.

"Whose car is this?" I slide into the passenger seat.

"Mine." She slips into the driver's seat. Josie, Aislinn, and Zoe smile at me from the backseat.

"Where's everybody else?" I look around for another vehicle. There's no way we would all fit in one—I just hadn't thought about the possibility of taking two.

"They went ahead with Hannah," Aislinn tells me. "But we're the cool group."

"Photo to document this amazing evening!" Isla holds up her phone.

I smile, happy butterflies dancing around my stomach. I don't remember the last time I was so excited about something.

Goosebumps prickle my skin and I glance at Isla's AC. Before I can ask about the temperature, she's saying, "Smile!"

My eyes dart up to the screen and I grin as she snaps the photo.

All of a sudden, my goosebumps go away. We barrel down the cobblestone path. Isla passes her phone back to Josie, who hits shuffle on a playlist. I think it's the same one we listened to in the bathroom because the speakers blast girl power anthems and soon, we're all singing at the top of our lungs.

We go past the Camp Swallowtail sign and down the streets of the town.

"What's first on the agenda?" I shout over the music.

"Coffee hopping!" Isla grins at me.

I laugh. "But it's already past dinner!"

"Who cares?" chimes in Zoe. "When coffee calls, I answer."

"Amen, sister." Aislinn offers her a high five.

It doesn't take us long to pull into the first coffee place, open still for crazy people like us. As I step out of the Jeep, I look around the town for the first time with new eyes. Instead of hating every square inch of it, I appreciate it for its quaint charm.

Aislinn holds the door open, and I'm immediately overwhelmed with the warm, toasty smell of coffee. Though I've always preferred tea, there's something about the smell of coffee that feels like being wrapped up in a warm blanket.

The woman at the counter has her brown hair pulled back into a tight ponytail. She smiles as we file into the space, Hannah's group not too far behind us. Judging by the bags they clutch in their hands, this isn't their first stop.

We trade greetings, though not all of them give me the nicest looks, but I'm okay with it because I enjoy my group. We stick with each other.

"Hey, y'all must be the Swallowtail counselors this summer!" the woman at the counter says cheerfully. "We've been wondering when we'd see you gals around here! Finally gave you the night off, huh?"

"Yes, ma'am!" Mia says cheerfully, pulling a purple wallet from her purse. "A vanilla latte, please?"

"Make that two!" adds Ginny, fishing around for her own wallet.

I clutch my backpack, grateful that I didn't forget my wallet. I squint at the menu, written on a chalkboard hanging about the woman's head. Not having ordered much coffee back at home, I'm uncertain what all of the terms mean. Who knew coffee had so many different names? I listen to what each of the girls get, trying to figure out if I know what any of the things are. A vanilla latte is the only thing that sounds familiar, because that's what Quinny usually gets. I tried it a couple of times, trying to like it, but it was far too sweet—I felt like I was drinking straight syrup. That said, black coffee isn't my cup of tea either.

Isla comes to the back of the line where I'm standing, holding an iced coffee that she stirs around with a paper straw.

"Whatcha getting?" she asks.

I tilt my head. "I'm not sure. I'm not much of a coffee drinker. All I know is that a vanilla latte is too sweet for me. Any recommendations?"

"Wanna try this? It's a lavender latte." She holds out the plastic cup.

"Won't that just taste like drinking a plant?"

She rolls her eyes. "Try it."

"Mm, okay." I take a sip and my eyes widen. "Whoa."

Her eyes go wide and she nods. "Good, huh?"

"I'm getting one of those."

Aislinn comes to the back of the line, clutching a brownie wrapped in brown paper. "I also recommend the dark chocolate brownies. Amber makes them and they are to die for."

"Coffee *hops*?" I shake my head dubiously. "No way I'll want anything after this. That latte is crazy good and that brownie looks heavenly."

Isla's grin grows wider. "You haven't even seen anything yet."

I order my lavender latte from Amber, the woman at the counter, and add a brownie.

"You won't regret that." She winks at me.

When she hands me the brownie, I bite into it almost instantly.

I don't regret it. Not one bit.

We pile back into Isla's Jeep and I'm feeling jittery with caffeine, but I can't stop sipping this latte. Zoe offers to let me try some of her white chocolate mocha, but I am hooked on my own. I do offer her a bit of my brownie as a thank you.

Hannah's group pulls away quickly and barrels down the street, windows down.

Josie sighs loudly. "Didn't realize they were too cool for us."

Isla smirks in the rearview mirror. "They only *think* they are."

"Where are we going next?" I ask in between bites of brownie.

Isla pulls out of the spot, only to jerk to a stop. Her face pales as the Jeep jostles unevenly. She exchanges a quick look with Josie and jumps out of the car.

"Is everything okay?" I unbuckle my seatbelt and slide out of the car, rushing to the other side where Isla is kneeling by her tire.

"Dang it!" she groans.

I kneel beside her in the gravel and gasp. Right beneath her tire is a collection of sharp nails. They don't look old or rusty and they couldn't have been there earlier. They almost look intentionally placed.

"I bet it was Hannah," Zoe says gravely. She stands right behind me, arms crossed over her chest, shaking her head scornfully.

"We don't know that." Isla drags a hand down her face in frustration.

I glance at Zoe and she nods at me, mouthing, *It was her.*

Personally, I could see it. But I don't say anything.

A bitterness tugs at my stomach. Our perfect evening has come to a crashing halt. Isla's tire is deflating by the second.

"Do you have a spare?" I ask hopefully.

She cringes and shakes her head. "No...my dad needed one a few months ago and I forgot to get another."

Perfect.

I blow out an irritated breath. Why would Hannah do such a thing? Surely she doesn't dislike us enough to ruin our time together. That's just so mean.

Josie plops down beside Isla. "We could call someone to see if we can get a fix?"

Isla shakes her head, shoulders slumping. "No one would get out here until the morning."

"Where are we supposed to stay?" An edge of panic creeps into my voice.

Aislinn looks around, spinning on her feet lightly. Her gaze lands on something and she taps Isla's shoulder and points.

"What about Hart Inn?" she asks, gesturing to a building just a few feet away. "Surely they've got a few open rooms."

Isla frowns but nods. "We could try it. I'm so sorry, guys." She lowers her head. "This night was supposed to be really fun."

"It has been fun!" Zoe throws her arm around Isla's shoulder. "We got coffee!"

"And brownies!" adds Aislinn.

"And girl power music!" Josie grins.

My bitterness falters. How can they be so positive about this? Our night is *ruined*.

But then, all of a sudden, Isla is smiling with them.

She shuts off her engine and grabs her stuff from the Jeep, gesturing for everyone to do the same.

"To the inn!" she says.

I stare at the three of them incredulously.

Aislinn smiles at me. "It's all part of the adventure!" I glance down at the plastic coffee cup in my hand and swirl the liquid around, watching it slosh against the edges. They're just so *okay* with this. Maybe I should be too?

Isla leads us toward a building, presumably the Hart Inn that Aislinn suggested a few moments ago. All of the girls carry their bags, talking and laughing loudly, swaying underneath the starry sky.

I watch them, working to take it all in.

Josie lags back and walks with me. "Is everything okay?"

I give a little dry laugh and turn my attention back to my coffee cup. "I just sort of feel like nothing bothers you guys. How do you do it?"

Josie stuffs her hands into her pockets. "No, stuff bothers us. I guess we just learned to let it roll off? There are too many good things and opportunities presented when things go "wrong" to feel upset about it all the time."

I look at her suspiciously. "So, you just let it go? Just like that?"

She smiles. "Just like that."

"Easier said than done I think."

Josie nods and chuckles. "It's easier to do here, when you're away from the world for a little while."

I nod. I believe that.

The windows of the building emit soft, yellow light that washes over us when Isla opens the front door. She holds it open as we file in and I look around the room. It looks like an old-fashioned lobby, with a roaring fireplace and dated rugs. There is a leather sofa and a coffee table. The walls are a deep red with antique lighting fixtures around the walls, resembling sconces. It's a weird sort of aesthetic but it feels homey all the same.

The room smells like honey and tea.

"Mrs. Hart?" Isla approaches a sweet looking woman at the front desk, a long wooden thing with a plate of cookies and a guestbook. The woman has gentle blue eyes and wrinkles lining her soft face. Her gray hair is woven into a braid—a long one that rests on her shoulder and trails down to her waist. This little detail makes me smile. I don't see many older women with long, gorgeous hair.

She's wearing a long nightgown with a fluffy blue robe belted at her waist.

"Can I help you ladies?" She smiles and folds her hands on the desk.

"Yes, please." Isla sets her bag down and pulls out her wallet. "We had a bit of car trouble and couldn't make it back to Camp Swallowtail this evening. We were wondering if you had any available rooms? Two should do it," she adds, glancing over and counting us.

"Camp Swallowtail?" Mrs. Hart's expression falls.

"Yes, ma'am," replies Isla, frowning a little. "We're counselors there this summer."

Quickly, she nods and puts on a smile. She rubs the back of her neck and turns around, pulling something out of a drawer. When she places it on the counter, I see that it's a thick book. She reveals a pen from another drawer and scans the open book in front of her.

"I believe we do have a few open rooms, if you would like to choose."

"Anything is fine with us. Thank you so much."

Mrs. Hart scribbles something in her book and then grabs two keys from the wall behind her, lined with pegs which are mostly vacant, but a few hold the remaining room keys. She passes them to Isla and says, "You may pay in the morning."

"Thank you, Mrs. Hart," I say, smiling at her.

She blinks and tilts her head when she meets my eyes. My smile fades. *Why is she looking at me like that?*

But before I can say anything, her smile is back. "Please, call me Elise."

insomnia
June 21-22

I'm tossing and turning for what feels like hours.

Beside me, Isla rolls over and groans a little bit in her sleep. It seems like she and Josie have had no trouble sleeping, but I have not been able to doze off at all.

I roll over on my side and stare at the wall. My brain won't shut off. Something about this place just *feels* strange, wrong even, to me. Maybe it's just my anxiety about leaving for volleyball camp in a few days. Maybe there's a part of me that is worried about what Quinny will say when she sees me.

Maybe I don't really want to go?

I sigh. Tonight, while not what I anticipated, was so much fun. Definitely more fun than I'd had with my friends back at home in ages. It was a simple evening but filled with carefree laughter that lifted my spirits in a way I didn't know I needed.

Quietly, I slide out of bed, cold air instantly wrapping around my bare legs. My giant t-shirt falls past my sleep shorts when I stand. I slip my feet into my Birkenstocks and grab my button down and throw it over my clothes—the same ones from earlier since we didn't anticipate staying the night.

I wonder if Elise has any cookies downstairs in the lobby at this hour. I could snack and bring a book, reading by lamplight down there so I wouldn't disturb anyone.

I close the door to my room behind me quietly and find the stairs. It's almost eerie how quiet everything is.

The fire is no longer going when I return to the lobby, my book clutched under my arm. The cookies have been left out on a plate, so I snag one and then curl up on the sofa, flicking on the lamp beside me.

I open my book.

"You're a bit young to be an insomniac, aren't you?" I jump and my book falls to the floor. Elise stands behind me in her robe, with an amused expression painted across her face.

"I-I'm sorry. I couldn't sleep," I stammer, hiding the cookie behind my back.

"You don't have to hide anything from me, child. Those cookies are left out all night for people like you."

"P-people like me?"

"The dreamers, the wanderers, the wide awake." She gives me a knowing look.

"No, I just couldn't sleep. I didn't want to wake my friends."

She nods. "Yes, yes, I understand. Would you like me to start the fire?"

I nearly protest but give in at her expectant expression. A fire *would* feel really nice.

As she walks over to the other side of the couch, kneeling towards the fire, I wrap my button-down around me tighter. I feel so sloppy, standing in front of this classy older woman in an oversized t-shirt with my hair thrown back in a bun and no makeup.

"Can I help you with that?" I ask her, pointing at the fireplace.

She raises an eyebrow. "Young lady, I may be advanced in years but am fully capable of starting a fire in my own inn."

"O-of course. I'm sorry."

She adds another log to the fire from the brass container to her left.

The silence feels awkward. I sit down on the couch and then feel weird because she's starting a fire for me, so I stand back up again. She turns around to look at me, so I quickly blurt out, "Do you work here alone?"

And then I bite my lip because what if that brings up bad memories?

Geez, Maeve.

The light does dim in her eyes a little bit and I feel like I might start crying in humiliation. But she shakes her head and says, "No. My husband, Thomas, works here with me. We opened this inn years ago when we decided this was the place we needed to live."

The fire roars to life and soon, the lobby is filled with warmth and a gentle campfire smell. I take a deep breath and find my mouth curving up into a smile. The flames crackle and dance while Elise gets to her feet and takes a seat in the chair diagonal from me. She crosses her legs and folds her hands in her lap.

I tug my button-down tighter and try for a smile. "Eat your cookie."

"Yes, ma'am." I take a bite and try to look nonchalant, but my eyes go wide because this is the best chocolate chip cookie I've ever eaten in my life.

"Oh my gosh," I say through a mouthful. "This is insane."

Elise chuckles. "You're not like the others."

I swallow, but the cookie tastes bitter now. "What makes you say that?"

The way she's looking at me makes my stomach clench. I hope she'll just say something that at least doesn't make me feel like I'm seeing things that normal people don't see.

Like ghosts.

"There's just something in your eyes that seems aged. Like you've been through things that most girls your age haven't."

"Isla's been through way more hurt than me," I protest, swallowing the last of the cookie. I dust my hands off on my legs. "I've never lost anyone the way she has."

"Maybe not," Elise agrees. "But you see things differently than she does."

I shake my head quickly. "I don't know what you're talking about." I reach for my book and start to stand up, but Elise keeps talking.

"I had a son and a daughter once."

I take a deep breath and look at her. "Once?"

Elise nods slowly. "Yes. I lost them both far too early in their lives."

Slowly, I sink back onto the couch, clutching my book to my chest. "H-how did you lose them?"

"Accidents just waiting to happen," she whispers, her eyes staring off to a place I can't see. "I suppose that's what most deaths are. One little thing goes wrong and brings on a domino effect. You catch a virus that you shouldn't have. You take a road you shouldn't have gone down. You trust someone you were better off staying away from."

I look down. I've never thought about death that way. To me, it has always been a monster or some kind of phantom, hovering over us until it decides we've had enough time on this planet.

"Accidents can't be avoided." My voice matches hers. "But I've heard that there are three ways to get over grief."

Elise laughs dryly. "Honey, you don't *get over* grief. You learn to live with it."

"What were their names? Your children?"

She shakes her head. "It doesn't matter now. But they went to Camp Swallowtail once, just like you."

My eyes go wide. "What?"

She laughs a little at my expression. "Child, every kid in town has gone to Camp Swallowtail at some point. But they loved it so much. That's why Thomas and I decided to stay here and start this business of ours." She gestures around the lobby and turns her gaze back to the fire. "We stayed for them."

"It must be really special," I say, at a loss for any other words that will make it better.

She studies me. "Camp Swallowtail *is* special. There's a lot that happens there that people don't understand."

When I open my mouth to ask, she waves her hand and stands up with a sigh. "I best be getting some sleep. It was nice chatting with you...What is your name, love?"

"Maeve." My grip on my book tightens. "Maeve Everbrill."

She purses her lips and closes her eyes briefly. Then she looks up at the ceiling, as if the universe is playing a trick on her and she can hardly believe it.

"Ah," she says. She walks away without another word, disappearing into a dark hallway, which I watch until I hear the shutting of a door.

I bring my knees up to my chest and rest my chin on them, arms wrapped tightly around myself as I stare at the raging fire.

But in my head, all I hear are her words.

Camp Swallowtail is special. There's a lot that happens there that people don't understand.

welcome home pt. 1
June 28

"Maeve!"

Quinny smothers me in a hug so tight I can hardly breathe. I clamp my mouth shut so as not to inhale the sharp notes of faux vanilla and spice. It's been so long since I've been around a cloud of heavy perfume.

"Quinny, hi," I say, when she's finally pulled back. "How are you?"

I try to find the old rhythm we used to swing to—the old way we used to talk. But something inside of me feels different. It's not something I can easily explain. Quinny looks like a stranger to me. Talking to her feels foreign.

"We've missed you *so* much!" She squeals. "You were really cutting it close, flying in on the day before camp starts! Especially with the dinner plans we have tonight."

I'd decided to stay at Camp Swallowtail longer than I'd intended, because the girls hadn't wanted me to leave. I'd found myself having such an amazing time over the last week that my lack of insistence to leave had surprised not only me, but also my parents.

"You don't have to go," Mom reminded me at dinner last night. "You can stay here. We've seen so much growth in you, Maeve. We really think you could be happy here."

A small, rebellious part of me wanted to go just to prove them wrong. I'd like to think I'm above pettiness like that, but in reality, I'm not. While my bitterness toward my parents has ebbed, it hasn't evaporated.

Maybe that's really why I'm here, I admit to myself.

Isla helped me pack when the girls were at rec. We folded my clothes neatly into the duffel bag I'd brought specifically for Volleyball Camp. As we prepared to zip up the bag, Isla stopped me.

"The girls made these for you." She rummaged through her backpack leaning against the wall and pulled out a fistful of friendship bracelets.

My wrists had been pretty bare up until this point, with only my green swim band and a limp, braided thing I attempted to create at the barn to offer any kind of decoration. I held out my wrist and watched Isla's slim fingers tie knots into the edges of the bracelets until a nice little row of them covered my wrists.

"Now you're really one of us." She backed up with a smile.

I admired the bracelets—the handiwork and time each one of our campers put into them.

"What are you hoping to get out of going back, Maeve?" Isla studied me. "Do you still regret coming here?"

No. I shook my head. "I don't regret it."

"Why are you going back?"

Isla pushes me. She keeps me accountable and asks me hard questions that no other friend has ever asked me. But instead of feeling repelled or annoyed, I find myself wanting to answer her hard questions, proving that I can. When she asks me these hard questions, I feel like she genuinely cares about me.

I hesitated, twisting the bracelets around my wrists. "I don't know. I guess I feel like I have to. To show my parents." I flushed.

"Go on. It's okay," Isla encouraged gently.

"I don't want them to think I'm just okay with all of their choices they spring on me. I want them to know that I do have a life and commitments. There are things I value and care about in my own life and it's not their right to just take it away from me when they feel like it."

"But do you wish they never moved you here?"

No. The word surprised me as it echoed through my head. I thought of Isla and her hard conversations, of Addie and her sweet, quiet spirit, of Hayes and the gentle protectiveness he offers me, even though I hardly knew him. I thought of all the other girls in our cabin and the small little things that make me care about them.

"I just need to do this," I told Isla. "I need to see which life I really belong to."

She nodded, like this is the answer she was searching for. A weight lifted off of me, knowing I answered her question honestly and correctly.

She hugged me before I left, standing by Mom's car. I'd be dropped off at the airport and meet Quinny there. She'd drive me to the gym where I'd meet up with Coach and the rest of the team.

Mom waited for me in the car while Isla hugged me once more. "The girls will be so sad they missed you," she says.

"Tell them bye for me."

"I will. And, Maeve?" She pulled back. "I really hope you find what you're looking for."

My lips turned up in a sad smile. What an interesting thing for her to say. "Me too."

She waved and left me standing by the car with my bags. Gripping the handle of the duffle bag, I lifted it to slide it into the rear end of Mom's van.

"I can help you."

I turned, seeing Hayes standing there, sunglasses covering his eyes.

"Where did you come from?" I asked, shielding my eyes with my hand, trying to block out the garish sun. I felt sweat beading on my forehead already.

"I do work here," he reminded me.

"I never see you working," I laughed.

He took my duffle bag and slid it into the car as I turned away to grab my backpack. "I heard you were leaving and wanted to say goodbye."

Joy blossomed through me like flowers on a spring day. "You did?"

"Is that so hard to believe?"

"I just haven't seen much of you lately."

He scratched the back of his neck. "Yeah, things have been crazy. But we're talking now, right?"

"Right." I smiled. "Look, I finally match the rest of you." I show off my bracelet clad wrists.

"Finally getting the hang of things." He smiled back.

For a moment, I thought he was about to hug me and it's embarrassing how hopeful I felt. I hated to be the kind of girl I always roll my eyes at in stories, who finds herself dreaming of the guy she hardly knows. But he stood there, sun shimmering off his tan skin with an almost transparent quality, with eyes that seem to light up when they look at me. His low voice, with the tiniest hint of a rasp. And he was amazing to me.

"I should let you get going." He reached up and shut the tailgate of the car. I tried to tamper down my disappointment.

"See you when you get back," he said, waving, watching me climb into the passenger seat.

"See you," I said.

I saw him glance toward the driver's side quickly. I followed his gaze and saw my mom, but was confused why that would draw his attention. When I turned back to him, he was gone.

Now, standing in the loud, chaotic airport with Quinny, I can hardly believe that was only a few hours ago. She ushers me out into the parking lot, where her shiny, expensive car sits, waiting for us. She leaves me to throw my bags into the back, fiddling with the AC and the music until I climb into the passenger's seat.

"Who sings this?" I look at Quinny, who has her aviators perched on her nose, humming the pop song that blasts on the radio as she pulls out of the airport.

Her jaw drops when she looks at me. "Girl, where have you *been* for the past month? This is only the most popular song on the charts right now!"

"I guess I haven't been keeping up with pop culture much," I laugh nervously. I guess now that I'm back, I have a lot to catch up on.

I whip out my phone and open Instagram (which I haven't done in weeks) and am instantly bombarded with posts and comments within seconds. I try to absorb it all so that I won't be so out of the loop when we get to dinner, but it's hard to make myself care about all of this.

"So, what's camp been like?" Quinny turns onto the freeway.

I conjure up an image of the last time I saw her— fighting before I left for camp. The normal way she's talking to me makes me think that argument is in the past and long forgotten, but if I know Quinny the way I know Quinny, there's no way this is over. I scan her face for any sign of an ulterior motive, then feel guilty. She drove here to come pick me up so I could participate in Volleyball Camp. I need to stop being so paranoid.

"It's been fine," I tell her. If I tell her I love it, she'll make fun of me. If I tell her I hate it, she'll try to find some way to get me to stay here, even if she wants my volleyball spot. "I have a cabin of freshman girls. The girl I'm co-counselors with is sweet."

"Oh?" Quinny says.

"Her name is Isla," I begin. "She's in college and I feel like I've learned a lot from her."

"Would I like her?"

I hesitate. *No, and she wouldn't like you much either.* "You guys are very different," I decide. "But I don't think that's any reason to dislike someone, you know?"

Quinny gives me a tight smile. "She sounds like a peach."

I slump in my seat a little and narrow my eyes, staring out the window.

Quinny continues to play songs from this artist I've never heard of. She knows the words to every single song. She jumps in with stories about Hazel, Jolie and her adventures this summer. She tells me about the parties they've gone to and the boys they've gone out with. She tells me about the lazy days spent at the pool, tanning and sipping strawberry lemonade.

"You're pretty tan, too, Maeve!" She raises her sunglasses. "Catching rays at the pool?"

My gaze falls to my skin. It has taken on a healthy, bronze glow that I hadn't even realized before she mentioned it.

"Something like that," I hold up my arms and flip them to check the difference. Definitely tan.

"Oh, those are kinda cute." Quinny keeps one hand on the wheel but reaches the other over to tap the bracelets adorning my wrists. "Gonna have to lose 'em for practice, though."

My stomach sinks at the thought of taking them off. I feel like I just became an official member of Camp Swallowtail, these being my badges of belonging.

"Not a big bracelet girl myself," Quinny continues, turning her attention back to the road. "I think it's because I used to wear so many when I was little that I associate them with being childish. Isn't it *so* weird how your brain just does stuff like that?"

"Yeah," I mumble. "Weird." I push away the sting. I wish Isla were here.

I step out of the bathroom in Quinny's house, dressed in denim shorts and an off-the-shoulder, loose fitting shirt. It's incredibly comfortable and the shade of blue sets off my tan and the different shades of sun-kissed highlights in my hair. I did subtle makeup and decided to wear my glasses because I feel cute when I wear them. I smile at my reflection.

That's a Maeve who knows how to be.

Quinny gives me a once over and claps a hand over her mouth.

Which isn't really necessary. As if her eyes didn't say enough.

I slide the hair scarf from my hair and take out the little crystal earrings I stole from Mom's jewelry collection.

"What are you wearing?" she shrieks. "Stop, stop, stop. Do you *want* people to think you sell drugs and crystals on the side of the road or something? *Geez*, Maeve you have been spending way too much time with camp people...and your parents." She smiles apologetically. "All I'm saying is that we are going to get you back to the way you were!"

She holds out her hand.

Quietly, I slide the glasses off my face and hand them to her.

"Ugh, these must go. I don't know why you're so intent on wearing them. You know that in all the movies the girls are only pretty when they take *off* their glasses."

When she snaps them in half, a little part of me snaps with them.

The pieces fall to the ground.

She smiles at me, encouragement written all over her features. She quickly grabs something from her closet and shoves me back into the bathroom. "I really am just trying to help you, Maeve. I want what's best for you. You know that."

"I know that," I repeat quietly. She closes the door.

I stare at the broken glasses on the floor, numb.

I look at my reflection again. Quinny's right...*what am I wearing?* I look ridiculous.

I feel ridiculous.

Without another glance in the mirror, I tear off my own clothes and throw them in a pile on the floor angrily. Then, I yank on whatever this tight, black outfit is that Quinny handed me. It makes me feel like I'm wearing a straitjacket, but this is who she wants me to be.

She's just trying to help me.

I stick contacts in my eyes. I slick my hair back with gel, taming the curls into a tight, high ponytail and then I grab gold earrings from the little dish by her sink.

When I walk out, she looks over me with a satisfied grin. "Much better."

the game
June 29

After changing into my black shorts and practice jersey, I stand in the locker room in front of the mirror, trying to tame my hair into a ponytail. Standing here with the light hitting my reflection, I feel like I'm back in the bathroom with Isla, moths fluttering overhead, except this bathroom is much nicer. I study my appearance, green eyes skeptical. Freckles have popped out across my nose from so much sun exposure and threads of golden-red weave throughout my hair, bleached by the summer. Even though I've gone most of the summer without wearing much makeup, I brought my makeup bag with me, knowing all the girls I'd be hanging out with would be reapplying lip gloss every ten minutes.

I reach for my mascara and concealer, but stop myself, and not because I'm heeding my parents' warning about chemicals. I kind of like the way I look without a whole face of makeup and at this point, I'm used to it. But I remember Quinny's reaction to my glasses last night and hesitate. But I hear Coach blow her whistle, so I don't apply the makeup anyway.

Coach has all the girls lined up beside the volleyball net. I feel their eyes follow me as I toss my backpack on the sidelines and line up beside Hazel.

"Welcome back, Everbrill," Coach directs at me. "Are you ready to get into it?"

I nod seriously, centering my focus on volleyball. "Yes, ma'am."

She blows her whistle. "Then let's get to work!"

It is instantly clear that a couple rounds of pool volleyball and a few nights playing by the light of the moon with Hayes were not enough to hold me over. It's lucky I'm gifted with some natural talent, otherwise I would be the laughingstock of the team. Unfortunately, I'm not the only one who notices my weakness.

Coach scowls as she watches me set the ball up loosely. I glance over at her with a grimace and catch Quinny's gaze. She smirks for a second, then dives toward the ball in an incredibly graceful move. I watch, irritated, as the ball soars over the net and smacks the floor on the opposite side, signaling a point for us if this were a real game.

I shake myself. Coach always said that a scrimmage *was* a real game.

I bend my legs and focus on the ball, adjusting my knee pads. All of those pathetic volleyball moments at camp need to clear out of my head right now. I've got a game to get into.

Suddenly, I'm overwhelmed with this determination. I have to prove myself.

To Coach. To Quinny.

To me.

If I do this right—if I give it my all, Mom and Dad have to let me stay here with Alivia.

I don't have time to mess around anymore.

I narrow my eyes and watch Jolie serve the ball over the net. A girl on the other team hits it to another girl, who sends it soaring over the net.

Hazel sets it up in my direction.

This is it.

I take a deep breath and rush over in perfect form, ready to spike it over the net. I catch air, ready to slam the ball down because I am *Maeve Everbrill, captain of the varsity volleyball team—*

I'm on cloud nine for just a few seconds, likely less than a few seconds, because just as the ball is about to make its descent, my hand gets tangled in the net.

When I fall to the ground, my face burns with shame. I can't even look at Coach. How many times has she told us *not to get our hands caught in the net?*

The whole gym seems silent, but I know it's just my imagination.

Coach angrily blows her whistle. "Go get water!"

Quinny saunters up to me and tightens her ponytail.

"It must be so frustrating to have worked so hard and then lost so much skill at that camp." She shakes her head sadly. "I suppose it can't be helped. But I would feel *terrible* if I were you."

I ignore her and slink over to the bench, my mind reeling. I collapse on the cold metal bench and fish around my bag for my water bottle. Before I can take a sip, Coach beckons me over with one dangerous finger.

Here we go.

I wish I could go back in time and show Coach that I am better than that. She knows I'm better than that. It isn't fair that all these other girls have had the whole summer to train, and I've been stranded in Nowheresville, Texas. Surely, she can't fault me too much.

But she props a hand on her hip and watches me as I sulk over.

"What is going on with you?" she demands.

I bite my lip. *I cannot cry in front of her.* "I'm doing my best—"

But I realize instantly that is the wrong thing to say.

Her face flames and in her eyes are everything unspoken that I still understand. She's given me a great honor by offering me this position *just like that* and here I am, acting like it doesn't matter.

Playing sloppy because I know I'm going to get it. At least that's how it seems to her.

I shake my head vehemently, trying to get her to understand. "Coach, I have been gone all month to a place where I am unable to practice. But I swear, if you keep believing in me and give me just another chance, I will wow you—I swear."

She laughs drily. "Wow me? That's a high bar to set, Everbrill."

I take a deep breath and stare her dead in the eyes. "It's one I can meet."

I have to do this.

She studies me and then sighs. After she blows her whistle, she narrows her eyes at me. "No fooling around, Everbrill. This spot can go away."

I nod. No fooling around.

I jump back into the game.

I don't play well. But I don't play as bad as I had before. It doesn't take too long for my body to get the swing of things and fall into the patterns of volleyball, something that once felt like second nature to me.

Just like old times, the rest of practice passes by in a blur, no thoughts in my mind except getting the ball and making Coach proud. My vision is fixed, like I'm wearing blinders.

I startle when Coach blows her whistle, half expecting her to reprimand me again. But she waves us all over and shouts, "We're done for the day! Tomorrow, come ready to work on drills. This was an easy day to get you girls back into what I expect of you. Don't expect tomorrow to be as easy." Her piercing blue eyes land on me and I flinch.

Everyone disperses toward the locker room. I moodily grab my gym bag and sling it over my shoulder, trudging over toward a stall.

I close the toilet lid and sit down, dropping my head into my hands. *What am I doing? I'm not fooling anybody—I don't belong here.*

But I have to, I tell myself fiercely, gripping the fly- away curls that dance across my forehead. I shuck off my shoes and my knee pads are soon to follow.

A couple other girls file into the locker room—I can tell by the sudden burst of giggling and tossing off of shoes.

"Is she in here?" Quinny's voice whispers.

It doesn't take a genius to guess what "she" Quinny refers to.

Quickly, I pull my feet up onto the toilet and hold my breath. I almost laugh when I realize I was in a similar situation a few weeks ago—with Isla and the girls at camp. I clamp a hand over my mouth, swallowing my laughter until it turns into bile because I know the conversation I'm about to overhear won't be quite as encouraging.

I squeeze my eyes shut. Do I even want to know? "Haven't seen her." I recognize Jolie's voice.

"I gotta show you guys something." There's the sound of rummaging around and then some shuffling. Underneath the stall, I watch a bunch of girls' feet crowd around Quinny's.

"I found this on Insta because Maeve was tagged in it. It's a photo of the new girls she's been hanging out with."

Confusion furrows my brow.

"Get a load of these weirdos," Quinny laughs. "No wonder she looked like a total hippie when we tried to go out to dinner last night!"

"What is in their hair?" asks Hazel disdainfully. "Are those beads? And thread? They look like total druggies."

I can't take it anymore. I throw open the stall door, angry tears pricking my eyes.

"Shut up, Quinny."

She stares at me incredulously and then barks a cold laugh. "What did you just say to me? You should be thankful for how I've helped you. You're so ungrateful, Maeve."

I grab my gym bag, shoes, and knee pads and sprint out of the locker room, tears pouring down my face— angry, hurt, lonely tears.

I don't even think about where I'm running...I just run. Because if I don't have this, what's left?

When I'm out of breath, I find a bench in one of the school hallways and collapse on it, drawing my knees up to my chest and holding on tight. Before I can fall into a pile of self-pity and hurt, my phone starts to ring.

It's Alivia. I answer. "Hello?" she asks.

"Alivia," I sob.

"Oh my gosh, what's wrong? I was just calling about the Sonic outing later today and if you still wanted to go. Did something happen?"

I wipe snot away with the back of my hand. "I can't stand her, but I can't stop wanting her approval at the same time. I hate it."

"Oh," Alivia makes a sympathetic noise. "She got you bad today, huh?"

I nod, forgetting she can't see me.

Alivia understands anyway. "Tell you what, why don't you take all your stuff from her house and just spend the rest of the week with me?"

"I don't have a car," I whimper. "I won't be able to get back and forth to the gym and I don't want you to have to drive me around."

"I work during your practice times, or I would offer, sorry! Catch a ride with Quinny on your way home if someone else can't take you," she says. "Pack up your stuff and have it ready in her car. I'll pick you up at Sonic."

"What if she sees?"

"Just be honest with her. That girl needs to know she doesn't rule the world."

"Easier said than done," I mumble.

Alivia hangs up and I hold myself into a little ball, leaning my cheek against my knee. Where did everything go so wrong? Quinny never used to call me out in front of the group before this summer—I was her right-hand man.

Being back here makes me feel like a puzzle piece that doesn't fit.

Angrily, I wipe away my tears.

I have to show her—I won't let her get under my skin.

I belong here. I do.

ocean water
June 29

"Ocean Water," I say when it's my turn to order. I toss a glance behind me, waiting for Alivia to show up. She told me she would be a little late, having just gotten off her shift, but I hoped it wouldn't be too much longer.

The car ride over was nearly stifling. Hazel, Jolie, and Quinny simply pretended like the fiasco in the locker room hadn't occurred, so I did the same, keeping to myself and blocking out their gossip-filled conversations.

Now, I step back and let Hazel, Jolie, and Quinny order behind me.

"Three cherry limeades," Quinny says.

I stare at her. "When did you stop getting the Ocean Water?" It's been our tradition forever.

Quinny says, nonchalantly, "We decided cherry limeades taste so much better. The Ocean Water feels young, you know?"

"Right, for sure." I curse myself for not letting them order first. I've never even tried a cherry limeade. Maybe it is the best thing on the menu.

The underclassmen don't help things; all the girls order cherry limeades, desperate to impress Quinny. I hate that they treat her like a goddess and am reminded of Madysen back at Camp Swallowtail. I noticed it more at the beginning of the summer, but something about girls like that creates this idea that to be liked by them, you can't be an individual. I'm quickly realizing the hold Quinny had on me and loathe myself for trying to climb back into that little hole.

The Ocean Water syrup hits my tongue. I force myself to swallow it down, hating the way it's suddenly so sickeningly sweet. The other girls chat and laugh like everything is so hilarious, slurping the slushies down. I watch them quietly, noticing the way Quinny bites on the top of her straw when she's listening to someone, her lips curving up into a smile as she does, knowing how cool it makes her look. More than one freshman girl tries to mimic this action, but it comes across as awkward.

"I'm here!" Alivia whirls over, dropping her stuff on the table beside me. Quickly, she rummages around for her wallet and peers at my drink. "What did you get?"

"Ocean Water," I mumble. "But I've heard the cherry limeades are better."

Alivia looks at me with knowing brown eyes. "Please. I'm here for a strawberry cheesecake milkshake."

I snort. "Ever a black sheep, huh?"

She grins. "I just like what I like."

I think of Isla and that she and Alivia would probably get along.

"So!" Alivia plops down beside me. "Aside from that boring dinner at the Vanilla Pig last night, we haven't had much time to chat about how things have been going for you. I want details! I want stories!"

I feel my pain drifting away like a cloud on a sunny afternoon. "I love my cabin. And I told you about Isla, I think."

"Yes. Tell me again about some of the girls?"

"Addie is really quiet, but she's coming out of her shell a little bit," I say thoughtfully. "I think going to camp has been way outside of her comfort zone, but it's having some pretty good impacts on her. Well," I amend. "Mostly."

Alivia frowns. "Mostly?"

"There's this one girl there I may have mentioned... Madysen?"

"You mentioned the name."

"She's kind of like..." my voice trails off, but I jerk my head toward Quinny. "A bit manipulative and mean-spirited at times. But a lot of girls want to be here. It's kind of funny though," I break off with a chuckle. "Isla and I can put her in her place every now and then and remind her to be kind to the other girls. But really, it's only Addie she picks on."

Alivia glances at Quinny. "They like to find the girls they think are weak, don't they?"

My heart stutters at what she's inferring. *Quinny thinks I'm weak?*

Quickly, Alivia shakes her head. "Not what I meant at all. I didn't mean those girls *are* weak—the mean girls just like to prey on the ones they think don't have claws. The ones who won't fight back."

Sighing, I nod. "I suppose that's true. Other than Madysen and a few squabbles between counselors not liking my parents, everything has been...really good."

I'm surprised by how much I mean that.

Alivia nods enthusiastically. "And the guys?"

I blush, giving myself away. "There's not *really* a guy..."

She slams a palm down on the table. "Let's hear about him!"

I pass my Ocean Water from hand to hand, thinking about Hayes' face. "Well...he has sort of messy dark hair and always wears a hat over it. Other than that, he's super tall and kind of dresses like he's from the nineties." I smile.

"What's his personality like?" Alivia stirs her milkshake with the red plastic straw.

"Sort of reserved, but really sweet and the sort of funny where you don't necessarily see it coming...sort of...goofy. His name is Hayes."

"What's going on over here?" Quinny saunters over, with a guy on each side of her.

"Just chatting about camp." Alivia shoots her a sugar sweet smile.

Quinny ignores her. "Well, Maeve, I wanted to apologize for the way I acted to you at the gym. It was uncalled for—I understand that now."

I raise an eyebrow. Quinny has *never* apologized. To anyone.

At least sincerely.

Alivia rolls her eyes.

Quinny glares at her but says nothing about it. "Anyway," she continues, "I invited someone I think might cheer you up!" She motions someone over and I exchange a worried glance with Alivia. There's no way something like this ends well.

A tall boy with short blond hair bounds over to me, extending his hand. "Hey." He gives me a big smile. "My name is Reid." He extends a hand.

Confused, I shake his hand, noting the differences between him and Hayes. "Quinny, what is going on?"

Quinny looks at me incredulously. "Maeve, that is so rude! Reid wanted to come meet you." She leans down and whispers conspiratorially, "Just between you and me, he thinks you're cute."

"She's not interested in a guy here." Alivia stands up. "Mind your own business?"

Reid holds up his hands. "Look, guys, I don't want to cause any drama. I just wanted to get to know Maeve." To me he adds, "I've seen you around school a few times. I love your curls."

Nervously, I reach up and tuck the flyaway pieces behind my ears. I'm still a wreck after practice.

It's nice of him to say, but he isn't the guy I want. "Alivia," I mumble.

"We're going to head out," Alivia announces, grabbing my arm and pulling me away from the table.

Why would Quinny do that? Why would she pick out a guy for me? There must be some ulterior motive because never in her life has Quinny done something without strings attached. She doesn't believe in random acts of kindness.

I make eye contact with Reid, who gives me a sad smile. "Sorry," he says, scratching the back of his neck.

"Wait!" Quinny grabs my other arm. "There's a party tonight. Reid will be there."

I shake my head. "I want to leave, Q. I'm staying with Alivia. I'll see you in the morning."

She scoffs. "You expect me to give you a ride to volleyball practice when you decided to stay with her instead of me?"

"I wasn't actually going to ask you for a ride," I mumble, rolling my eyes.

Reid raises his hand. *Why is he still here?* "I can give you a ride."

Quinny's lips turn up into a wide smile. "That would be amazing. She would really appreciate that, wouldn't you?"

"I..."

"It's settled!" Quinny claps her hands and leans back against one of the guys she brought along with her. "Reid will pick Maeve up at Alivia's house—8:30 on the dot!"

"Don't worry about it," I say sharply. "I'll get a ride with Jolie."

Alivia drags me away before anything else happens.

We don't talk on the way back to her house, until we're safe inside her room with the door closed. She has a bunk bed, thankfully. I smile at it sadly. I bet the mattresses are much more comfortable than the ones at Camp Swallowtail.

Alivia shakes her head and collapses on the floor. "What is wrong with her?"

"She's probably just trying to make up for what she said to me," I try feebly. I grab my bags from the doorway and start unpacking things.

Alivia looks up at me, brows furrowed. "You don't really believe that, do you?"

I sigh and yank my hair tie out, my curls tumbling down wildly over my shoulders. "No, of course I don't believe that. But what does it matter, Alivia? I'm not staying here and I'm not dating Reid, no matter how badly she wants me to."

"Did she hear us talking about Hayes?" Alivia asks quietly.

I shake my head. "It wouldn't have mattered. This Reid guy was in on it with her. I only have a couple days left here and I want to spend them having a good time."

Trying to fit back in is what I don't say.

But I think about Reid as Alivia hops into the shower. I collapse on her beanbag chair and stare up at her ceiling, wondering what on earth Quinny would be hoping to accomplish with this one.

I look at the time and get an idea. I grab my phone from my bag and dial Isla's number. It only takes a few seconds and a brief prayer on my end that my parents were honest about letting her have her phone this week so I could communicate with Misty Monarch, and finally, she picks up

FaceTime. Her eyes are bright and her hair is wet, a towel draped across her shoulders.

"Hey!" she exclaims. "We've missed you so much!" She looks over her shoulders and calls, "Misty Monarch gals! Get over here!"

"Maeve!" they cry, racing over.

I hear a sharp whistle in the background, and a lifeguard yells, "No running at the pool!"

Isla yells back, "Shut up, Jacob!"

Madysen's voice retorts sharply. "Don't tell him to shut up!"

I laugh and laugh, shocked to find tears pricking my eyes. I must be exhausted. It certainly has been an emotional day for many reasons.

"Guys! I've missed you so much!"

"Are you kicking butt at volleyball?" demands Kiara.

"Something like that," I laugh.

I miss them so much. My cheeks hurt with how big I'm smiling, leaning back in Alivia's bean bag chair. All the girls crowd into the screen and Isla holds it up higher, helping them all fit in the frame.

All of that noise. I miss that too.

"It's so good to see you girls," I say.

"We miss you!" they all call back.

"Alright, give Maeve and I a few moments alone," Isla laughs. "I want to talk to her about some things." The girls all wave and tell me they miss me and can't wait for me to come back. Then Isla takes the phone to a slightly more secluded area of the pool, one by bushes and wildflowers. She sits down and her gaze turns serious.

"How are things going?" she asks quietly. "I want the real answer."

I bite my lip. How did I know she would ask me that? "It's been fine."

"Maeve."

I sigh and glance at Alivia's bathroom door. Still closed. The shower is still on.

"It could be worse. Quinny is trying to hook me up with some weird guy I've never even seen before named Reid."

Isla chuckles—which shocks me. "What?" she asks defensively when I stare at her. "Is he cute at least?"

I shake my head. "Why is that all anyone cares about? For your information, I've got my eye on someone else and it sure isn't Reid."

"Who?"

"Have you met Hayes? He works around camp."

She frowns, shaking her head. "No, I guess I haven't. The name doesn't sound familiar. What is his job exactly?"

I shrug. "Maintenance? Stuff that sounds boring."

"Can't say I know him. I'll keep an eye out though. Camp romance, huh?" She raises her eyebrows with a smile.

I scowl but it doesn't last. "The point is, I'm still trying to make it work here. I'm just not into this specific guy."

Her eyes are sad. "Don't try to force what isn't meant to be."

"I know," I say, a little sharper than I intend to. "That's not what I'm doing."

She studies me and then her eyes go away from the phone. I hear voices on the other end and Isla nods to them before turning her attention back to me.

"I have to go," she says. "It's nearly time for dinner. We'll talk soon, okay?"

"Thanks for picking up. I really enjoyed seeing everyone. Tell the girls I miss them!"

Isla nods. "Bye, Maeve. Remember, you have a place here, okay?"

"I know. Thanks."

The screen goes dark, showing me my reflection. It's something so much more complicated than it used to be.

it's not halloween
July 1

I whirl around to find Coach jumping up and down, hooting like a lunatic, yelling for all the world to hear, "And *that* is how you jump serve!"

So much warmth fills me til I'm nearly bursting with it. I could dance under Coach's praising eyes.

The remainder of practice goes accordingly, with me showing off to impress Coach. I don't think about how this impacts the other girls until I turn around and see Jolie looking at me, an eyebrow raised and her arms crossed over her chest.

"Seriously?" she asks.

Heat floods to my cheeks. My smile fades. "What?" She rolls her eyes and walks away.

Quinny watches and stalks over the second Coach pauses us for a water break. "You aren't cute," she says.

"Not trying to be." I take a sip of my water.

"Look," she says. "There's a party tonight."

"Another one?"

She scowls. "Don't be lame. Come. Reid will be there."

"What an incentive."

She props a hand on her hip. "Are you coming or not? Are you too chicken?"

I scoff and slam my water down on the bench. "Are we in middle school, Quinny? Chicken? Really?"

She narrows her eyes. "Are you?"

I lock eyes with her. If I tell her no, I'll walk away doing what I want but I'll also give her the satisfaction of knowing she scared me away.

If I go, who knows what I'll be walking into? But at least she won't think she won.

Since when did it become a competition between the two of us?

I lift my chin. "I'll be there."

The second her lips curve up into a sly grin, my stomach drops, and I wish I could rewind and get over my pride. I should've said no.

"See you then." Quinny turns on her heel and flounces over to grab her water and chat with Hazel and Jolie.

I jump into Alivia's car right after practice and fill her in on the situation. Before I even get all the words out my mouth, she is shaking her head vehemently.

"What?"

"Do not go to that party."

I pull my phone out of my bag. "Why does it matter?"

She stops at a stoplight. "Maeve, it's so obvious that she invited you because she has some hidden agenda. This is not a happy-go-lucky, we're-all-in-this-together sort of party."

I wrinkle my nose and force a laugh. "Have any of the parties ever been that way?"

Sighing, she shakes her head. "Do what you want, I guess. I'm just saying that I don't think this is a good idea."

"Come with me?" I clasp my hands together. She scoffs. "Please, Alivia?"

"Why do you care so much?"

I drop my hands and stare out the windshield. Why *do* I care so much?

"I just have to do this," I finish. "I did really well in practice and if I stay here, I need to prove myself."

Alivia sighs deeply. "I really thought we were past this."

I raise an eyebrow. "You sound just like Isla."

"I'll take that as a compliment."

Relief rushes over me when she smiles, and I know she'll be there to back me up tonight. I have an inkling that she's right about this party, but going back on my word to Quinny is not an option at this point.

Last time, it started with a ghost story.

This time, when I walk in, everyone surrounds me, practically begging for my attention until I'm wide-eyed with confusion. I thought that after volleyball practice, Quinny would've spread the world around that I was a show-off and the outcast of her group.

"Oh my gosh, we've missed you!" seems to be the cry from everyone, which seems especially odd because I saw them all a couple nights ago at the Vanilla Pig for dinner. Dancing and food and laughter fill the room and I soon forget myself and get lost in the ebb and flow of the crowd. Alivia frowns at me but I tell myself I just need this one night. Just this one night to finally feel like old Maeve again.

I don't know what I'm searching for. All I know is that I'm *searching*.

"You came!" Quinny shouts over the music, clad in a pink skirt and black tank top. Her blonde hair is coiled into perfect curls and there is pink glitter flecking her eyelids.

"Obviously!" I shout back. "Wouldn't have missed this for the world!"

"And look who's so popular!" Quinny adds, nodding to all the people flocked around me.

I realize what feels weird: she's not jealous. If anything, she nods encouragingly at all the people who are trying to dance beside me, which causes a strange feeling in my chest, but I ignore it because maybe she decided to be nice?

Stop being so naive.

But I can't help it. Tonight, I just want to have a good time.

Someone taps me on the shoulder. I spin around with a grin, loving the way my loose curls fly through the air, but my smile falls when I see Reid, matching my earlier grin.

"Wanna dance?" he asks, holding out a hand.

If I look past him hard enough, I can almost pretend he has dark hair and hazel eyes, a lazy, goofy sort of smile that leaves me wanting more. I can almost pretend he is tan and tall with toned cords of muscle running down his arms.

"Sure!" I take his hand. I can pretend. What's the harm in pretending?

"Okay, Maeve. I hope someday you realize that being liked isn't all that matters in the world. You can make perfectly good friends without pretending you're so cool and have it all together." I hear Alivia's words from so long ago ringing in my brain.

Reid is an incredibly good dancer; I have to give him that. He knows all the right ways to spin and dip me, the right way to look at me and make me feel like I'm the prettiest girl in the room. His hand is warm around my hand with the other firm on my waist. We look a dozen times better than all these other teens who just head bob or sway to the music. Reid is clearly a practiced dancer and this is something I could get used to.

Get used to?

Alivia beckons me over to get some snacks. I part from Reid with a breathless promise to dance with him later and take the cup of Sprite she passes to me.

"What the heck is wrong with you?" she demands. "Have you forgotten about Hayes?"

"It's just a dance, Alivia." I can't disguise the annoyance in my voice. "What's so wrong with that? And it's not like I'm dating Hayes so does it matter?"

"I guess not, but—"

"You're acting like I'm cheating on him," I raise my voice. "And I'm not."

She holds up her hands. "Okay, do what you want. But let me know when you're ready to leave."

"We just got here."

"Just saying." She walks off, shaking her head.

I huff. Why does she have to be so judgmental all the time?

Leaving my drink on a nearby counter—I don't even know whose house this is—I return to the dance floor where Reid is waiting, along with all the other people who are suddenly my new best friends. Reid takes my hand as the next song starts, an upbeat love song, and twirls me around while I shout answers to the questions the people around me ask. I feel like some sort of celebrity.

The night passes by in a blur of music, sweat, and dancing.

Reid and I dance and dance and while we don't talk a lot I find myself captivated a little by his bright-eyed gaze and open smile.

The music turns slow, and I glance up at the DJ, who gives me a big smile. I don't even know who that guy is. But I smile back and draw closer to Reid, inhaling the sharp woodsy scent of his cologne and loving the way his eyes lock on mine.

Our dance is gentle and slow, the kind that makes me forget about everything except this moment. Reid is smiling at me and I smile back.

"You're pretty," he says. "I really wish we'd met sooner."

"So do I," I whisper back. *Do I?*

He tugs me aside, away from all the crowd, toward a small hallway with hardly any people. My heart skips a beat. I take his hands in mine.

He leans down slowly and presses his lips to mine.

My first kiss.

I close my eyes.

And it feels...

Wrong? Can a first kiss even feel wrong when I have nothing to compare it to? I should be thinking about how good he smells or how gentle he is with me or how kind he's been but all I can think about is that I feel like a stranger in this body of mine, kissing a boy I don't even know. But this would be my life here. This is what I'm missing while being at Camp Swallowtail.

Oh my gosh, I don't even know him.

I back away and smile really quickly. "Thank you," I fumble. "That was really..." my voice trails off.

I scurry away, my mind reeling and hating myself that I had my first kiss with a stranger. A stranger, to make it worse, Quinny picked out for me. She orchestrated my first kiss!

I'm burning with fury and humiliation.

Humiliation. Fury.

The people in the crowd all stare at me as I walk away, only...they aren't staring at me like normal. They all tilt their heads at an almost unnatural angle, and suddenly have dark eyeliner rimming their eyes, with streaks coating their cheeks.

"Maeve!" I hear someone cry, but I'm stunned by what's going on.

They all slink with jerky movements toward me and goosebumps prickle across my skin. One girl reaches out with a heavy arm and drops it onto my shoulder, slowly digging her nails into my skin.

"Hey," I plead, backing away. "You're hurting me." She grips on tighter and then suddenly all these other twisted arms are reaching for me and I'm breathing faster and faster, wondering what on earth is going on, scanning the crowd for the ghost girl from Camp Swallowtail because everything has come crashing down on me—

"Maeve!"

I think it's Alivia's voice, but I don't see her.

There are shrieks and cries all around me. I clamp my hands over my ears and bite down on my tongue to keep from screaming.

The disco lights are flashing around me, and I wonder if this is what it feels like to have a seizure. Everything is bright, loud, and all my classmates are hulked over, wearing grotesque makeup and clawing at my skin.

Layer by layer they pull me apart until I'm nothing more than a little girl, lying in the fetal position on the ground of some stranger's house, screaming and crying at the top of her lungs because she's living in a ghost story.

It's little Maeve when she was seven, locked in a storage closet in a cabin at Camp Swallowtail, screaming and crying at the top of her lungs because she... she...

I don't believe in ghosts.

Yet here they are, clawing at me and breaking me apart.

"MAEVE!" Finally, Alivia's voice is louder. Or is it Isla on Fright Night? I blink and the girls around me are graveyard girls. I blink and they're just my classmates.

Alivia kneels and pulls me up, screaming at everyone else to back away. The next thing I know, blinding lights flicker overhead and everyone is laughing hysterically, wiping away the makeup and slapping each other on their backs. High fiving Quinny and high fiving...

Reid.

He smirks at me, arms crossed over his chest.

Oh my gosh. *Oh my gosh.*

"Maeve is a lunatic!" Quinny laughs, throwing her stupid blonde head back.

There are tears in my eyes, but the hot, angry kind.

The kind that burns into my skin and heart and soul and tells me that I will never forgive her for as long as I live, no matter how many more parties she tries to throw for me or how many boys she persuades to kiss me, just for a sick joke. Just so I can believe that I'm liked.

With Alivia's help, I stand and glare at them all, as they laugh at me and try to make me feel weak. I wipe away my smeared mascara and stalk over to Quinny, who smirks at me. She lowers her phone, which I realize was *taking a video.*

Before she can open her mouth, I wrench her phone away from her and throw it as hard as I can onto the ground, where the screen shatters into a million little pieces.

There's a collective hush as everyone realizes this isn't a game anymore.

As I realize *I don't want this anymore.*

Her jaw drops and her eyes get deadly as she screams, *"What did you just do?"*

"I am sick and tired of the way you treat me!" I scream back. "The way you treat other people? This isn't fun anymore, Quinny!"

"You're such a child!" she retorts, angrily falling to the ground to collect the shattered pieces of her phone.

"You can take your volleyball captain spot. I don't want it anymore. Cling to your stupid parties and idiotic friends who think it's okay to join in on stuff like this!" I snatch a cup of soda from the counter and throw it, reveling in the way they screech as the dark liquid meets their pretty clothes.

After that, I stalk over to Reid, glowering at him, hating how he smirks.

"How was your first kiss?" he goads.

I slap him across the face, feeling extraordinarily violent but justified. "You call that a kiss?"

The crowd exchanges gasps and wide-eyes and I watch with satisfaction as Reid's face goes red.

I look at Alivia. "We're done here."

She nods with a huge grin. "I'm with you, sister."

It's the first time, with such freedom, driving down the streets with Alivia's windows rolled down, blasting music, that I can say that I don't belong here.

And that's okay.

apple juice
July 2

About an hour into the plane ride, a stewardess pulls up beside me with a refreshment cart. Her dark hair is coiled into a perfect bun and her matte red lipstick is as pristine as her uniform, which has a name tag fastened to it: Courtney. I pull out one of my earbuds and pause the folk mix I'd created before boarding the flight.

"Can I get you something to drink?" She smiles.

"Apple juice, please?" Sipping apple juice and listening to folk music feels like such a mood for some reason.

Cheerfully, she unscrews the lid of the Minute Maid apple juice and begins to pour the amber liquid into a small, plastic cup. Her eyes stray to my t-shirt, the teal shirt from Camp Swallowtail, and she raises a perfectly waxed eyebrow.

"Are you headed to Camp Swallowtail?" She sets down the juice container on the cart.

I glance down at my shirt, pulling at the fabric.

"Yes. I'm a counselor there. My parents just bought the camp at the beginning of the summer. You've heard of it?"

She nods vigorously. I had no idea its name extended much past Texas.

"I had a relative that went there, back in 1996, the year everything went down," she says thoughtfully, capping the bottle. She passes me my apple juice and quickly asks the lady next to me what she'd like to drink.

"Coke. Everyone has heard of Camp Swallowtail, doll," the lady beside me looks at me like I'm crazy. "Your parents bought that place?" She shudders. "Hope you don't believe in ghosts."

The air suddenly turns cold around me. "What do you mean?"

Courtney tips the Coke into another small cup. "My aunt— the one who attended back in the 90s," she clarifies, "said that the death of that one little girl was due to this dangerous slide they had down by the river."

"What?"

"You didn't know?" the woman beside me scoffs. "Thought your parents bought that wretched place."

"They did. But I didn't know the rumors. They must not have known about the slide, either." Why would Mom and Dad buy the camp if it had such bad publicity? It's obviously bad that a girl died there, which I'm sure hurt Camp Swallowtail's reputation. But if the death was by an unknown cause, it didn't necessarily have to be the fault of the camp. If the girl died while on a camp activity, however...that makes the ghost stories feel more real.

"Your parents would've known," Courtney assures me. "The old directors would've had to tell them about that incident before they bought it. But kudos to them for buying it anyway. People think that place is haunted, but it's really not. All it needs is a little love. I'm sure your parents have given it more than enough."

"It's never been as popular a place to spend your summer as it was before 1996 is all I'm saying," insists the lady beside me.

"Do you know anything else about the story?" I grip the tray table in front of me.

Courtney shakes her head. "Not much is known about the incident, really. The only thing my aunt told me was that a little girl died on the slide at the river. I believe one of the clasps or something came undone and set the whole thing off. I also heard that part of the reason the details haven't really been released was that the girl's parents didn't want their daughter's death to go too public and become something everyone was involved in."

"Something bad went down with their son, too," chimes in the lady beside me, taking the cup of Coke from the stewardess.

"Their son?" I ask. *Brother Bane?*

"Can I get my drink, please?" the man behind me asks with annoyance.

"I'm so sorry," Courtney apologizes, flustered. She leans down close to me and whispers, "Please don't worry too much about it. If your parents are confident in the camp, I'm more than sure everything is fine now." She smiles at me and continues to serve the other passengers aboard the flight.

I turn to the woman beside me, sipping her drink, unbothered.

"The son?" I repeat.

She waves a hand at me like I'm nothing more than a pesky fly. Usually, such blatant rudeness would irk me, but I'm way too invested in this story to be bothered.

"Maybe this is something you should ask your parents about, girl," the lady replies shortly. "If it's not something they already talked with you about, you probably shouldn't be hearing it from me. I do hate to gossip."

I raise an eyebrow. Something tells me this woman *lives* for gossip. But I respect her dismissal and turn back to my apple juice. I slip my earbuds back in and unpause the playlist on my phone, but the music falls on deaf ears. I'm too busy thinking about all the information I've just been given and how it fits with what I already know about the camp.

Within seconds of stepping out of the airport, I feel sweat dripping down my back like hot rain. It's sort of unpleasant, but at the same time, I know it means I'm back in Texas, where Camp Swallowtail, Isla, Hayes, and Addie are.

Second, I see Mom, standing there in front of her van, holding a sign that says WELCOME BACK, MAEVE. It's colored with paint and adorned with lots of glitter that I know came from the Art Barn at camp. Mom smiles at me, holding it up to make sure I see.

Third, I see Addie, Kiara, and Lena all poke their heads out from the van windows and yell, "SURPRISE!"

I run to Mom, lugging my bags with me and hug her so tight. She drops the sign and grasps me, as if she never wants to let go. I feel tears prick at my eyes and look up at her, her green eyes just like mine, pouring into me with overflowing love. Her hand is on the back of my head, smoothing my hair down.

"I missed you, chickadee," she says softly, smiling.

"I missed you, too." I hug her. "I'm so sorry. For how horrible I've been. I see now where I was wrong. I was wrong. And I don't want to live my old life anymore."

"Maeve, honey. I hope you think we didn't send you back to prove a point of ours. We sent you to volleyball camp because we thought that's what you wanted."

"I know. It *was* what I wanted, but not anymore. That's why I wanted to come back early."

"We're glad you came back early!" cheers Lena from the car.

I laugh, wiping away tears with my arm. I grab my bags and the sign and stuff them into the car. The girls all sit in the second row, so I climb into the passenger seat beside Mom. She cranks up the AC to the coldest it can go, and within moments, we're pulling out of the airport and heading back to Camp Swallowtail.

"How was volleyball camp?" Kiara asks.

"Tell us all about it!" chimes in Lena.

Addie smiles and nods, quietly agreeing.

It means so much to me that they came to pick me up. I feel wanted and appreciated—it only makes me want to value my relationship with the Misty Monarch girls more and more.

"Honestly..." I raise an eyebrow, drawing out the suspense. "It sucked!"

At first, they look sad for me, but when I laugh again, they begin to laugh too. I tell them all about Quinny and the rude things she said. When I talk about the slushies at Sonic, Mom shoots me a look, no doubt horrified at the food dye I ingested, but she doesn't say anything.

I leave out the kiss and the party.

Both those things still ache a little too much for me to laugh off yet.

welcome home pt. 2
July 2

I don't realize how much I've missed Camp Swallowtail until I'm staring at the wood that makes up Misty Monarch and the front porch and the little light that shines over the doorway, swarming with flies. But instead of towels and swimsuits draped over the banisters enclosing the porch, there are streamers and tinsel.

I glance back at Lena, Addie, and Kiara. "What...?"

They burst into a fit of giggles and leap out of the car, quickly racing to the back and pulling all my stuff inside the cabin before I can even respond.

"Go!" Mom urges me, pushing me out of the car with a grin.

"Addie, what's going on?" I shout at their bubbly figures. I follow them into the cabin and am instantly bombarded with loud music, food, and the rest of the Misty Monarch girls all shrieking and rushing to me excitedly.

Isla is last, barreling at me. "You're back!"

"I am!" I relax into her hug, smiling as I catch a whiff of the scent of earthiness, sunshine, chlorine, and a tinge of sweat—it smells like camp. It's by no means glamorous, but it's real and it's good.

"What is all this?" I gesture around, unable to keep the smile off my face.

"We wanted to throw you a welcome back party." Addie ducks her head with a little smile. She motions to the food set up, a table draped with a plastic tablecloth and heaps of glorious food from Anita, the chef.

"Also..." Isla strolls over toward her little plastic dresser and dramatically points to a bowl with a ladle, plastic cups to the side of it. "Coffee punch!"

I raise my eyebrows. "Coffee *what*?"

"Coffee *punch*!" she accentuates the last word by throwing her fist up in the air. "It's chocolate and vanilla ice cream mixed with coffee. Like a root beer float, but coffee."

"And way better," adds Madysen, twisting a strand of hair around her fingertip. She reaches for a plastic cup and looks at Isla pointedly. "Now that she's here, can I *finally* have some?"

I smirk and lean over Madysen, giving her a tight hug like she's my annoying little sister. "Awww, I'm *so* glad to see my little ray of sunshine! Have you become a glass half full kinda gal while I was gone? Or are you still smitten over Jacob?"

She shoves me away, scowling. "Geez, I liked it better when you were at that stupid camp. You're just jealous the guys like me better, okay?"

I nod seriously, folding my hands in front of me. "You saw right through me there. You should really consider a career in psychology with how accurately you can just see straight to someone's very soul and deepest desires."

"Shut up." She rolls her eyes and pours some coffee punch into her plastic cup.

Isla gives me a thumbs up behind Madysen's head and the other girls giggle.

They all take turns telling me about any new inside jokes or funny things that happened the last few days and I absorb all of it—their faces, smiles, and laughter. I'm here to teach them something, but I really feel like I'm learning more from them than they ever could from me.

We snack on chips, crackers, cookies, and before long, all the food is devoured. I want to have a moment to talk to the girls all individually, to try and be more intentional, but the cabin is so small and their voices are so loud, there's hardly any point in it.

Isla comes up to me quietly at one point, while the girls discuss guys and stories from back home. I'm sitting on her bed, so she plops down beside me, holding a cup of coffee punch in her hands. She passes it to me, and I take a sip, letting the bitterness of the coffee mingle perfectly with the sweetness of the ice cream. "Didn't find what you were looking for back home?"

"No." I shake my head. "But I'm glad I went because it made me appreciate this place more. I realized how much I had changed. And I just decided that my old life isn't what I want anymore."

Smiling, she slings an arm across my shoulder. "I'm proud of you for figuring that out and letting it be a good experience, even if it didn't feel like it at the time. Sometimes you have to go through something rough or irritating just to figure out what you really want."

"Camp is what you make it," I say with a smile.

"Darn right." She smiles back.

star tipping
July 3

My wet hair is dripping down my back when Hayes finds me walking back from the girls' bathroom. The second I see him—the first time since I've been back—my brain takes me back to the party and the hallway, dancing with Reid and giving him my first kiss. My cheeks redden with mounting frustration. There was deeper meaning to what I said to him: to me, that wasn't my first kiss. It doesn't count.

Those moments with him are disgusting and they belong to a girl I no longer know.

Still, pieces of me feel guilty when I meet Hayes' hazel eyes, bright and glad to see me.

"Long time, no see." He stuffs his hands in his pockets.

I shift my toiletries bag and towel, wincing as he always seems to catch me at bad times. Like now, when I look like a half-drowned rat. But I smile at him anyways.

There's only you, my mind says, as if that can make up for the impetuous actions of two days ago.

But what if I'm making another mistake?

"It's been a while," I say finally, continuing my walk back to Misty Monarch. All the girls have already gone to sleep, and Isla wanted to give me time for a nice long shower.

He steps in front of me and starts walking backwards, an easy grin on his face. "I don't know about you, but I sure am bored."

I stop and tilt my head. "Bored? It's midnight. Why aren't you asleep?"

He scoffs. "What a ridiculous question. C'mon, I have something fun for us to do."

"Hayes!" I hold up my shower stuff. "I can't go messing around. I just showered and now I'm going to bed. I'm a counselor—I can't just be off gallivanting."

"Oh, like you didn't do plenty of gallivanting last week?"

My jaw clenches as the color drains from my face. "What are you talking about?"

Please tell me he doesn't know about Reid. That would be so humiliating. But it's very possible—Quinny videoed the whole party and while I haven't checked social media, I'm positive she ended up posting it. If she got her phone fixed, that is. What if Hayes somehow saw that I was tagged in it or something? Does he even have social media?

"Relax!" He crosses his arms and laughs. "It was only a guess. Don't worry, I didn't go sleuthing into your personal life. That said, it hasn't escaped my notice that you haven't participated in what is possibly the most important Camp Swallowtail event."

"What? Fright Night wasn't enough for you guys?" I step around him and continue walking.

Chuckling, he hops back in front of me, stopping me in my tracks. I blow out a breath. I like him, but he is exasperating and I'm ready to go to bed.

"We'll need a flashlight," he says.

"Hayes, whatever it is, I'm not participating."

"It doesn't have to take long, I promise."

Reluctantly, I sigh and hug my shower stuff closer to my chest. "I guess...Where should I meet you?"

He wrinkles his nose.

"I'm taking my stuff back to the cabin first! You want me to leave all of this on the ground?"

He starts to walk away, his hands back in his pockets, sort of skidding his feet against the gravel ground as he goes. "Meet me by the kitchen. We'll walk to the open field. Make sure that you grab a flashlight!"

A combination of giddy and nervous, I follow the path back to Misty Monarch, carefully opening and shutting the door. I drop all my stuff on my bed, careful not to wake anyone before grabbing my backpack, double checking that the flashlight is in the left side pocket.

Isla snorts in her sleep, rolls over a little, but stays oblivious to the world. I take a deep breath and hold it as I shake out my hair a little and run a brush through it quickly, trying to give it some definition. I scrunch it up with my fingers a little. At least it'll dry nicely this way.

Trying to be as quiet as a mouse, I shut the cabin door and walk briskly down to the kitchen, gravel crunching under my feet and wind whistling through the trees like a gentle melody. I see the soft glow of the kitchen light and hoist my backpack higher.

The nervous part of me continues to glance around in a lighter version of paranoia to ensure that I'm not being followed. I'm not too keen on getting into trouble with my parents for breaking curfew, especially if it was because I was out with a guy. Especially after I apologized to Mom about my poor behavior and we seem to be on relatively good terms.

I see the outline of a person by the kitchen, shadowed by the flickering kitchen light by the back door, near the heaping black trash bags and wash bin. He's bouncing on his toes a little bit, waiting for me.

"Well?" he asks expectantly.

I hold up the flashlight.

"Okay. To the field!"

Following him is like taking the first step into something so new and exciting. I almost wish he would lead me by the hand, like a boy and a girl in a movie, but he moves so fast I have to shove the thought aside and run to keep up with him. Finally, when we're in an open spot, far enough away from the soccer nets and other rec equipment, Hayes motions for me to throw down my backpack.

He holds his arms out wide and stares wistfully at the sky. "This is the most beautiful sky on earth."

I glance up and understand what he means.

My first night at Camp Swallowtail, I knew that this night sky was like nothing else I had ever seen. Now, I feel like I know so much more—having seen some of the ugliness of this place and glimpsing this beauty again, which almost feels like a haunt in itself. It shouldn't be real—this is far too glorious. Like it should be impossible for something this splendid to be glimpsed at by the fickle human eye.

It's mesmerizing, these stars. Wide and open and sprawling—a sky made for lying under, for first kisses and sharing secrets in the dark. Stars people swear by.

"I think you're right," I breathe, coming to stand beside him.

I feel his eyes fall down on me and when I turn to meet them, the corners of his mouth quirk up. Mine do the same.

I long to reach for his hand. It's this ache building inside of me, to be close to him in that way and share this moment together, hand in hand.

Instead, Hayes lets his smile go devilish as he tosses the flashlight up into the air and catches it, flicking it on. He waves it around in my face a little and I squint, swatting at him but missing.

"Let's star tip," he says.

I shake my head. "I don't know what that is."

He graces me with a long-suffering sigh and plants his feet in front of mine. "It's simple. Pick any star in the sky to stare up at. Then, you spin in a circle for twenty seconds while I shine this flashlight in your eye. After the twenty seconds are up, you run as far as you can until you fall."

There's a beat of silence.

"What?" he asks.

"This is fun to you?"

Enthusiastically, he nods. "Absolutely. You'll love it."

"I don't know..."

"I'll go first if you want."

He drops the flashlight and kicks it across the grass to me. I pick it up and shine it right in his eyes.

"No!" He jerks away. "I haven't picked a star yet."

"Sorry." I stifle a laugh as he rubs his eyes and then squints up at the sky. "Okay...I picked one."

"So, I just..." I hold the flashlight up. "Higher."

"Okay."

"Now you count."

Hayes begins his first quick rotation as I count to twenty. His feet whirl around in an impressive fashion, far more graceful than I anticipated for someone of his height. But manage he does.

"Twenty!" I wrench the flashlight away and he sprints off, feet tangling, limbs catching, until he wobbles with a grunt and falls to the ground.

I burst out into laughter, tucking my curls behind my ears.

When he gets up, he stumbles back over to me, lost in his own laughter. He straightens his hat. "Pretty fun, isn't it?"

"Are you sure I should try? It looks dangerous. And you were just so good at it that I wouldn't want to steal your thunder."

He snatches the flashlight from me with a grin. "Try to do better. You won't."

"I probably won't," I admit, tucking my hair behind my ears. I plant my feet and look up at the sky, wondering which stars I should choose. I guess it doesn't really matter, but I pick an especially bright star anyway.

"I got it," I say nervously.

He shines the flashlight in my eyes, and I begin the rotation.

One, two, three, four...

As I spin, I see Hayes' face in my peripheral, going round and round, shadowed by the garish beam from the flashlight. But I keep my eyes locked on that start, spinning and spinning and spinning and spinning.

Eight, nine, ten, eleven...

It suddenly feels like the world is spinning around me, like I'm not the only thing moving. My head feels light and this warmth comes up to my cheeks as my stomach begins to churn and before I know it, Hayes has said "Twenty!" but I'm still spinning and spinning, and then running and running, and collapsing —

And then I'm sick.

I clutch the grass in my fingers, throwing up everything I can, the world still morphing by like a kaleidoscope before my eyes. I squeeze them shut and bring my knees to my chest, heat flooding my cheeks, but for an entirely different reason now.

Hayes sprints over. "Maeve, are you okay? Oh my gosh, I'm so sorry, I didn't know being dizzy would make you sick."

I move away from him, humiliation staining my entire body. After taking a deep breath, I stand up, feeling slightly woozy still, but walk over toward my backpack on steady legs. Hayes trails after me, attempting to ask how I am, but I ignore him. This was a dumb idea. I can't believe I just did that.

"Maeve, look at me." But he doesn't reach out for me. He just steps in front of my bag.

"What?" I demand, wiping the residue from my trembling lips.

"Are you okay?" He tries to meet my gaze, but I duck my head.

"Fine."

"Is there anything I can do?"

I shake my head. "No. I'll just go get some stomach medicine from the little nurse's office by the kitchen."

Hayes widens his eyes. "Maybe...maybe we shouldn't go by there."

I throw him a frustrated look. "I thought you wanted to help."

"I do, yeah, I just..."

"Then what's the problem?"

He drags his hand through his hair. "No...no problem..."

"Great." I grab my backpack and slide the flashlight into the side pocket, storming off. My stomach still clenches, and I feel like at any moment, I might hunch over and puke again. Hayes walks beside me and there's this weird space between us, where it's like we both know he should reach out and pull my hair back or hold my hand, but he doesn't.

And it's so, *so* painfully obvious.

Finally, we get to the nurse's office. I reach for the door handle. But Hayes is standing there, glancing over his shoulder uncertainly.

"What?" I ask again.

"Nothing." He stuffs his hands in his pockets. Then pulls them out to scratch the back of his neck. "Go get the stuff."

But I follow his worried gaze to the side of the building.

"Maeve," he protests in agitation.

I ignore him and turn until I see it. My jaw goes slack and I back up slowly.

It's just like Hawkmoth Haven. On the wall, in red that looks suspiciously like blood, is a message. For me? For my parents?

"As we await a payment for your sins
The ghost's fun finally begins..."

The hair on the back of my neck stands up, as if someone is breathing right behind me, their breath touching my skin. When I whirl around, there's no one, except for Hayes and me. Though I swear the air gets colder and there's something like a little girl's laugh haunting the breeze, gently whispering through the tall trees.

He shakes his head. "It's...I saw it earlier. I didn't want you to be frightened."

I whirl around angrily. "Well, obviously I am! Look at this! Someone is intentionally trying to freak out my parents *and* me!"

He holds up his hands. "I know, trust me, I know. But I don't want you to get involved in this because it isn't about you, okay? I'm serious. This stuff is dangerous and I can't stand it if something..." his voice trails off and our gazes lock.

"If something?" I whisper.

"If something happens to you," he finishes quietly. "Ugh." He tears a hand through his hair again. "This is bigger than you think. Please go back to your cabin. It was stupid for me to ask you to come out tonight."

I'd nearly forgotten about star tipping and emptying the contents of my stomach in front of him. But suddenly, neither of those things matter very much when I glance back at the writing on the wall.

"I'll walk you back to Misty Monarch, okay?"

I nod numbly.

We walk in complete silence, both of us trying to puzzle through these events. My stomach still feels a little bit off, but at this point I can't tell if it's from the vomiting or the panic.

Hayes walks me to the front porch steps. If this were any other situation, maybe we'd be dating, and he'd walk me to the door of my house and kiss me goodnight with a smile. But it's not and we're not and there are ghosts haunting this place.

If not ghosts, people. People who mean to scare my family.

For what cause? Do they want to hurt us?

Every new thought pounds a new nail of worry into my skull, until my head is aching with them and I long to bury my face in my pillow, sleeping off the anxieties until the morning.

Hayes' hand twitches as he raises it toward me and then lowers it quickly.

"I'm so sorry..." he whispers. "I wish I could explain it all, but I can't."

I open my mouth to ask him what he means, but he quickly turns away, stuffing his hands in his pockets and hulking his shoulders. I clutch the doorknob tightly in my hand.

After everything that has happened here so far, what on earth could this supposed ghost do to make things worse?

A better question—what did my family do to deserve it?

greater good?
July 3

My hand never turns the doorknob.

I stand there on the front porch, biting my lip, worrying about this whole situation. Hayes is long gone, but something tells me there is a bigger issue going on here.

That last question keeps echoing in my mind.

What did my family do to deserve this?

Maybe I should tell someone.

A deep breath fills up my lungs and I start back down the Misty Monarch stairs, intent on waking up Mom and Dad. They have to know about this. Even if it is some harmless prank, they have a right to know. Just in case it becomes something bigger. Just in case this helps.

My strides are quick and long, desperate to get to Mom and Dad's lodge as soon as I can. The night seems to grow colder with each step I take, with each crunch along the gravel. My thoughts develop as I walk.

Mom and I had a good moment at the airport when she picked me up from volleyball camp. Surely, she'd have told Dad and they would know that I recognize what a horrible daughter I've been. I know I have much more to apologize for and the time will come for that. But we're on decent enough terms that this feels like something I need to share.

I stop in my tracks when I hear whispered voices.

My eyes go wide and I look around desperately for somewhere to hide, my heart pounding furiously. I scramble over to a tree on the side of the lodge, gripping onto the bark and cramming my body behind it. The whispered voices grow louder and the air turns colder, chills rippling across my arms.

I shiver.

"There is no excuse for what you're doing!" hisses a voice. It belongs to a girl. It chills me to the bone, but I can't place where I've heard it before.

The second voice, however, I know for sure. "What you're having me do isn't right," Hayes insists. "I can't keep trying with her like this, making her feel a certain way anymore. It's not fair."

I flinch, inching closer to hear. Who is "her"? Am... am I "her"?

"You are doing this for the greater good."

"Who's greater good?" Hayes snaps. My eyes go wide. I've never heard him *this* angry.

"Our greater good!" snarls the girl.

What girl is he talking to? I want to look around but am worried they'll catch me.

"I'm not leading her on anymore for you," he says flatly. I hear a shuffle and hide further behind the tree, my heart falling to my feet. I know for sure they must be talking about me, hating the way tears prick my eyes.

Leading me on?

He doesn't care, does he? Star tipping was a trick— this was all a trick.

The voices finally go away, and I'm left standing in front of my parents' lodge, gripping the bark of the tree in front of me like it's the only thing keeping me from screaming out loud.

Hayes' words penetrate my heart and take the air from my lungs.

I shake my head. Maybe this is just my life now. Maybe severing certain relationships is what's meant to be.

I throw open my parents' door and storm through the hallway until I get to their bedroom door, which I pound on, tears pricking my eyes, until Dad throws it open, hair rumpled, and eyes half closed.

"Maeve?" he mumbles, dragging a hand down his face. "What's going on?"

"I need to talk to you." I barge into their room and sit on the edge of the bed, shaking Mom awake gently. She moans and reaches over to turn on the little bedside lamp. Her blonde hair is wrapped up in a braided bun, little tendrils curling around her face and deep bags under her eyes. She draws the covers up to her chest and smooths out the space beside her.

"Chickadee, what's the matter?"

I crawl up into that space, feeling like a little girl again.

"Something dangerous might be going on here," I whisper. "I...I was out tonight and saw something written on the wall of the nurse's office."

"Why were you out?" Dad demands, waking up more by the second.

I cringe. "I..."

I could totally throw Hayes under the bus right now, but I'm not sure it's wise to let them know I was out with a boy. Especially a boy that I don't even want to think about right now.

"I was just showering late and then my stomach started to hurt." This makes me think of star tipping and I bite my lip in frustration, growing hurt rising up in me like some kind of beast. Quickly, I swipe away the beginnings of tears. "It's a message like the one found on the wall of Hawkmoth Haven."

Dad lowers himself down beside Mom and me. "What does it say?"

Mom tenderly places her hand on my arm.

My brain conjures up an image of the bloody letters, dripping down the side of the wooden wall.

"Something about sins that need to be paid for." My words are shaky. "And that the ghost's fun will begin in the meantime. I don't know what it means."

Mom and Dad exchange panicked looks.

"What does it mean?" I whisper. "I feel like there are so many secrets and things that people won't tell me. Why is someone doing this to our family?"

Mom is shaking her head sadly. "We can't explain everything to you, but we wish we could."

I jerk away from her touch. "Yeah, I keep hearing that."

My feet find the ground as I slide off the bed, my heart growing cold and frustrated. People won't tell me anything about the camp or whatever is going on around here. Why? Am I going to mess something up by knowing?

It hurts not to be trusted. It hurts really bad.

"Where are you going?" Dad demands as I reach for the door.

"I'm leaving."

"Maeve, please stay!" Mom pleads. I glance over my shoulder and her green eyes are wide. "It's not safe out there during the night. And this message is a very big deal, chickadee."

Resolutely, I shake my head, knowing I'm being childish, but not caring.

"We'll explain everything," Mom promises. "Just... not right now."

A deep breath. I turn. "You will?" Maybe that can be enough.

Mom nods while Dad shoots her an irritated look. "Yes," she promises. "Please, stay."

a fatal fourth
July 4

I bump into Isla on my way to the bathroom the next morning.

"Where have you *been*?" she demands. "We were all worried sick when you weren't in your bunk this morning!"

I grimace. "I know, I'm so sorry. There was an incident last night and I stayed with my parents. It's no big deal, I swear."

She doesn't look convinced, but doesn't push the situation. I'm grateful.

I'm intentional with the girls all morning, disappointed in myself for causing such a fright. They, of course, want to know all the details, but I tell them nothing, instead trying to divert the conversation back to them and what they're excited for the rest of the summer. Many of their statements seem to revolve around the 4th of July parade coming this evening, which leaves me with a nauseous stomach and a bad feeling in my mouth.

After Misty Monarch goes through the breakfast line, loading our plates up with gluten-free pancakes (with real syrup, though!) and freshly squeezed orange juice, we plop down at the table, ready to discuss what we're doing for our float.

We don't actually get to make a float exactly. We *are* the float—we dress up a certain way and hold up signs and banners based on our cabin's chosen theme.

"I vote for a Hawaiian theme," Kiara says. She holds out her hands. "We could wear leis and flowers in our hair and decorate the signs in bright colors!"

Addie nods encouragingly. "That sounds like a really good idea! We could each draw flowers on the posters and whoever has the best handwriting could write 'aloha' really big on the leading banner."

"No, no, no!" Madysen disregards all of that with a wave. "Hawaiian is incredibly basic. We have to do something bold and fun! What if we did retro?"

"Don't shoot down ideas—everyone is encouraged to share their opinion respectfully," Isla rebukes her lightly.

"Retro could be cool," Charlie adds thoughtfully. "That would also incorporate a lot of bold colors."

Emily wipes away some smeared eyeliner with her napkin. "I'm only down if we have the Bee-Gees on in the background."

Madysen wrinkles her nose. "How is that patriotic?"

"I'm not sure it really has to be patriotic," I laugh. "I really think the idea is to come together as a cabin to celebrate unity and that we get to express ourselves! Like a small representation of American freedom."

Lena applauds me. "Well said! Everbrill for president!"

"I really liked Kiara's idea," says Charlie. "Retro might be cool though, too." She bites her lip, glancing back and forth between Kiara and Madysen.

Kiara smiles. "We don't have to go with mine." She stretches and yawns. "No big deal."

"So, mine?" Madysen says.

The girls all glance at each other and nod. They look to Isla and me after.

"Whatever you guys want to pick," Isla says.

Just then, Dad walks into the center of the dining pavilion and all the other cabin tables go quiet. I catch a few counselors trading uneasy looks with others, including Josie.

"Good morning, Camp Swallowtail. I hope you've all had a lovely breakfast so far. I just wanted to let you know that there has been a...change made to the schedule for today. Typically, we have a grand 4th of July parade, but Winnie and I have decided it would be best to...forgo this event, as disappointed as many of you might be."

A wave of irritated and upset shouts rise from all the tables, including mine.

I sink lower in my seat, shaking my head. *What is he doing?*

Dad raises his hands calmly. "I know, I understand how upset many of you may be. However, it is for safety purposes that Winnie and I think it would be best to avoid this event."

"What safety purposes?" Hannah demands, standing up and propping a hand on her hip.

"It's never been a dangerous event!" adds Hendrix.

Dad frowns at them. "There have been new circumstances brought to our attention. Trust me, it's the last thing we want to do. Unless anyone would like to come clean about causing these commotions, this is what must be done."

Isla leans down to whisper, "Are these commotions at all related to why you didn't come back to the cabin last night?"

I nod reluctantly. At her expectant look, I fill her in. "Someone left another message on the wall of the nurse's office last night, warning us that the ghost's games are just about to begin. Do you have any idea what that means?"

She rolls her eyes. "My guess is it's another knucklehead like Jacob trying to give your parents a hard time. Hardly something to cancel this event over, don't you think?"

I glance at Dad. "But what if it isn't a counselor writing these messages, Isla?"

"You don't seriously think..."

"I don't know what to think."

The other cabins have risen, demanding that Dad allow them to keep the 4th of July parade. I see sweat beading down his forehead and feel a pang of guilt. I know this isn't what he wants to do but I think this summer has been a lot more than they signed up for.

"Alright!" He holds his hands up again. "I'll discuss it with Winnie and come back with a final word."

A cheer erupts from the tables.

"Can you get me more water?" Madysen asks, shoving her water bottle at me.

I frown at her, but take the bottle to the cooler, bringing mine as well.

The excited chatter has grown again as Dad wearily walks away from the pavilion. I watch him as I fill Madysen's water first, but I almost drop the bottle when Hayes comes up to me.

The anger and hurt I felt toward him come rushing back like an angry wave.

"What do you want?" I retort.

His eyebrows jump up. "Why the aggression? Is this about throwing up still? I seriously don't care about that, okay? It didn't bother me, and I just wanted to see that you were doing fine."

"Well, I am," I say quickly, slamming Madysen's lid on her water bottle with a sense of finality. "So, there's no need for you to feel like you have to talk to me anymore."

He shakes his head. "I don't get what you're saying."

"I heard you last night," I snap. "I went to find my parents and I heard you and your *girlfriend* talking about what a pathetic little thing I am, being led on like I'm in elementary school or something."

He blanches. "Maeve, that's not...You shouldn't have heard us talking. It's not what you think at all."

I shake my head, filling my water bottle now. "I don't want to talk to you, okay?"

"Hey." He bends down toward me, his breath cold on my face. "Don't go to the parade tonight, alright?"

I laugh drily. "Whatever."

"No. Maeve, I'm serious." His voice is firm, dangerous. "Something bad might happen. It shouldn't be happening at all, but if your parents can't stop it, find a way not to go."

I shake my head. "So, you want me to leave my cabin there alone? Really?"

"Don't go."

I snatch the water bottles. "Don't tell me what to do."

death by swallowtail
July 4

When evening falls and the sun begins to set, all of Camp Swallowtail is lost in festivities. I see some of the other staff members setting up fireworks out in the field, but Hayes isn't with them. I shift uncomfortably, remembering what he warned me about.

Why should I trust him?

For all I know, he could be the one who wrote those messages.

The girls decided to switch back to Kiara's Hawaiian theme when we realized Painted Lady—Heather and Zoe's middle school cabin—called dibs on all the retro paraphernalia before we could get our hands on it.

Isla brings out the plastic container with Hawaiian odds and ends from the skit closet to where we all crowd around our usual breakfast table outside. Charlie plunges her hand into the bucket and starts handing out hula skirts and fake hibiscus flowers to clip into our hair. Everyone decided to wear their hair down and we used Isla's curling wand to bring some life and body into any straight hair.

Addie brings her costume over to me, fidgeting with her curls.

"I really like them," she says fondly, twisting one around her finger. "I wish my hair was always curly."

I laugh and pin the hibiscus to her hair. "No, you don't."

She grabs a yellow hibiscus and pins it into mine. "Yes, I do!"

Kiara caps a marker and tosses it across the table. "I think I'm done with the banner."

Lena runs over and gasps. "Kie, it looks so good!" She wraps her arms around Kiara and gives her a quick squeeze. "Your handwriting is incredible."

Kiara laughs and shakes her head. "No, I only did the drawings! I wish I could take the credit, but Emily actually is the one with good penmanship."

We all crowd around the white banner with the word 'aloha' written across it in bright pink. The word is done in gorgeous, bold calligraphy and we all gape at Emily.

"This is the best handwriting I think I've ever seen," I observe. "Beautiful."

Emily hides behind her hair a little bit, which is almost funny. She's not the type to seem shy about things, especially accomplishments.

Isla places a hand on her shoulder. "Really good job, girl."

I glance around to see the progress of the other groups. Painted Lady wears colorful sweatbands and brightly colored leotards. All they're missing are the roller skates.

My snags on my parents, walking around practically twiddling their thumbs. I smile a little bit, almost endearing, until I notice the way they watch everyone, as if waiting for something to explode. Mom tucks a loose strand of her blonde hair back into her bun and it's only then that I notice the dark circles under her eyes.

She notices me watching and sends me a weak smile. I beckon her over and she comes.

"How are you girls doing?" Mom folds her hands in front of her politely. She's barefoot, wearing a long maxi dress with yellow flowers.

Lena points to the banner. "What do you think of this, Winnie? Emily made it."

Mom's smile becomes real, lifting at the corners and reaching her eyes. "This is truly beautiful, Emily." Her eyes light up for a second. "Actually, would you be interested in making different signs for places around camp? Some of the signs have faded with age and George and I were hoping to create some new ones. However, we want them to be appealing to the eye—my thoughts were calligraphy on different slabs of shaved wood?"

Emily tucks her hair behind her ear and nods voraciously. "Yes, ma'am. That would be perfect. I would love to do that."

The girls all cheer, except Madysen who snorts a little, crossing her arms.

Mom notices and gives her a big smile. She plucks a purple hibiscus and pins it to Madysen's blonde hair.

"Lovely," Mom says. She backs away from the table. "I'll let you girls finish."

"Wait." I grab her wrist gently as she begins to walk away, pulling her aside. I see Dad watching us with a slight frown and lower my voice. "What's going on?"

Mom keeps her smile on, but it no longer reaches her eyes. "What are you talking about, chickadee? Everything is fine."

I give her a knowing look.

She reaches to tug on one of her dangling earrings. "There are just a lot of factors at play. And your father is worried that with some of the...other issues going on, this parade might be the perfect opportunity for certain *entities* to express their desires, even at the expense of the campers."

I drag a hand down my face. "Mom, *entities...*"

Mom's eyes close briefly as if she's in pain. "Maeve, I know you think your father and I have some outlandish ideas but trust me—there is value to what we're saying." When she blinks, her eyes plead with mine. "I'm not asking you to believe me...but I am asking you to trust us. We just want to do what's best."

I bite my lip. *I don't believe in ghosts.* But how much longer can I deny that I'm seeing them?

I don't have to respond because Isla calls me back to the cabin. Mom nods and gives me a little smile before turning back to Dad, her dress blowing around her ankles.

I take a seat beside Isla at the table, the rough wood biting into the back of my thighs. Mom and Dad talk quietly to each other. He grips her hand and looks over at me sharply and Mom shakes her head.

"Hey." Isla snaps me out of my reverie. "Is everything okay?"

"Yeah." I slowly take my eyes away from Mom and Dad. "I think so. I just wanted to make sure everything was okay."

"And is it?"

A beat of silence passes. "Yes," I say finally.

Misty Monarch finishes getting ready for the parade when Josie runs over, wearing an eyepatch and clip on hoop earring.

"Nice getup!" I tell her.

"Thanks, buccaneer." She grins. "Just came to tell y'all that everyone's about to start lining up for the parade." She hooks her thumb over to where many other cabins have lined up behind Caterpillar Corner, the youngest girl cabin. Aislinn waves at me, cat ears resting atop her head. The Bitty girls are all dressed as animals, with faces painted with whiskers or spots. Behind Caterpillar Corner are the boy Bitties— Hawkmoth Haven. Alex and Hendrix have donned superhero capes and wrangle their little boys. Had Hendrix not gone behind my back and expressed his true thoughts of me, I'd almost feel bad for him.

"C'mon, girls!" I stand up and wave my arm. The shuffle behind me towards the back of the line. Kiara and Addie carry the banner above their heads, grass skirts swinging around their legs. Isla coaxes a smile out of Madysen when she points out Jacob, wearing a leather jacket and sunglasses.

The hanging porch lights flicker on as the sky darkens and there's a moment of silence before the first bout of fireworks erupts. The sudden pop startles us all but we cheer when the sky is painted in sparks of blue and red and white. The fireworks fizzle into the night, mingling with stars. A huge smile bursts across my face and Isla giggles beside me.

Caterpillar Corner begins the parade, marching in their animal costumes and holding up their banner proudly. Hawkmoth Haven follows, hooting and hollering as Mom and Dad blast patriotic music over the speakers in the dining pavilion.

The smell of kettle corn, hot dogs, and funnel cakes wafts through the air. It was surprising to know that Mom and Dad approved these snacks—I guess they were feeling especially patriotic and decided to go all out if they were going to do this at all. I can't wait to get my hands on a funnel cake after this parade.

No one notices much when the first couple of butterflies land on shoulders, on heads, on hands. I brush one of them aside, hardly noticing the yellow and black wings. It's only when the first Bitty girl screams that people start to panic.

The butterflies are *everywhere*.

Crawling on skin, clinging to hair, and they don't go away. One little girl sits on the ground and cries, butterflies crawling up her face. Hannah sprints over to her, screaming, "Lyla! Lyla!"

I shoot Isla a terrified look, the sky darkening with butterflies. Thousands of legs and eyes and beating wings, beating so loud it seems like the whole camp is resonating with the sound. My skin crawls with bugs and I want to claw my way out of my skin.

I want to open my mouth to scream but I'm too scared a butterfly will crawl in.

"They're swallowtails!" shouts Isla, swatting them away. Her eyes are wide with fear. "Where did they all come from?"

The girls in our cabin huddle together, swatting and shrieking.

Between the thousands of bugs, I see Dad sprinting through and trying to usher people into the Great Hall. Mom clutches his hand, wailing. I run through the butterflies to get to them and shield my mouth. "What's going on?"

"It's the ghost!" Mom screams. "This is all her doing!"

Her? The pieces click together. During Fright Night, the little girl ghost conjured up hallucinations of swallowtail butterflies to terrify me, along with the various characters in Fright Night. If these really are her doing, they are nothing more than hallucinations, unable to truly inject their venom into any of us.

It's a vision meant to terrify, but not to harm.

"One of my favorite things about ghosts is that we're able to use powers that are mostly closely tied with the emotions we harbor in death...I'm able to create illusions, hallucinations, if you will, that make you see the things I want you to see."

"Swallowtail butterflies are some of the most deadly known to mankind...And they aren't particularly native to this area. Don't you think it's strange that Bo and Abigail would name their camp after something so dangerous?"

"Get everyone inside!" Dad shouts to me.

He understands—these are illusions. If they were created in this space, maybe they won't be able to get inside the Great Hall. Or maybe if we separate people from the hallucination, they won't believe them.

I nod to Dad and sprint over to Misty Monarch. Just our cabin name makes my stomach clench—I am so tired of butterflies.

"Get inside the Great Hall!" I scream to them over the dull flapping of wings. Nausea rolls within me when I feel the spindly legs of a butterfly crawling into my mouth. I fight the urge to spit it out because it feels *so real* but it's not, it's not, it's not.

Then there's the crunch in my mouth and I throw up all over the ground.

I wipe the sick off my face. That part is certainly real. I want to scrape my tongue.

The hallucinations feel so real.

Isla stares at me with wide eyes and pulls Madysen and Charlie over to the Great Hall. I grab Addie and Lena, who grip onto Emily and Kiara, pulling all of them to the safety of the Great Hall. We slam the doors closed and the butterflies stay outside, pounding against the window, hundreds upon hundreds, likely *thousands* trying to claw their way into the Great Hall, flinging their ugly little bodies at the glass doors. Addie huddles against me, shaking like a leaf.

"Maeve, what's happening?" she whispers. Her eyes are filled with tears.

I clutch her tightly. "I have no idea."

Between the flapping wings, I see something that makes my heart drop to my toes. I release Addie and start banging against the glass.

"Hayes!" I scream, the sound shredding my throat. "Hayes!"

"Maeve, get back!" barks Dad, yanking me away. "Don't you *dare* open those doors."

"But Hayes is out there!"

Isla runs over to me and clutches my shoulders. "What's going on?"

I fling my finger to where Hayes stands in the midst of all the butterflies, staring at me with sad eyes. He's not moving or walking or doing *anything*.

"Hayes is *out* there!"

Isla shakes her head. "I don't see anyone."

"He's *right there!*" Standing there, staring straight at me with sad eyes.

Why isn't he moving? Why isn't he walking towards us where it's safe?

Dad pulls me back and locks his arms around me. I gawk at him and see him glance at Isla and exchange a worried glance. "What are you doing? Let me *go!*"

"Maeve..." Isla whispers. "There's no one out there."

dead bugs
July 4-5

All night without ceasing, the swallowtails pound on the windows, desperately seeking a way to come in. My suspicions are that the ghost girl isn't present or that she's grown weak with exerting so much power, otherwise she could have easily made the hallucinations pour into the Great Hall.

I remember her saying ghosts possess the ability to draw from whatever emotion they harbored the most during death. For the girl, she held tightly to madness. But why? If she's the same girl everyone seems to talk about—the one who died here in 1996—wasn't her death an accident? The stewardess on the plane said the slide came untied. I don't understand why that would cause someone to go mad in death.

She was a little girl. What would she know about madness?

Mom and Dad gathered a few counselors to go out and grab every piece of bedding they could find so that everyone could stay the night in the Great Hall together. Most campers were too afraid to leave and screamed at anyone who tried to make them. Although the cabins are untouched by the swallowtails, Mom and Dad decided it wouldn't be the worst thing to keep everyone together. Just in case, they said.

Just in case.

The two of them have been whispering most of the night. They try to keep their voices down as a lot of the campers fall asleep, curled up with blankets and pillows on the floor.

Isla leans against the door, nodding off every now and then. When she jerks her head back up, she tucks her hair behind her ears and glances over the Misty Monarch girls to make sure everyone is okay. She needn't bother. I'm wide awake and have my eyes on all of them. Mama bears must feel this way—I won't let that ghost touch any of my girls.

I don't know what happened to Hayes. I haven't been able to stop thinking about him and that's bad enough. Though Dad held me back, I watched as the swallowtails swarmed him. At some point, I must have blinked because the next second he was gone. Warning bells rang in my head, telling me I should be more worried about this. However, there was something about the calm way Dad and Isla stood beside me, insisting that they couldn't see anyone out there and they didn't even know anyone named Hayes that made me go almost numb to the entire situation. Realistically, knowing a boy I like vanished in thin air is concerning—but it's like my system is so overwhelmed that I physically am unable to process another thing.

A cough to my left startles me. Jacob sits in a similar position with his cabin, watching them all with a guarded expression. His eyes shift to mine when he feels my gaze on him and his jaw clenches. I look away with a twinge of guilt. I've been accusing him the entire summer of doing things to cause trouble for my family. He had nothing to do with any of this.

Addie stirs in her sleep. Her red hair fans out on the borrowed coverless pillow. My brows draw together when her fingers tighten around it and she inhales sharply. Beside her, Madysen rolls over and sits up, fists clenched.

I open my mouth to stop her, but she shakes Addie, eyes narrowed.

"Would you *shut up*?" she hisses. "Some of us are trying to sleep and we can't when you're sitting there having dreams about your *ghost friends.*"

But Addie doesn't wake up. She lays there, muscles in her face twitching and her eyes fluttering under her closed eyelids. Slowly, I rise to my feet and creep over to Madysen. She stares at me. Despite her unkind words, I know she's just scared.

"Leave her be," I whisper, lowering a hand on Madysen's shoulder. "If she's keeping you awake, take my spot."

Madysen shoots one more fearful glance at Addie and then nods, moving her stuff over to the spot I vacated. I slide down to the floor beside Addie, smoothing back sweaty strands of her hair. Her body tenses at my touch and I freeze. When her eyes rip open, I can tell she's not really awake. Her eyes shift back and forth, back and forth while my heart skips a beat. My hand hovers over her skin as her eyelids snap closed again, but now her mouth gapes open.

Suddenly reminding me of the ghost girl. How she unhinges her jaw like a snake when she talks. That gaping black hole of a mouth.

Dreams about your ghost friends...

I turn back to Madysen, but she's already letting her breathing slow.

Addie's gasps turn into groans. I slide back. *What should I do?* Something in my gut tells me this is more than a usual nightmare.

Should I wake Isla? I lean over, but stop when Addie's arm flings out, grabbing my arm with great force, fingers digging into my skin. Slowly, she begins to sit up as I sink down, wide-eyed and jaw going slack. Does anyone else notice what's happening?

What if it's all in my head? A lump rises in my throat. I scramble back and bump into someone but don't check who. It doesn't matter because no one wakes up, no one seems to notice, but Addie crawls closer toward me and a scream builds in my throat.

Nausea rolls in my stomach and my heart pounds so fast.

"A life for a life, peace for a ghost," Addie croaks in the ghost girl's voice. *"Better act fast or suffer the most!"*

Slowly, all the other sleeping campers in the room twitch and look up at me and the scream finally breaks free. I curl up in a ball, screaming and crying and scratching at my head. This is worse than the butterflies, than the ghost stories, and I just want to go away.

Something fiercely shakes me, but I don't want to look up. If I do, I know the only thing I'll see is the ghost girl looking at me through Addie's big eyes, wearing a smile that doesn't belong to her.

"Chickadee!"

That's not the ghost.

Timidly, I raise my head to find Mom with her hand covering her mouth. Many other heads stare at me, but not to scare me. Campers have big eyes and cling to one another, and it takes me a minute to realize *they're scared of me.*

Mom lowers herself down beside me and grasps me tightly, rocking back and forth with her chin pressed against the top of my head. I cry and cry and hold her arms against my chest, breathing in her warmth and lavender smell.

It's only when my tears subside that I see my whole cabin awake, watching me. I've woken everyone up with my screaming.

It was all a dream. A hallucination.

"It's okay, Maeve," Mom whispers, smoothing my curls. "It's okay."

Addie reaches out a tentative hand and rests it on my knee. Isla throws her blanket around my shaking shoulders.

"It's going to be okay." I don't know who says it, but someone does. It could even be me. In the end, it doesn't matter where the words come from—just that we believe them and try to make them true.

Still, eyes watch me somewhere in the dark. I feel them. When I look past the comforting hugs and gentle words, I know they're there.

Waiting. Watching. Promising.

Better act fast or suffer the most! The words are almost gleeful.

scrapbook bunk
July 5

Despite everyone being a bundle of nerves, Mom and Dad wanted us to continue with our activities as normal as soon as the swallowtail hallucinations died off. They reminded all of the counselors that parents paid for this summer and when threats weren't immediate, we should do our best to pretend like nothing is wrong. Their words are so reminiscent of what Alivia said to me at the first party of the summer: why does everyone keep pretending?

Misty Monarch's activity today is apparently one of the best ones in Camp Swallowtail history. Everyone's a little tired and groggy, but spirits perk up at the mention of Scrapbook Bunk.

"It's better than the high rope courses?" Addie asks dubiously, staring up at the tall wooden building.

"I don't think so, personally," Madysen butts in. "And I've been to it before. But who knows—maybe *you'll* find it fascinating because it's full of a bunch of dead people."

"Girl, really?" Isla plants her hands on her hips. "Can you stop?"

Madysen sniffs and reaches for her water bottle, continuing the bracelet she's working on, tied to the bottle. It looks like a hot pink version of the chevron pattern.

Addie looks down, biting her lip, reaching for the tips of her red hair to fidget with. Pain for her ripples through me, wedging itself into my heart. I try to be patient because I know everyone is tired and grumpy.

Isla and I exchange glances.

Scrapbook Bunk is an old cabin that no longer houses campers— real ones, anyway. This cabin is floor to ceiling with bookshelves instead of bunk beds. Each bookshelf is wooden and smells like time and memories. An ornate rug is laid down across the floor, bringing color to the room. Resting on the rug is a large table—I'm impressed it fits in here, even though this cabin is a little bigger than most. The table is surrounded by chairs and topped with a little green table runner with a stained glass lamp on top.

Filling up the bookshelves are scrapbooks, nearly bursting with photographs. There's one for each year the camp has been open, dating further back than I expected. One scrapbook lies open on the table, a blank page staring up at us.

"This is the scrapbook for this summer." Isla sits down at the table, slinging her backpack across the back of the chair and flips through the pages. It's clear that a few other cabins have been here because they've pasted their pictures inside, on specific pages. White space is filled with their names and cabin inside jokes.

"Wow." Kiara's brown eyes are stretched wide, taking in the whole room. "I forget how magical this place is every year. And every year I'm even more amazed."

"It's my favorite spot at camp." Isla smiles sadly. Her eyes flick over the spines of the scrapbooks lined up along the shelves, landing on one from only a few years ago. It's only when I see her eyes sparkle with tears that I realize her fiancé, Josiah, is probably encased within that book. I want to ask her about it, but not in front of our campers.

"There should be a stack of photographs taken of our cabin in one of the drawers over there." Isla blinks roughly and points to a wooden dresser that I didn't even notice until now. My footsteps thump across the wood floor. But something atop the dresser catches my eye.

It's an old photograph of an old couple, sitting in front of the Camp Swallowtail sign, looking very much in love. They both wear bucket hats and have bare feet.

"Who is this?" I hold up the photo.

Isla glances over, smiling when she sets her eyes on the picture. "Oh, the old owners. They were the cutest couple. Bo and Abigail Simmons. You would've loved them."

My eyes linger on Bo and Abigail but my mind flashes back to the question the ghost girl asked me—*why would such a sweet couple name a camp after something so dangerous?*

"Maeve, the photographs?" Lena drums her fingers impatiently on the table where the scrapbook resides. I stick my tongue out at her jokingly and grasp the packet of photos. Back at the table, I dump them all on the surface and spread them out so everyone can see.

"That's such a gross angle!" Emily clutches a photo of her and Madysen on the rock wall tower. "Please don't put this one in the scrapbook!"

"It's okay!" Isla laughs. "We only have room for about five photos, anyway. And look how many we have to choose from!"

Everyone agrees to glue in the group photo we took in the matching Camp Swallowtail t-shirts of this year.

My stomach clenches, remembering that day. It was around the second week of camp, when I was still defiant and angry. All the girls wear happy smiles. Isla looks thrilled to be a part of Misty Monarch.

Me on the other hand?

Not so much. My smile is fake and forced—insincere and empty. My eyes say *take me anywhere but here.*

Isla asks Charlie to grab a glue stick from the dresser. She swipes the deep purple stickiness onto the back of the photo and presses the picture into the middle of the scrapbook page. The girls continue to add photos around it—one of us at the pool, one of all the girls making bracelets at the breakfast table, one of Isla and me at a counselor late night, and one of the whole cabin right before the Fourth of July parade.

Since the photos take up the right side of the book, we have a blank page to the left. Isla fishes in her backpack for pretty highlighters and markers, dumping them all out on the table. Before we even decide what to write, the girls are already reaching for their favorite color, Charlie and Emily fighting over who gets the teal.

"Who has the best handwriting?" Isla asks over their arguing.

"Probably me," Madysen says in a bored tone. She flips the hot pink highlighter around in her fingers, her chin resting in her other hand.

"Emily, how about you write it?" Kiara suggests. She pushes the leftover markers and highlighters towards her with a smile. "Your handwriting for the 4th of July parade was glamorous."

Addie tucks her red hair behind her ears and nods.

Madysen sighs loudly and leans back in her chair, narrowing her eyes at Addie and Kiara. Pausing, everyone waits for the snappy retort that's sure to follow, but we're met with only silence.

"What color should I do?" Emily opens the question up to the group.

"Do black," suggests Lena. "And then we can add pops of color around it by adding our names and the date and inside jokes!"

The girls nod in agreement.

Emily takes the thickest black marker she can find from Isla's stash and does her best calligraphy. She writes "Misty Monarch" in loopy cursive and goes back over the downstrokes, darkening the edges and bringing more flow into the lettering. She holds her hand up to admire her work, impressed.

The girls huddle around and "ooh" and "aah" over it. Isla nods, satisfied.

The next step is writing our names. Each of us grab a color —if we haven't already—and sign our first and last names around the cabin lettering. In olive green, I write "Maeve Everbrill" right beside the names "Isla Monroe" and "Adeline Bennet".

"I didn't know your name was Adeline." I look at Addie.

Nodding, she says, "After my grandma."

Lena and Emily work on filling the empty space of the page with inside jokes and song lyrics. Charlie doodles little animals and pieces of nature along the edges, humming to herself quietly.

Lena drums her hands against the table. "Can we look at the scrapbook from 1996? I want to see what Cora looked like!"

The other girls nod, suddenly looking interested. "Cora?" I ask.

"The girl who died in 1996," Kiara reminds me.

Isla shrugs and strolls over to the shelves. She runs a fingertip across the spines of the scrapbooks, searching for the one labeled "1996". Finally, her finger stops, and she pulls the book from the shelf. Dust tickles my nose when she drops it on the table, and I sneeze.

Mesmerized, the girls push her toward the table and crowd around the open scrapbook. Isla looks up toward the ceiling, like she's trying to remember something.

"I think she was in Painted Lady..." her voice trails off as she flips through the pages, searching.

The cabin name sounds familiar. I think it was the first cabin I was in.

Painted Lady's cabin name is written in exquisite cursive on the page, with names signed all down the sides. I scan the names—no last names are recorded. Sure enough, in black ink and a young girl's scrawl, I see the name "Cora".

But what sticks out, possibly even more, is the name "Winnie".

Swallowing feels wrong. I squint.

"Where's the picture?" I breathe. I follow Isla's finger to the next page, where there is an old, faded photograph. She points out Cora, who smiles big at the camera, brown hair in two twin braids.

The girl. The ghost girl.

The breath whooshes from my lungs like I've been kicked in the gut. *Cora is the ghost girl.* Cora is the girl I keep seeing. She's real.

But even more terrifying?

Standing behind her, is a tall, college-age girl, all blonde and long legs, smiling with her mouth closed. Her eyes are green, like mine.

She is a familiar stranger. Betrayal lingers on my tongue, although I'm not entirely sure why. I haven't really been betrayed, but somehow this feels personal.

"That's my mom," I whisper. My finger trembles as I trace the outline.

"What? You're joking." Isla squints and then her jaw drops. "Your mom was Cora's *counselor*?"

The girls begin to whisper and point and gasp. Cora's story has suddenly gone from something distant to something I have a direct connection to. For all their talk about not believing the ghost stories told around campfires, my parents are hypocrites. There's no way Mom could've been Cora's counselor and then doesn't believe in the rumors.

I carefully study the faces again. *Was Mom there when Cora died?*

"Maeve, look!" Isla taps a photo vigorously. I squint, trying to make out what she's so desperate to show me. But I see him. It's a photo of the Painted Lady cabin at the pool, but in the picture, Mom is in the background chatting with a guy around her age, instead of smiling with her cabin.

I'd recognize that man anywhere.

It's my father.

"It's George!" gasps Emily. "Maeve, did you know your parents went to this camp the same year that Cora died?"

"No." I grip the table. "I knew they'd gone to a camp when they were young, but I had no idea it was this one. I didn't know they knew Cora."

"You *have* to ask them about this." Isla shakes her head, dumbstruck. "This is bizarre."

My parents belonged to this place. I don't know how many summers they spent here, but I doubt it was only one. This was probably where they met, like some summer rom-com. I thought I knew my parents so well. I thought I was the enigma in this family. It never occurred to me that they could have stories I hadn't heard yet.

Or that they'd hid from me.

I know for a fact they didn't tell me they went to Camp Swallowtail when I came here at age seven. That's something I would've remembered.

I open my mouth to say something, when a clatter and the sound of breaking glass fills the room. My heart skips a beat and we all whirl around. Addie and Madysen stand near the dresser, wide-eyed.

On the floor is the broken photo of Bo and Abigail.

"Guys," Isla grimaces. "Please be careful in here. What were you two doing?"

"It wasn't me, it was Addie!" Madysen cries, flinging a hand in Addie's direction.

Addie's jaw drops and she looks at me pleadingly. "It wasn't. Maeve, it wasn't."

"Stop your whining," Madysen retorts. "It was you and you know it."

Isla holds out her hands. "Guys, it doesn't really matter. The point is an important piece of this room is broken and it's because we weren't being careful. Would the two of you please step away from the glass so I can get it cleaned up?"

Timidly, Addie takes a step away, but she looks at Isla with teary eyes. "Isla, it wasn't me. I promise. I didn't."

Isla squeezes Addie's shoulder. "It's okay. I'm not blaming you guys; I'm just reminding everyone that we need to be more careful."

Addie stares at her feet.

I watch Madysen's expression quietly. She smirks at Addie, then dons a startled look when the other girls crowd around her. Anger boils in the pit of my stomach.

She is such a fake. How could she be so nasty to Addie? How could she be so nasty to *anyone*?

I kneel on the ground to help Isla pick up the pieces of broken glass. The photo lies, abandoned, on the ground with the back of the frame. I set it delicately on the dresser. As I reach down to grab a piece of glass, I jerk my hand away and scramble back.

Isla does the same, screaming.

I clap my hands over my mouth and blink about a million times, certain that I must be dreaming or hallucinating. But the girls see it too.

Somehow, against all scientific possibility, the shards of glass begin to levitate in the air, slowly, shaking. A violent image floods through my mind, of all of us being sliced up by these ghostly pieces of glass, leaving us here to bleed out.

It makes me tremble more. My vision has tunneled on those enchanted shards of glass.

The shards, jagged and fractured, float towards the wall where they begin to carve harsh words. The very first letter is an "I".

Charlie begins to cry.

The pieces continue carving until the words "I am here" are permanently etched into the wooden wall of Scrapbook Bunk. When the final curve of the "e" is finished, the shards tremble and sling through the air by some invisible force, making a beeline for the open scrapbook from 1996, still on the page depicting Cora.

With a horrible, bone-chilling sound, the glass pieces shred up the Painted Lady page, leaving nothing but shreds of paper. It's completely unrecognizable.

I'm dreaming.

There is no way anyone can deny this—something is making the shards of glass float.

Or someone. The hallucinations. The ghost.

Cora.

The pieces clatter to the table, inanimate once again, and the girls begin to scream and wail again, clinging to each other. Except Addie.

She's watching the pieces, a mix of fear and wonder on her face. The lack of terror worries me, but I see I'm not the only one who picked up on it.

Madysen has too.

"Calm down, everyone!" Isla shouts over the roar. "Everyone just needs to calm down!"

"It's the ghost!" wails Lena. "She's haunting us!" She drags her fingers through her hair, tears stream down her face.

"Guys, listen to Isla!" I press my hands to my temples.

"Everyone please just take a deep breath." Isla's hands are trembling. "We're going to go outside and then Maeve and I are going to talk with Winnie and George." She shoots me a look. "It's all going to be fine and I'm sure there's a logical explanation for this. There is no ghost."

Incredulously, I gawk at Isla.

"I know what it was," Madysen announces. She turns on Addie. "It was you. You summoned your little ghost friends because you were mad about the picture frame. You're trying to scare us. And it's not going to work." She shoves her against the ground and Addie falls.

I consider Madysen's words. Addie did mention a few weeks ago that she sees things that aren't always there, and she shut down when I tried to ask her about it. Truthfully, I have no way of knowing what goes on inside that girl's head, but I know there must be more to it than I'm realizing.

What if Madysen's right? I've been discrediting her opinion because she reminds me so much of Quinny, but Quinny didn't lie about *everything*. Is Madysen onto something? Could Addie be communicating with ghosts or even be possessed by one herself?

"I didn't do it!" Addie's voice rises, a flash of anger I've never seen in her before rising to the surface, like a volcano about to blow. "I don't summon ghosts, Madysen."

"How would we know?" Madysen counters, hands on her hips. She's trying to act brave, but I know she's scared. I don't think she's just trying to be mean anymore; she genuinely believes Addie communicates with ghosts.

She's afraid.

And so are the rest of the girls. They begin to move closer to Madysen, away from Addie.

Afraid. They're all afraid.

Isla looks at me, loss for words. For the first time, she doesn't know what to do.

Little Maeve is in my head again, pulling me back down into the past, when my cabin mates thought I was communicating with ghosts and with magic, all because my parents were crazy and superstitious. I remember the pain, like a void in my chest that nagged at me and wouldn't go away. I remember feeling like I was about to cry every second, like one comment by one mean girl would set me off and I would fall captive to my sadness. Pounding against the closet door hurt my fists back then, but I did it anyway because I was so afraid they would never open the door and let me out.

And I see the similarities. I look at Addie, and I see Little Maeve inside of her, trying to tell me something.

But it's not only Little Maeve that I see.

I see *her*. She's smaller than I thought, but she looks *real*. There's just a small outline of something ethereal around her that makes me realize that she isn't real, even though her dark braids are ratty and messy and she has dark circles under her hazel eyes.

Cora.

She tilts her head eerily to one side, watching me. Slowly, she raises one pale, skinny finger to her lips, instructing my silence. I try not to let shock register on my face, but I must fail, there's no way that I don't.

She's a ghost. I'm seeing a ghost. The same ghost I saw when I was seven. Locked in a closet. Afraid. And I know for a fact that Addie is seeing her, too. Addie meets my eyes and a tear slips down her cheek.

I glance around at the others, but they must not see her. The only person they fix their eyes on is Addie. *Why do she and I see Cora, but the others don't?*

Bitter cold air settles into the room and I feel goosebumps prickle along my skin.

Has she been writing all those messages around the camp? If she is, she must have something out for my parents or something to call this place Camp Evil instead of Everbrill. And what about the message by the kitchen?

What sins need to be paid for? Who is paying? And how are they doing it?

"Maeve!"

I jolt and blink. Cora isn't there anymore. Did I imagine the whole thing?

Addie doesn't look at me. She continues to stare tearfully at the floor.

Isla is shaking me, eyes worried. "What happened to you? Did you just zone out or something?"

"I...I..."

"Probably put under some spell from sixth sense Addie," Madysen snarls.

Addie covers her ears with her hands and brings her knees up to her chest. Her tears become loud, ugly sobs that fill up the whole room. I don't know if she's trying to block out

Madysen's voice or if Cora is telling her things that the rest of us can't hear.

I want to reach out and pull her away from whatever haunts are taking over her mind and body. Ghost stories are meant to give you sympathy for the dead, but a red rush of hatred for Cora pulses through me.

She lost her life and it's a sad thing. But she needs to leave the rest of us alone.

As soon as I think the thought, I feel a thousand little pinpricks racing up and down my arms and legs. I know that it's her, so I bite my lip so hard to keep from screaming that I taste blood, metallic and tangy. My eyes snap shut.

She's messing with my mind. She can't actually hurt me.

It's not real it's not real it's not real—

But before anything else happens, Addie stands up with a grating scream and sprints out of Scrapbook Bunk, leaving the rest of us behind, gaping in silence.

The coldness vanishes. Cora is gone.

drowning
July 5

Isla asked Josie to watch the girls while the two of us split up to find Addie. My pulse is pounding through my ears, while everything else around me sounds slightly distorted, as if I'm underwater.

Drowning.

Addie's horrific expression as she ran out is cemented in my mind, flashing before my eyes every time I turn around as Isla and I sprint to the Great Hall, hoping to make heads or tails of what's happening. Because Addie didn't go back to the cabin. And she wasn't in the bathroom when we sent Kiara to look.

The girls wanted to come look for her with us, which was a shock. I thought for sure that Madysen's comments freaked them all out enough to turn Addie into someone they should be afraid of. But it seems as though Madysen's comments only truly hurt Addie.

Beads of sweat slowly trickle down my back, despite my goosebumps. I'm worried that if whatever this is doesn't get addressed, things will get a lot worse.

"You go look for your parents near the Great Hall!" Tendrils of Isla's hair stick to her forehead with sweat. "I'm going to make rounds around the road!"

I nod, veering to the left. Splitting up will help us cover more ground quickly. The thought of Cora haunting Addie right now, while she's alone and vulnerable, is almost too much to stomach and gives me the willpower to run faster.

Isla and I should've stopped Madysen before it got this bad and before Addie had this breakdown in front of all of us. Her quiet demeanor was just so impossible to see through—I knew she was haunted in some way, I just didn't know by what.

The poor thing was suffering more than she let us see. Bullying is its own kind of ghost, dancing around your heart and mind, gripping its claws in you until all you see is the person that you aren't—the person that you should be. If only you looked this way, acted this way, lived this way, maybe you wouldn't be treated so poorly.

Madysen's words have haunted Addie. The same way that ten years ago, the words of those girls who locked me in the cabin supply closet haunted me.

I never had someone to stick up for me, even with the subtle jabs Quinny would give.

If I let myself realize that my parents weren't freaks, I could have learned how to get over things like this. Then, I'd have been better equipped to support Addie during my time here.

I could have helped her, if I hadn't been so freaking *selfish*.

I don't realize I'm crying until I see Hayes in front of me, standing by the door of the Great Hall, like he's been waiting for me this whole time. My tears blur his figure and against the sunset, it looks like he's glowing.

He's here. He's alive.

I gape at him, loss for words and reach to throw my arms around him but he backs up nervously, squinting when he sees my face.

"Maeve? What's going on?"

"Hayes..." I don't want him to see me crying, but at this point I can't do anything to change that. "Hayes, I *really* need your help. How...how are you okay? What happened to you? I saw you with the...with the swallowtails and I thought—"

He shakes his head. "Focus on this, okay? Are you hurt?"

The emotion in his voice makes me cry more. I wipe my eyes. "Addie is missing."

"Your camper?"

My chest tightens. *My* camper. *My* responsibility. "What happened? When did you last see her?" Shakily, I point back toward Scrapbook Bunk, tears beginning anew. "We were adding our page to the scrapbook for today's activity..." My voice trembles. "And the girls wanted to see what Cora looked like, so Isla found that page and then this old picture frame broke. I know it sounds crazy, Hayes, but *I saw Cora*. I saw her and so did Addie—one of the girls said something mean and Cora started to hurt me and Addie ran."

His jaw tightens and something flashes across his eyes. Does he go pale or is that just my imagination? "Cora did *what* to you?"

"I know, I know." I take a deep breath and lower my hands. Close my eyes. "I know how it sounds, but I swear to you—"

"No, I believe you. What did she do, Maeve?"

I shake my head. He doesn't understand. "This isn't about me! This is about *Addie* and she's *missing*—"

His jaw clenches. "Have you looked by the river?"

"I...no? Why would I look there?"

"C'mon. Let's go." I want him to reach out and hold my hand, and show me a physical response to what he's saying, showing me that he really believes this is going to be okay. But he doesn't touch me.

Adrenaline courses through my veins, giving me tunnel vision and a ringing in my ears that blocks out all the attempted comforting words Hayes shouts at me as I sprint.

Everyone was right. Camp Swallowtail *is* cursed.

Hate, black and strong, rises in me because I'd finally found a home in this place. Now I'm not sure what about it I can trust. Camp Swallowtail has always been a part of my life, even before I knew it. My parents met here. Maybe I was always destined to come back.

I have to get to Addie.

I have to.

Fingers of tall, long grass itch my legs and bugs jump up from the ground, disturbed. The ringing in my ears has calmed down to a faint sound that is almost easy to ignore by the time we get to the river.

The last remnants of the sun are sinking.

There's a chill in the air.

Cora is here.

Crickets chirp and cicadas buzz, the only thing that fills the silence, save for the humming of the wind in the trees. Every now and then, it stirs up a lot, blowing my hair back and stinging my eyes.

Hayes approaches the river cautiously. I follow him, wringing my hands together, nerves buzzing in the back of my mind.

"Check the slide," I whisper. Squeeze my eyes shut. Swallow the lump in my throat.

Addie is halfway in the river, half laid out across the sand and grass. Blood trickles down the side of her head and her eyes are shut, her mouth slightly open. Her skin is pale and glistens with river water.

The slide blows free in the wind.

Untied.

Did she know? She wouldn't have gone on the slide if she knew it was untied, would she? Addie may have been frightened but she didn't have a death wish.

The air is cold again. Bitingly cold.

Frigid.

Slowly, almost too slowly, Hayes approaches Addie like she's a dangerous predator about to pounce. He squats down beside her, observes her still body. I tear my hands through my hair and fall beside her, kneeling in the wet sand and grass, not even bothered that it clings to my skin.

One of my hands shakes as I reach for her wrist, checking for a pulse. It's faint, but there, and I breathe a huge sigh of relief, feeling so much tension immediately evaporate from me.

At least she's alive.

"We need to get to my parents," I say urgently. I brush my hands off on my legs, pull my hair back from my face. "Do you think you can carry her?"

Quickly, Hayes shakes his head. "No, I don't think carrying her is a good idea."

"Why not?"

"We don't want to jostle her around too much—it's clear that she has some kind of head injury." He points to the dark stain across the pale skin of her forehead.

I wince.

"I know it seems cruel, but we're going to leave her here and find your parents, okay? I promise that we'll come back, but the two of us shouldn't carry her, Maeve."

Shivers rack my body. I wrap my arms around myself, working so hard to stay altogether. I hear that ringing again, faint, but there, mingling with the songs of the cicadas and crickets.

And the air is still cold. If we leave her, what will happen? What if someone finds her and sees us leaving and thinks that Hayes and I hurt her?

Surely, that wouldn't happen. Isla and the other girls knew she was missing before we went to search the grounds for her.

"Maeve," Hayes says softly, his voice like a calm sea breeze

"You're right." I tuck the wild strands of hair behind my ears and clench my fists.

I hate to leave her.

But I know Hayes is right. I have to trust him.

"I just hate this ghost," I whisper. "She *is* evil." Hayes shakes his head vehemently. "Stop, Maeve, don't say stuff like that."

Addie's silent body flashes through my brain and fear and anger dig claws into me, spiking my heart rate and breathing. Trying to focus and stay calm, I concentrate on taking one step at a time but can't because I'm suddenly so overwhelmed.

Blood splatters the side of Hawkmoth Haven. Camp Evil.

Blood splatters the side of the kitchen. Someone's sins.

Blood splatters the shards of glass in Scrapbook Bunk. My mom, Cora's counselor.

Blood splatters the otherwise flawless skin of Addie's forehead. She's lying by the river all alone.

Hysteria builds and I shut my eyes. Dizzy.

Little pinpricks of pain pierce my skin, like the sensation I experienced in Scrapbook Bunk after mentally ridiculing Cora. But as I think more angry thoughts about her, the pain increases until I've fallen to the tall grass and am writhing, dark clouds shifting through the sky with the promise of imminent rain.

"Maeve, stop thinking about her!" Hayes yells,

I wish he would carry me out of this storm and back to the Great Hall or Misty Monarch, where I could sleep and cover myself in blankets until this whole nightmare ends. But he doesn't. He curls his fingers and drags them through his hair. He doesn't touch me.

"Leave her alone, Cora!" he screams at the sky.

The pain jerks my body like some kind of broken puppet. Tears stream from my eyes and I scream so hard my throat burns.

Pain, pain, pain, pain, pain is all I can think of. It's excruciating and I wish Cora would just kill me.

"STOP!"

It suddenly ceases, just as quickly as it began. I'm shivering and heaving on the ground, waiting for the next strike of cruelty.

"I'm so sorry," Hayes whispers. He holds out his hand but pulls it back and then looks angrily at the sky, either because of Cora or because for some reason he can't touch me.

I'm haunted. I must be.

Hayes' eyes well up when he looks at me, helpless and defeated.

"I can't save you," he whispers. "But I can try to help Addie."

I shake my head feebly. *What?*

Before I can fathom what I'm seeing, Hayes' body pulses with a strange glow, something dull that slowly brightens. It radiates off his body in a completely unnatural way and I scramble back.

What is he?

Somewhere, there's a little nudge in my mind, telling me what I always knew. But before I can put words to it, Addie's eyes flutter open and Hayes is gone.

the office
July 5

There's always a moment in good movies where the heroine hits rock bottom. She feels abandoned by the people she's invested in or finds herself in a situation that can't get worse. The scene is usually encompassed by dark lighting and tears, something to portray the vast chasm she feels splitting inside of her—tearing her apart at the very marrow and bone.

There have been many times in my life when I thought I understood this feeling. This panic and complete lack of knowing what to do next. But this moment tops them all.

Addie's eyes are still fluttering but Hayes is gone. I don't know if I can move her or what to do and I have no phone. I should feel hopeful, but I feel inadequate and unequipped to handle this situation in the right way.

"Addie," I sob.

Before I have to say anything else, Isla is running over to the rescue and the tears come anew. I wish I knew where Hayes went or what just happened between them. It wasn't human but I don't have any better way to describe it.

"She's okay," I reach out to Isla, and she throws her arms around me.

"I have my phone," she breathes, dialing 911. "Go find your parents. Tell them what happened. I'll stay here with her."

I nod quickly, scrambling up and casting one last anxious glance at Addie before sprinting off towards Mom and Dad's office. The grass itches my bare legs as I sprint, but I hardly notice it. There's this deep fear that I'm being watched and it's prickling the back of my neck. I just want to get to the office as fast as I possibly can.

The dark front porch steps finally come into sight, and I jump up them as fast as I can. I throw open the door, thinking of nothing but Addie and Hayes and Addie and Hayes and Cora, Cora, Cora...

My skin is clammy when I get to Mom and Dad's door, closed, but with light pouring out from underneath. Something stops my hand from turning the doorknob.

Voices.

Quietly, I calm my racing heart and listen against the wooden door.

"This isn't what was supposed to happen when we bought this place," Mom wails. "We decided this would be a good way to make amends for the past!"

I slowly lower my hand to the doorknob but don't turn it.

"Winnie, how were we to know this place was really cursed? Couldn't this still be some kind of coincidence? Or Adeline Bennet could be a very clumsy, accident-prone, young girl."

He knows about Addie?

Mom's sobs get louder. "George, you *know* I don't believe in coincidences! Everything that happens happens for a reason. This is payback; no amount of reconciliation could fix what we did."

"Hush!" Dad whispers harshly. "You have to be careful what you say."

"It's in the past! Who would even hear me anyway? We both know this is our punishment for our stupidity years ago. We never should've bought this wicked camp."

I shake my head, lost for words. I have no idea. I didn't know they had any history with this camp before today at Scrapbook Bunk. All of this solidifies the idea that Camp Swallowtail and I are far more connected than I ever imagined.

Part of me wants to barge in and demand that they give me the full story of whatever the heck it is they are talking about. Realistically, however, I know doing that would be the very last way they would confess any past horrors to me.

"We made a mistake," Dad continues to Mom, his voice soft and comforting now. "It was wrong, and we know that. But this *is* us making amends, Winnie. Cora's ghost may be real, but she's not haunting us for anything that we did. And she's not punishing us for it right now either. You know spirits don't work like that."

"But they *do*. And if we're not careful, she could harm Maeve, too. We already had the incidents of the painted messages and the swallowtails! If this is the work of Cora, it means that she is after vengeance. Who knows what else might happen? Ugh. I wish I had been a better counselor. I wish...I wish so many different things."

"We can't change the past, Win," Dad says grimly. I finally can see his figure through the crack in the door, approaching Mom slowly and wrapping his arms around her shaking body, folding her into one of his warm bear hugs. "There's no number of tinctures or concoctions can heal this wound."

Mom shakes her head sadly, looking up at him with teary green eyes.

And looks over his shoulder.

Right at me.

I scramble backward and thud to the floor. "Dang it!"

"Maeve?" Mom calls out. I hear the gentle slap of bare feet hitting the wooden floor and before I know it, the door swings open, orange light blinding me. I hold out a hand, trying to block the garish glow.

"Uh, hi."

Dad stalks out beside her, quiet anger burning. There aren't many things I can do to really irritate Dad, but eavesdropping has always been one of them. Unfortunately, it's been one of my favorite pastimes, up until this point.

I figure I might as well explain. "One of my campers, Addie, went missing. I thought Isla was here, but I guess she didn't come? But it sounded like you already knew about Addie..." my voice trails off. I cock my head suspiciously. "How did you know? Did Isla make it here somehow?"

Bracelets clank around Mom's wrists as she fiddles with her flowing dress. "We somehow received an anonymous tipoff."

I gasp. "Somebody did this to her on purpose?"

"We don't know that." Dad turns his warning stare on Mom, but unlike the rest of us, she doesn't falter. She raises a blonde eyebrow at him, dishing it back.

"Why would someone intentionally hurt Addie?" I demand, looking back and forth between both of them. "Is there something that the two of you want to explain? There's no point in lying," I add when Dad begins to defend himself.

Just as I was beginning to feel comfortable here, with my cabin and with my parents, I find out that there's been something huge they've been hiding from me, possibly all my life.

Firmly, Dad shakes his head. "That is none of your business, young lady."

"George, she already heard us," Mom contradicts.

Her eyes watch me. "What harm does it do for her to know the truth?"

My heart softens at her words.

Dad isn't so easily persuaded. He stalks over to his oak wood desk stained a dark shade of brown and thumps his fist on the top, sending a stack of papers flying across the floor, echoing his frustration.

Mom's eyes glisten again with unshed tears. She grabs Dad's arm tightly. "Just tell her, George!" she sobs. "Just tell her!"

Finally resigned, Dad covers Mom's hand with his own.

"Dad?" I whisper, looking back and forth between the two of them.

Mom, teary-eyed, her chemical-free mascara streaking down her cheeks like oil.

Dad, holding Mom's hand like it's a delicate butterfly, his eyes soft on me like he knows he's already let me down.

"You might want to have a seat," he says.

summer
1996

Once, there was a love—the wildest kind, young and naive.

Winnie, age twenty, was hopelessly in love with George Everbrill. On their nights off from counseling cabins full of preteens, they talked about the potential of their future—of what it might look like. They talked about dropping out of college and forgoing the ideas their parents had for them, which included respectable things that left no room for creativity or adventure.

And the only thing Winnie and George craved more than each other was adventure.

"What if we opened a summer camp?" George asked Winnie one evening, lying beside her in the grass.

She turned towards him, blinking her big green eyes that he adored. "A summer camp? Where would we get the money?"

George's gaze strayed toward the moon, full overhead like a bowl of milk. "We could make it. But it would have to be quick. You know my parents are going to be really hard on me about a business degree when fall rolls around. So, if we're really doing this, it needs to be now."

Excitement blossomed like rosebuds in Winnie's stomach. She sat up, planting her arms on either side of her. "You mean it? We could do this?"

"Why not? I have money saved and with what we both make at camp, maybe we could do it."

She let her eyes flutter shut for a moment, imagining a life filled with wonder and George. It wasn't what her parents had in mind, but she couldn't picture anything more splendid. She wanted to run off with him. Start their own camp.

It sounded perfect.

But George's older sister found herself in a bad situation, in which George had to pay her bail to get her out of trouble with their parents. He was angry but couldn't leave her on her own.

"We could ask Bo and Abigail to raise our pay," Winnie suggested quietly one evening, sitting by the pool after sneaking out when her cabin had gone to bed.

George splashed the water moodily. "They'll say no." His insistence in this plan had grown since July had begun. Soon, it would be August and his life would no longer be his own.

Winnie felt for him. Her parents were sending her to an IVY league school, which she'd worked hard for, but at the same time, didn't care about. She understood that it was a blessing but knew that life wasn't for her.

More than anything, Winnie wanted to live.

So she asked Bo and Abigail one morning, pleading their case, presenting it honestly.

And left with a broken spirit, rejected and told to grow up.

"Running a camp isn't easy," Bo retorted. "And I'm not sure you and George have what it takes."

George and Winnie were crushed. Without thinking, they began to cause little bits of trouble around the camp—

nothing dangerous, just things that were found to be annoying.

Their perception of Camp Swallowtail was tainted by their anxiety and bitterness.

Anger took hold of George, and he decided that Bo would pay. He wanted to talk to Winnie about it, so he knocked on the window by her bed and pointed down toward the river. She rubbed the sleep out of her eyes and threw a sweatshirt over her head.

Rain began to fall as the two of them walked toward the river, tall grass itching their legs and housing all kinds of night bugs that chirped in the emptiness of the evening.

"We have to do this. I've never been so passionate about anything. I'm just so mad at him that I can hardly think!"

Winnie held out a gentle hand. "You need to take a breath."

Red burned in George's vision. He couldn't go to business school. He couldn't. He wouldn't fit in there and it would lead to a boring life where all he would care about was money. He'd rather live on the streets with Winnie.

Winnie glanced back over her shoulder, spooked like a deer. She almost swore that she heard a twig crack as though under someone's foot.

But no one was there.

The river was a much needed source of white noise; it calmed Winnie's mind.

She slipped off her sandals, laying them beside her in the sand, and submerged her feet into the cool river water, watching the way the moonlight danced across the streams, reflecting on her painted toes. A pleasant chill ran through her, a combination of the night, the cool water, and being here with George which was against the rules.

"I need to do something, Win," George whispered to her, burying his face in her blonde hair. He shook when she wrapped her arms around him.

"Then do it," she heard herself saying, not really realizing what she was giving him permission to do. If it was even her permission that he needed.

But they both glanced over at the slide and then back at each other.

George loosened the knot first.

Winnie followed with the second.

Slowly, the slide slid free from the contraption supporting it and blew with abandon in the gentle breeze, the end flapping up like a kite. George and Winnie watched, awestruck at the massive blue and yellow tarp blowing around. It felt good to do something so wrong and rebellious —it felt like the first taste of freedom, of revenge for Bo and Abigail's harsh words.

When the wind died down, the slide sank back to its position but remained far from safe. Winnie realized that one kid descending the slide with the knots undone could result in some kind of serious injury.

A lump lodged in her throat. Surely this would only be a warning, not actually something that would cause a problem.

Especially when she heard an all-too-familiar voice.

"Late night slide!" cheered one of Winnie's campers, from the top of the slide.

Winnie clapped her hands over her mouth. George was beside her in a minute, gripping her arm tightly.

"I thought you were alone." His voice was strangled.

"I thought I was too," breathed Winnie, wide-eyed.

But there was Cora, illuminated faintly by the moonlight, getting situated on the slide. She was even in her swimsuit—

a blue one-piece with lots of tiny purple stripes. Winnie recognized it immediately.

"She must've heard you tap on the window and point toward the river," Winnie paled. "And then she followed me here, but was careful that I wouldn't see her."

"Get her off the slide!" George raced toward the steps, leading up to the slide. He began to climb, but Cora protested loudly.

"No, no!" she cried. "This is going to be so much fun!" She gave a laugh that chilled Winnie to the bone. Something about it...wasn't quite right.

Maniacal.

Cora was having one of her fits again, prone to schizophrenia and sudden changes in personality.

"Cora, get down, please!" Winnie ran to the edge of the slide, standing ankle deep in the river.

The wind picked up dramatically and the slide danced in the wind.

"Whoa," Cora breathed, mesmerized. "It's extra fun tonight. All my friends are saying so. Do you hear them, Winnie?"

And then she let go.

"NO!" Winnie screamed as Cora's little body flew up, up, up into the air.

She doesn't know what she's doing, Winnie thought, panicked.

She reached her arms out helplessly as Cora plummeted down, down, down, and smacked her head against the metal bar.

Her eyes fluttered shut and her head went slack as she collided with the ground and Winnie screamed.

Everything moved in slow motion for Winnie. Her eyes stretched so wide that it hurt, and her screams echoed *throughout the trees, bouncing off the bark and surrounding Cora's broken body.*

A massive wound split across her forehead and her eyes were staring unseeingly at the sky. One of her arms was bent in an unnatural angle and a tiny trickle of blood traced down the side of her face from her mouth.

What have I done? Winnie panicked. What have we gotten into?

George's body shadowed Cora and Winnie. His hands were shaking violently. He was making these little gasping sounds, like he couldn't get words to form. Finally, he fell to the ground beside Winnie, the gravity of the situation weighing on him.

Things had instantly gotten so much worse. He'd let his anger get the best of him and he saw the consequences immediately. Agitation bubbled up inside his chest and he began to pace, tearing his hands through his dark hair and gripping the fabric of his t-shirt.

Winnie looked at him with empty eyes and he could see the heartbreak broadcasted all across her face. A pang of guilt ripped throughout him. There had been many things his parents taught that he didn't agree with, but one thing his dad always emphasized was that men are supposed to take care of their women. Winnie was his—and he had failed to take care of her.

She pressed her forehead down against Cora's body, sobbing broken, painful sobs. The sound tormented George's heart and he fell beside her, wrapping his arms around her trembling body.

But they couldn't tell.

They were too afraid of what would happen, so they left, letting the guilt eat at them for years and years to come.

Leaving Cora, dead, by the river.

everbrills
July 5

Blinking doesn't clear away the fuzziness in front of me. My parents shift and bleed like watercolors, blurry and ever changing. It's sinking in that this has never been simple or easy—nothing they've ever done has been.

I swallow.

Mom sobs. Covers her face with her hands and rocks slowly back and forth on her feet.

She didn't *mean* for this to happen.

They were in the wrong place at the wrong time. At least, Cora was. And she had much more going on than people realized.

"We want you to know that we feel bad," Dad's voice breaks. "Do you think we just went on our merry way, never giving another thought to the poor girl?"

"We were *heartbroken*," Mom wails.

"It haunts us to this day." Dad puts an arm around Mom. They're broken people.

"Maeve?" Mom whispers, blinking at me with watery green eyes.

Eyes like mine

"Mom," I whisper back.

"What are you thinking, chickadee?" She braces herself like I'm about to tell her that I hate her and never want anything to do with either of them again.

It was a terrible, terrible thing that they did. There's no excuse.

But when I look at their faces, I know how much they've grieved. I understand how so many things they've done have brought us to this moment where they hoped they could make amends for what they did.

"You made a mistake." My words are soft and they ring true deep inside my bones. "What you did was horrible. And there's really no excuse."

She bows her head. Tears fell from her face and onto the ground, staining the wood floor a darker shade of brown.

"We would reconcile with whoever we need to," Mom promises, her voice trembling. "We truly do wish we could've done it all differently. I know how shocking this must be for you, but please understand. We know we don't deserve forgiveness for our sins, but..." she shudders through a sigh. "We will do whatever else we need to do to make this right."

We know we don't deserve forgiveness for our sins...

I blink.

The nurse's wall.

The ghost's fun finally begins, while we wait for someone to pay for their sins.

Frosty air enters the room. What will she do to Mom and Dad?

"Speaking of Cora," I whisper.

Mom closes her eyes. She feels her too.

"Winnie." Dad's voice is tight. He points to the rocking chair in the corner, made of old oak wood, rocking softly, even though there's no one in it.

That we can see.

Within seconds, a ghostly form appears, exactly the way I saw it in Scrapbook Bunk.

There stands a little girl, with a tilted head, watching us all with hazel eyes that have a darkness inside of them. Her dark hair is twisted into two braids, resting on her shoulders. She's wearing a pale pink nightgown with lace across the shoulders. Her feet are bare, but muddy and stained with faded blood.

She skims over my parents and settles her chilling gaze on me.

I stare back. I don't want to be afraid of her.

She opens her mouth unnaturally wide and I flinch, torn between covering my eyes from the grotesque sight and feeling like I can't look away. For a moment I think she's about to take a bite out of my parents. A sick feeling rolls up within me.

A voice, ghostly and unearthly, pours forth from her mouth, but she isn't *speaking*. Her mouth doesn't move as the words take form and become a sentence.

"My parents always believed that my death was an accident and they never received closure for what misery you thrust upon them."

My parents both flinch.

"Dad instantly shakes his head. "No, Winnie, we can't do this. They could sue us more than we can pay. We could go to prison. The risks are too great."

"George," Mom wails. "Don't you see? We have to do what is worth the risk because we already messed up too badly! We have to do this."

"The only person she's harming is us," Dad argues. "The situation isn't as bad as you think."

A dark scream erupts from Cora's gaping mouth. Blackness pours forth, stealing the light from the fixtures in the room until we're left in darkness, lit only by the faint glow around Cora's body.

"Ask your daughter if that's true." Cora's voice takes a nasty tone. *"Ask if she's willing to suffer for you anymore."*

I close my eyes, my heart pounding so hard that I hear it in my ears and am certain everyone else in the room can hear it just as loud.

"What does she mean?" Mom's voice is hushed.

Cora's eyes dare me to lie, to not be honest about what happened, about what she did to me that summer.

"You're wicked," I whisper, tears pricking my own eyes. I can't believe her. "You really are. I don't know if you always were a little devious, or if holding this grudge made you this way."

"What does she mean?" Dad's brows are drawn together as if he's in pain.

"Before you continue," Dad butts in. "We should be honest with you about *why* we sent you. It was only *partly* to give you that good camp experience."

"We wanted a reason to come back and see the state of the place." Mom's voice breaks with shame. She tucks a strand of gray-blonde hair behind her ear. "And we saw that it wasn't doing too well."

"Bo and Abigail remembered us," Dad scoffs. "They never liked *us* as campers, so they didn't think you'd be any better."

"Well, I'm not surprised," I snort. "Everyone hated me."

"They did?" Mom flinches "Because of us?"

Reluctantly, I nod. Fidget with the hem of my shirt. I *really* don't want to hurt them. But Cora might hurt me if I don't tell them the truth.

Mom's eyes soften around the edges, sorrow creeping into her expression.

"I used to be so proud to be your daughter." A teardrop falls off my nose. "I bragged to the kids in my cabin about all the interesting things you guys were always learning and discovering. I told them about the teas and Dad's mushrooms. About the butterflies we studied together as a family. About the recipes I would make with Mom every night."

Little Maeve dances around me again, but this time she's not afraid.

She's wearing an apron that goes all the way down to her floor, belonging to her mother, who is happily spinning around the kitchen, a bowl and spoon, whisking away as she sings to Little Maeve. Little Maeve claps her hands, a cloud of almond flour puffing up into the air.

Again, a new scene: Little Maeve helping her dad observe butterflies, copying down the intricate markings on their wings into a notebook, sketching studiously with her tongue poking out of the corner of her mouth.

"The girls in my cabin made fun of me relentlessly." I wipe away snot and tears with the back of my hand. "They left me behind at events, moved away from me at the table during meals...Sometimes they wouldn't even *talk* to me."

I did everything I could to get in good with Quinny back at home so that I would have security. So that I would *always* have a place at the lunch table.

Looking at it now, I see the parallel between Addie and me. But Addie knows herself better than I ever did.

"One night..." I pause. I close my eyes because the screaming in my head is so loud and jarring that goosebumps prickle my arms.

Everyone waits for me to continue. Cora watches with knowing eyes, mouth still gaping open.

I take a deep breath "One night, they locked me in the supply closet in the cabin when my counselors both headed out to go to the bathroom. The girls said they wanted to quarantine my "crazy". They didn't want to catch whatever disease they thought you passed down to me." I avoid eye contact with my parents, fearful of the expressions they'll be wearing.

Little Maeve is back in the closet. Tears stream down her face like blood and she beats the wooden door with her fists, banging and banging, trying to get the door open because no one wants to help her.

"LET ME OUT!" she screams at the top of her lungs, Her sobs are loud and shrill, which should embarrass her, but she's too agitated to care, thrashing against the door.

"Please!" she begs someone, anyone. The darkness in the closet seems to close in and she suddenly feels a rush of cold air, striking her right to her very marrow.

"But, all of a sudden, I wasn't alone in the closet anymore."

Cora tilts her head at me, watching. The gaping hole that is her mouth turns up into a little grin, too wide to be natural.

I look away. "I felt this cold presence in the closet with me."

"George," Mom mutters, strangled. I glance up and see her gripping Dad's arm, agitation in her green eyes. Her tears are quiet now, but they remain present.

"What's the matter?" the ghostly voice had asked me.

Little Maeve looked around wildly, looking for the source of the shivering voice. When a faint glow around the body of a little girl appeared, she began to scream even more and bang against the door until her hands were bruised and bloody.

"LET ME OUT LET ME OUT LET ME OUT!"

"They're treating you wrongly, aren't they?" the voice continued, ignoring Little Maeve's screams. *"I was treated wrong once, you could say. An accident just* waiting *to happen."*

"I was so overwhelmed with what I saw," I choke on my words. My eyes flutter shut, and I try to calm my breathing. "I ended up passing out. When I woke up, I was back in my bed. My counselors had been told by the girls that I locked myself in the closet and ordered them not to disturb me as I performed my witch rituals. That's when they started thinking I was weird, too."

"Baby," Mom whispers.

Both my parents rush over to me and wrap me in

their arms, holding me so tight that I don't believe it's possible for any of my ugliness to spill out. The overwhelming love sinks into my core and I grasp them just as tightly, mingling my tears with theirs.

"Why didn't you tell us?" Mom whispers, smoothing my hair back. Dad touches my cheek lightly with his weathered hand.

"I didn't want you to be hurt." I'm hiccuping. "I thought it would be easier to pull away so that you could still do the things you love. But I couldn't be treated like that again...I just couldn't."

"We're not mad." Mom holds me tight. "We just wish you would've told us."

Dad leans down. "Maeve, no one is *ever* going to treat you like that again."

"I love you guys," I whimper, leaning all my weight onto my parents.

They made mistakes, like me. They're broken, like me.

But they're Everbrills. Like me.

beating harts
July 5
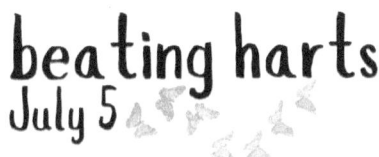

It's nearly midnight when Mom and Dad pull me toward the car. Everything is a blur of whispers and slamming doors and sirens from the ambulance that Isla called for Addie. My brain feels stretched, like it's being pulled in a hundred different directions, trying to figure out which aspect to focus on: Addie, Cora, or Hayes.

I buckle my seatbelt mechanically.

Cora vanished after my parents decided to make a visit to town. I have a sinking feeling that wherever we go, she will be there. Waiting.

This isn't over.

I know it isn't.

Driving through the camp gates brings new experiences every time I've gone through the open metal barricades this summer.

The first time, I was moving here, bitter at life for dealing me these impossible cards.

Mom cranks up the volume to whatever is currently blasting on the radio station, and I feel my jaw drop. All those times she scolded me for drowning out my emotions with music have finally come back to her. I could accuse her of being a hypocrite.

I guess that sometimes we just need a distraction.

I lean back against the soft leather and close my eyes, shutting myself off from the world and becoming as disconnected as I can possibly be in the moment. There's warmth in knowing my parents are on my side, even though I've spent years running from them. But as we drive to wherever it is that Cora's parents live, a knot forms in my stomach, reminding me that the worst is yet to come.

I don't want to see Cora's parents. I'm afraid of what they'll say and do to Mom and Dad. Will they be arrested?

My eyes widen when Mom and Dad pull up to Hart Inn. I grip the seat. "What are we doing here?"

Mom pauses unbuckling and glances back at me. "Maeve, we told you. We need to be honest with Cora's parents about what happened."

"We're hoping our honesty and the risk we're taking will bring Cora some sort of peace that will stop her from harming anyone else at Camp Swallowtail," Dad adds.

I point out the window. "But here?"

"Hart Inn," Mom says. "Cora Hart."

Cora Hart. Thomas and Elise's daughter.

"They went to Camp Swallowtail once, just like you."

Everything clicks into place about the way Elise treated me. Kind, but almost uncertain when she learned my last name. She's known all along that Mom and Dad did this. She must've.

But how? And why didn't she say anything?

My heart skips a beat when Mom and Dad slip out of the car, moonlight pouring over them as wind howls, rocking the Hart Inn sign ominously.

Cora has something planned.

The air smells like a dusty memory, like something you found in an attic that once belonged but has no place in this world anymore.

The front steps creak under our weight, the wood hard underneath my feet. Mom knocks on the door and takes Dad's hand in hers, squeezing it tightly.

I swallow. It feels so different to be here now that I'm not with my friends.

Elise's eyes peer around the curtained window and they widen when she sees me. Her gaze focuses on Mom and Dad, putting two and two together. Slowly, the doorknob turns and we're face to face with Cora's mother, clad in a nightgown and robe. Her expression is wary and guarded.

"Can I help you?" she asks.

Mom's breath catches. "Yes. We're—"

"George and Winnie Everbrill," Dad interrupts, holding out his hand. "And this is our daughter, Maeve."

"We've met," Elise says promptly.

Mom whips her head around to gawk at me and all I can do is shrug helplessly.

"Come in." Elise opens the door wider, eyes lingering on me for a beat too long, causing me to dig my nails into my palms, wracked with nerves.

I can't shake the feeling that this won't end well. Something isn't adding up.

This time when I step into the lobby, I notice the absence of cookies and fire. These small details carve out a hollow cavern in my chest. It's like all the warmth has been sucked out, replacing the kind woman I chatted with in the wee hours of the morning with an old lady who does not trust us.

And why should she?

Mom and Dad slowly glide over to the sofa in front of the fire, mirroring the way Elise and I sat that one night.

"You might want to take a seat," Dad suggests, scratching the back of his neck.

A shuffle of feet brings my eyes to Elise. A tall man looms behind her, gray hair on his head and face and deep pain in his blue eyes. He rests a hand on Elise's shoulder. "Who are these people?"

Elise gestures to us. "Cora's killers. And their daughter."

Mom's jaw drops and she shoots a panicked look at Dad. He grabs her hand tightly. "You knew?"

"We've always known," Thomas says, his bushy eyebrows coming together. "Bo and Abigail told us."

The color leaves Dad's cheeks.

I eye the distance between my parents and the door. Elise sinks to the loveseat. "Nothing ever happened because we felt no need to press charges. We know Cora had her hallucinations and problems and they sometimes drove her to foolish behavior. This was an accident, we've come to realize. What's done is done. So why are you here?"

Mom's voice trembles. "We wanted to open to you. We thought it would help things."

"What things?"

I gnaw on the inside of my cheek. There isn't really a way to go about this with delicacy. News like this surely evokes emotions that are impossible to process, which could be dangerous to my parents.

But Dad isn't known for his subtlety.

"Your daughter has been haunting Camp Swallowtail," Dad says, wrapping a protective arm around Mom. "A girl is on her way to the hospital right now because of her actions."

Mom and I wince.

Thomas' laugh is dry. "She's *dead*, Everbrill. What could she possibly do to a living girl?"

"She can haunt."

The words are out of my mouth before I can think. They all look at me. Dad shoots me a warning look.

"You're saying she's a ghost?" Elise's voice drops to a whisper.

I nod once. My arms wrap tightly around my body. Studying Elise's melancholy face, I try to picture Cora the way they remember her. Despite all the anger and bitterness I may harbor against the ghost, she's still a daughter, loved by her parents.

The splash of sudden sympathy surprises me. But it's hard to hate when you see someone through that sort of lens. When you strip away who people pretend to be and analyze the raw bones of what's really there.

Maybe Cora is putting on a show.

Maybe she isn't as mean and scary as she seems. Thomas narrows his eyes when I don't answer.

"What is your purpose in coming here? To dredge up old memories and cause us unnecessary pain?"

"No," Mom says quickly. "No, we just wanted to come and...apologize."

Thomas throws his hands up. "Well, clearly it's water under the bridge, isn't it? Now get out before we make you."

"Thomas," Elise mumbles feebly. Her eyes latch onto mine.

But before anything else can happen, a horrible shriek echoes throughout the lobby, shaking the walls, causing the picture frames to rattle. The impact is so strong many of them fall to the floor, shattering completely.

I whip around to find Mom and Dad clutching each other. Thomas and Elise do the same. *This is real.*

It's one thing for my family to see ghosts. It's quite another for outsiders to witness the same.

If Cora had the ability to be seen by her parents this whole time, the same way she's revealed herself to me, why hasn't she? Thomas and Elise had no idea she'd come back as a ghost.

The air in front of me shimmers, but it doesn't seem visible to anyone except me—everyone else is still focused on the shaking walls and resounding cry. I stumble a little, catching myself on the side table. The shimmer grows brighter, morphing into the outline of a little girl.

I open my mouth to call to the adults, but Cora's wide mouth gapes open and her voice stops me.

"This isn't between them, Maeve Everbrill. I'm here for you."

Goosebumps ripple across my skin and I back away slowly. When I try to shout again, no sound comes out of my mouth. Eye wide, I scratch at my throat with shaking hands.

When I blink, everything is gone.

oh, brother
July 6

There's something so romantic about the clock striking twelve.

Midnight should be a time for stolen kisses and girls in ballgowns who have a propensity for losing glass slippers. Like any other girl, I fancied myself a potential princess, even if I knew I'd never have a palace or a fairy godmother. The brightest wish is the desire to fall in love with a prince and find a fairytale.

Instead, I've been transported into the pages of a horror novel.

Mom, Dad, Elise, and Thomas are gone. Maybe they're still back in the lobby of Hart Inn, but I wouldn't know because any signs of the familiar fireplace and loveseat are long gone. Instead, I find myself sprawled out on a carpeted floor, smelling foul like mothballs and rot. My body is sore, as if I've been dropped unceremoniously to the ground. When I sit up, my head rushes and I grimace, slowly assessing my surroundings.

I'm in a bedroom, walls painted pale pink but appearing darker with the raging storm going on outside the window. A storm that had not been there when my parents and I got to the inn.

My hands are clammy, but I push myself to my feet. There's a made bed in the corner, complete with a slightly crooked teddy bear with a purple bow around its neck. Directly across from the bed is a small vanity, covered with cheap lip smacker and blue eyeshadow, among discarded Barbies, the kind that have marker on their face and hair shredded by scissors.

I had a few of those, back in the day.

I take a step toward the vanity, closer to the mirror, mottled and warped with age. Flinching, I take a good look at my face and wish I hadn't. My eyes are rimmed with dark circles, my green irises surrounded by bloodshot veins. My skin seems to have lost its summer glow replaced by a sickly pallor. Lanky curls frame my face.

I reach out to touch the reflection, strangely entranced by the way my pupils seem to grow wider and wider and wider and—

"It's a pleasure to see you have not become immune to my tricks," cackles a voice behind me. The hair on the back of my neck sticks up and I turn.

Cora perches on the edge of the bed, nightgown cascading around her swinging ankles. Apart from the shimmery aura surrounding her and the dark hole of a mouth, she looks like a sweet little girl, waiting for a bedtime story.

Snapped out of the trance, I hold my hands up in a placating gesture.

"Look," I say softly. "I don't want trouble. Hopefully you don't want trouble. I came here with my parents to help your family. To help *you*. I know you went through a lot—"

Cora snarls, jumping right up into my face, eyes swirling with madness. "DON'T tell me that you understand what I went through! You will never understand! Not even after I show your parents what they did to me!"

My breathing is quick. "Please," I whimper, shuffling back. "I don't understand, you're right. But I want to help. Is getting revenge really the best way to make up for all of this?"

She doesn't answer but her expression also doesn't soften at all.

"Let me help you."

A snort escapes her. *"Let's think about this little situation, shall we? How would you be able to help me, Maeve Everbrill? You are the spawn of the two people I hate the most in this world and while you like to pretend to be a good little girl, I know better than anyone how two-faced you are. That's what you always do, isn't it? Pretend, pretend, pretend!"* The last syllable breaks off with a shrieking laugh and Cora spins around in circles, arms flung out, laughing maniacally at the ceiling.

My blood turns to ice. "How would you know anything about me? You can't leave this town. This is where you died."

Cora's laughter continues as she speaks. *"You think I can't rummage through that loud mind of yours? I'm too young to understand the way humans work, maybe?"*

She stops spinning and stares me dead in the eye.

"I've got news for you. I understand humans better than anyone."

But you're a ghost, I almost say.

"And," Cora continues, tilting her head, eyes flashing with dark amusement. *"Though I'm able to fish through your emotions, I also had an inside source. Only for a little while, but a source all the same."*

I frown. "What source?"

Cora's gaping mouth widens into a grin. *"Oh, brother. This is about to get good."*

Black spools of writhing darkness pour forth from her mouth, encircling me with a sticky kind of warmth, something that smells like a combination of rotten nectar and geraniums. The solution climbs up my arms, tangling around my limbs like vines and ripping into my flesh like thorns. I cry out, throwing my head back.

Just as I think the fright is never going to end, I blink and find myself sitting in a small, country church, an open casket residing in front of the pulpit. I glance down and find myself clad in a black dress, Cora beside me wearing one resembling it. Her dark hair is tied up with a black velvet ribbon. I'm shocked to see tears on her face. The vulnerable expression makes me wonder if she's human, but then I catch a glimpse of the shimmering aura surrounding her.

Soft crying floats through the room as I look around, mourners clutching handkerchiefs and patting each other on the back.

"Cora, where are we?"

She nods toward the casket. *"My death impacted* more than just me. It impacted my brother."

"Brother Bane," I whisper, rising slowly. "This was his funeral?"

Cora inclines her head.

I walk through the crowd, unseen by the people in this memory. My feet hardly feel like they're touching the ground. When I get to the front of the line, the casket is open and overflowing with flowers, I peer in and lose my footing.

"I wish I could explain everything, but I can't."

Somehow, I knew. Ever since he miraculously healed Addie by the river, I knew.

Lying in the open casket is a boy I've grown accustomed to, a boy who appears at the most random moments, always when I need him. A boy who refuses to touch me, even when his eyes roam my face and his hands twitch. A boy who seems to glow every now and then and is unaffected by swallowtails.

I collapse into a pile of sobs, feeling betrayed. Cora must have been the girl he conferred with, the evening after we went star-tipping.

So many things fall into place.

Cora's laugh is bitter and cruel behind me. Glimpses of Hayes flicker through my brain like a kaleidoscope. In and out. In and out.

"What happened to him?" I whisper. A sharp pain bursts in my chest and I feel like I'm losing him, like this is the first time he died and I'm a witness.

"My death was too much for him to handle."

I clutch myself tighter. Pull my body into a ball. Breathe. Breathe. Breathe.

Cora brings us back to her old bedroom while I clutch my head and sob.

"He's been using me?" I whisper, rocking back and forth. Hating that my mind goes there because I should be grieving him.

He's dead. He's been dead for years.

Hayes is Brother Bane—as long as I've known him, he's been a ghost. And he's been working with his sister.

Cora inhales sharply. *"At first. Unfortunately, Hayes has always valued kindness over revenge, although he could have been much more productive had he listened to me. He found feelings for you, which led him to go against me."*

I hate that my brain snags on the words *found feelings for you.*

I quickly brush them aside. If what Cora's saying is true, Hayes' intentions had been against me in the beginning—but what does that entail? His presence at all of the sites containing ghostly messages was always a bit suspicious and is honestly something that had crossed my mind before. Why would he do something like that? For revenge? To get back at my family?

Had it been easier for him to stop joining in with Cora because *kindness* had been the emotion he held closely in death? Surely that couldn't be the case. Who holds *kindness* close to them in death?

"What my parents did was wrong," I whisper. "I'm sorry this happened to you and your family. But Cora, you must understand, something was messing with you long before they came around."

She lifts her nose and the darkness around her seems to grow so much sharper. *"The blame game is rampant with you Everbrills, isn't it?"*

I drop my gaze. "I want to help you. I want to help Hayes."

"Hayes is gone."

"What?"

Cora levels me with a glare. *"Didn't you see the way he sacrificed the final piece of his soul, the piece holding him down here, in order to save the life of that stupid little girl?"*

"Ghosts can...do that?" A surge of warmth floods through me, followed by sharp pain. Hayes sacrificed the last piece of himself in order to save Addie, a girl he didn't know. Why would he do that?

"He's too soft," spits Cora. *"A ghost should never do such a thing in kindness. Our lives were taken from us, we ghosts. And to save a human...it's the lowest thing you can do. Stooping down for a people who cut you off. I prefer to revel in the idea of taking a life."* Her eyes gleam with madness. *"They say to do it that way is to be brought back to life."*

I ball my fists, standing. "How could you be so *wicked*?" I understand a wrong was done to her, but why can't she, like Hayes, give that up? Why can't she find peace in saving someone instead of hurting them?

"What if I show you how it feels?" Cora snarls. *"Will you realize then the weight of what your family has done?"*

Pulsing light encompasses her body, expanding to every corner of the room, reaching tiny fingers of magic out, tinged with red.

An angry shade of red.

I bite down on my tongue to keep from screaming out. But who would hear me? Cora has surrounded me in a hallucination of her design, one apart from all natural things and one that separates me from the safety of my parents.

perfect poison
July 6

A bloody shriek rips through my throat, searing my vocal cords and ricocheting out of my lips with a violent force that I can't control. The pain starts at my extremities, working its way up into my core, shaking my bones and my marrow until every inch of me feels electrified, burned, beaten, hardened into a type of body that no longer feels like mine. It's a pain like I've never experienced.

But then my brain starts messing with me too.

Flashes of my past flicker in and out of the dark bedroom, dancing along, but jaded in different, horrific ways. I see my parents, watching me with angry eyes—eyes that don't belong to them. Weaving in and out of these moments, I see myself at seven-years-old, carefree with wild curls, but glaring dark circles painted underneath my big green eyes. This version of myself is pale, with a stony expression.

Not so carefree after all.

Somewhere, in the back of my mind, I know Cora is causing all of this, giving me a chance to admit that this is all my parents' fault—that she can do with us Everbrills as she likes, so long as she makes my instant pain go away. But I can't bring myself to find those words. Somewhere I know, if there was hope for Hayes choosing the right thing, maybe there's hope for Cora. Granted, she has a lot more to work through than her brother, but she can fix this. She can save me.

She can make the wrong things right.

The feeling of hot fire ripples down my skin and I claw at it, desperate for some sort of relief, but to no avail. Darkness crowds around my vision, until I'm no longer writhing on the floor of Cora's old room, but in a closet.

There's something so familiar about its smell. Woodsy, combined with something faintly antiseptic and clean. I roll my head to the side, coming face to face with a little girl.

Me.

"H-hello?" her voice trembles as she gazes at me, wide-eyed. She scoots back and hugs her knees to her chest. "W-who are you?"

"I'm you," I try to say. *"But older."*

Instead, what comes out is, *"I'm not going to hurt you."*

The voice sends chills racing across my spine. It's not my voice that comes out of my own throat.

It's Cora's.

Smaller me begins to tremble. "Please, don't hurt me. They won't let me out of here."

"You have nothing to be afraid of."

I wish I knew what I look like to her. Her shaking has intensified, and she begins to scratch at the walls of the closet.

I bite back the words, but they burst through anyway, *"Why are you running from me?"*

"LET ME OUT!" screams little Maeve. "GUYS, PLEASE LET ME OUT!"

I clamp my hands over my ears. My voice fights through Cora's and I'm able to say, "Get me out of here! I don't want to relive this memory anymore!"

"Don't you see?" hisses the real Cora. *"You were meant to be mine to deal with from the beginning. The universe has given me this chance to take back what was mine. Life."*

I struggle against her invisible torture. "But what if saving someone brings you life, too? How would you know unless you try? Cora, please, I'm *begging* you—"

She snaps. Her face is inches from mine and if she were human, I know I'd feel her hot breath lapping over my face. Instead, there's a faint smell of something acrid and bitter cold.

"I begged!" she snarls. *"I begged the doctors to fix me. I begged my parents to treat me like I was normal. I begged Hayes to stay with me at all times so I wouldn't feel alone at Camp Swallowtail. I begged your stupid mom to talk with me in the evenings, to help me calm down. But she was always off frolicking with your father, too busy to sit and listen. I begged and look where it got me."*

I close my eyes. A tear trickles down my cheek.

She's right. She did beg. She begged and she pleaded with people to help her, but no one ever did. No one understood. Why would my begging for my life mean anything to her? The only thing she can set her eyes on right now is hurting me, is getting revenge.

What she wants most is to be human. And when I look back on my life, I've wasted that precious gift by using my life for selfish reasons, for hiding away from the truth, for living under a guise that is fashioned from nothing but lies.

Her life was taken. And all I've done is waste mine. "Fine," I whisper. "My life is yours. I hope you do a great deal more with it than I have."

Cora's eyes stretch wide. The scene in front of me shifts and we're back in her old bedroom, the pain subsiding in my body. I gasp.

"What?" she demands.

"You're right," I say again, more tears falling. "You didn't deserve the fate you were met with and in a lot of ways, the blame belongs on my parents. But it's not them you want—it's me. So do what you need to do. I want you to have life." The words sound foreign even as I'm saying them. I can hardly comprehend what they mean, what I'm offering, but somewhere, deep in my gut, there's this feeling of *right*. Of *true*.

Of *free*. Of being honest and not hiding.

Cora's chest swells with a deep breath. I see the madness flicker in her eyes, but grow suddenly as she lifts her hands.

Alivia and Isla were right about everything. I think I've finally learned how to *be*.

Just as Cora's fingers gnarl in grotesque shapes and I feel my heart begin to palpitate, beating in a rhythm that I know is unhealthy, lethal. Two more tears trickle down my cheeks as I stare up at the ceiling.

This is the right thing to do.

I love you, Mom.

I love you, Dad.

I love you, Alivia.

I love you Isla, Madysen, Addie, Lena, Charlie, Emily, and Kiara.

I love you, Hayes.

Hayes?

Before I feel my lungs give out, there's a frighteningly loud yell. Cora jerks and as she does, my body twists violently and my head swings to the side. Standing there, is Hayes, flesh and bone, wearing his hat, arms out and eyes alarmed.

Death is peaceful—if I'm seeing him, I must've made it already.

"Cora, don't!" he shouts. "Don't!"

She screams and collapses to the ground, staring at him. *"You're alive."*

He runs to her, kneeling beside her. A frustrated sound escapes his lips when his reaching hands go right through her.

"You're alive," she whispers again in awe.

Vehemently, he nods. "Don't do this." His eyes stray to me and there's heartbreak inside of them. Feebly, I reach out my hand toward his. He grasps on to it and pulls me closer.

For the first time, I feel his warmth.

But I'm fading. Colors blur before my eyes and his words sound like he's in a tunnel.

"Save her," he pleads. "But you have to mean it. Otherwise, it won't work."

"I don't know how to mean it. Not after what they did to me."

I moan, weakness drifting to my extremities. "I said...she could take me."

"Cora!" Hayes says. His arms tighten around me. I hear his heart—a real heart—pounding and pounding and pounding and pounding.

My head is pounding and pounding and
pounding and
pounding.

"There's forgiveness in there somewhere, little sis," Hayes says softly. "Find it."

Cora shakes her head. *"I can't."*

My eyes flutter shut. But before they do, I see Hayes lean closer to Cora and whisper, feather-soft, "Find it."

Maeve

Beat, beat, beat, beat. Inhale, exhale.

My eyes open wide and I gasp, fresh air filling my lungs. I feel two hands holding me, a warm voice murmuring, "You're okay, Maeve. You're okay. Everything is okay."

But I don't see Cora.

Cora

I blink and stare up. I'm in a dark room. It's vaguely familiar, a place I've only been once. There are no people, but a voice from everywhere and nowhere speaks to me.

"Cora Hart," it says.

"Yes?" I whisper. I hold a hand up to my eyes, hoping to see flesh and bone, but there's still a translucent quality to my skin. It makes frustration boil inside of me.

What if Hayes was wrong? What if I won't become human?

"Do you regret what you did?" inquires the voice. I grimace that it can read my thoughts. I hate that. My thoughts should be my own. I didn't give it permission to peer inside my head, especially not when I've been alone for so long.

My nightgown pools around me when I sit on the floor, feeling defeated. I shake my head softly. "No."

"Why did you do it?"

"I...I wanted to be human," I say carefully.

The voice sighs. It sounds fatherly.

Then a second voice speaks up, this one delicate and distinctly feminine. "You must assess the heart and the true intentions to be granted personhood."

I recognize that voice. Quickly, I stand. "Mama? Daddy?"

Two white figures shimmer through the darkness, slowly taking the form of my parents. I take a trembling breath. It feels like it's been years since I've truly seen them. I'm able to appear to those who aren't family. Death is not a reward; I don't get to interact with my loved ones.

It's part of the reason I'm so desperate for humanity. I'd get to be with my family again.

"Sweetheart," Mama whispers. "We can't bring you

back to life if your heart's not in the right place."

I feel tears welling up inside of me. "But I saved Maeve! I healed her! Isn't that enough?"

Daddy shakes his head. "The heart speaks louder than the action, Cora."

Frustration explodes inside of me and I cry. "But I don't know how to forgive. I don't know how to make the wrong things right! I've spent so much time feeling lost and broken because of all the things wrong with my mind! And I'm so angry at what they did to me. I hate George and Winnie!"

"But it's not Maeve you hate," Mama reminds me.

I wipe away a tear. "Guilty by association." Daddy's lips turn up into a small smile.

Mama watches me affectionately. Deep sadness is still wedged in her features. "Until you learn true forgiveness, you'll stay here with us."

"You're not real," I whisper.

"But soon, we will be."

They reach out and each take one of my hands. I watch them both with a peaceful feeling beginning in my heart.

I don't know how to forgive—not yet. But until then, I will learn to be at peace.

I follow them into the dark.

a swallowtail song

Camp is what you make it.

Rubbing my eyes, I yawn as I sit up in my bunk bed, morning light pouring through the window. That little catchphrase repeats in my head—a mantra that seems to be murmured around Camp Swallowtail quite frequently after what is now being called "Addie's Accident". It started when people whispered those words to calm down panicked Bitties, reminding them to look on the bright side. But now it's become something that has become a promise.

Something that encourages all of us to keep on going. To finish the summer out well.

Sleepily, I gaze over all the other girls in the cabin, watching their quiet forms. Below me, Isla's bed creaks as she rolls onto her side and slams her hand down on the alarm. Groans and pleas for five more minutes ring out through the cabin.

I peer over at Addie, in the top bunk beside me.

Every time I look at her, I feel a rush of appreciation and gratitude for Hayes. If he hadn't saved her, who knows where she would be. Thankfully, she was back from the hospital only a day later, with a doctor's note that excused her from rec and commanded her to drink an abundance of water.

"It was only a minor concussion," they assured us. "But it's better to be on the safe side."

Although my parents have taken down the slide for good, we've been telling people that when Addie ran out of Scrapbook Bunk, she slipped and fell, hitting her head on a rock. Dad thought that if people knew the truth about the ghosts and the slide, fear would run rampant throughout the camp. Only my parents, the Harts, Addie, and I know what really went down.

Ghost sightings haven't happened since that night.

I rub my eyes. There's a fuzzy spot in my brain when I think of that night with Cora and Hayes—who is now a real person—and I know that Cora must have saved me. But because we haven't seen her since, neither Hayes nor I are entirely sure what happened.

As for him, my parents excused his presence as a recent hire. My brain still can't comprehend the fact that I'd discovered he was a ghost, Cora's brother, and that he'd come back to life all in the same day. It seemed impossible.

Then again, impossible things seemed frequent at Camp Swallowtail.

Sometimes, like now, when everything is sort of quiet, I think about the fact that Cora voluntarily saved me. That she chose to give my life back to me instead of keeping it for herself. I marvel at the fact that her heart softened towards me at all.

Addie sits up and blinks at me, rubbing the sleep from her eyes.

"G'morning," she says through a yawn. Her red hair is tumbling out of its braid.

I stifle a laugh, joy flowing through me. "G'morning to you, too."

My attention turns back to Isla when she sticks one of her tan legs out from her blankets.

With a groan she says, "Up at at 'em, Misty Monarch!"

"Five more minutes," mutters Kiara, stuffing her face back into the pillow.

Lena rolls over with a grunt and pulls her blanket over her face.

I lean down and share a smile with Isla. This is it. Our last day.

As she shuffles out of bed, tossing her blankets haphazardly, Isla reaches for a plastic bag by her portable dresser, filled with those ugly teal Camp Swallowtail t-shirts. She reads the names off the tags and flings each shirt out toward its owner.

Mine hits me squarely in the face and I laugh. I shimmy down the bunk bed ladder, overwhelmed by enthusiasm and joy I wish I'd harnessed all summer. Addie watches me, amused, and rips the hair tie out of her sloppy braid.

I shake the shoulders of each girl who is trying to sneak a few more winks of sleep.

"Get up, get up! It's Closing Day! You wanna look pretty for your parents, don't you?"

Madysen growls at me when I steal her pillow. I throw Isla a mischievous grin when Madysen snaps, "Shut up and give it back!"

I toss the pillow. Isla catches it, spinning around the room.

"Ugh!" Madysen flings her shirt on the ground and gets out of bed.

After a few more minutes of pestering, Isla and I finally succeed in waking everyone up. We're all headed to the bathhouse to get dressed for breakfast—clad in matching Camp Swallowtail t-shirts with that stupid slogan.

Camp is what you make it!

Everything up until the ceremony itself is kind of a blur. We've packed up all the luggage, leaving it out on the porch for male staff to come take to parents' vehicles once they arrive. Isla and I led the cabin to the dining patio for breakfast—an assortment of pastries, eggs, and cereal packets. There's freshly brewed coffee for the adults.

I meet the parents of the girls. Or meet them again.

But it feels like a first time. I was a different person back then.

After telling me they're so grateful for all the time and love Isla and I put into these girls the whole summer, we file into the Great Hall for a closing announcement from my parents. Everything seems to move so fast, and I wish I could just pause it and savor this moment.

I take a seat in the plastic fold-up chairs, lined up in a row. Someone catches my eye from the back. It's Hayes. He waves with a smile.

I smile back.

The lights in the Great Hall dim as my parents stroll to the stage for the closing ceremony. Stragglers find their seats and the talking dies down to a hushed whisper. I sneak into a back row with Isla.

The spotlight from the back of the room shines across my parents as they stare out into the crowd with nervous smiles.

"Welcome to Camp Swallowtail!" Dad announces. "Parents, we are so happy to have you join us for our closing ceremony. Your children have been treasures to spend the summer with."

"We've loved getting to know each and every one of them," Mom adds. "But before we brag too much on how incredible they are, we'd like to introduce ourselves."

"Of course!" Dad chuckles. "My name is George Everbrill and this is my wife, Winnie. Our daughter served this summer as a counselor for younger high school students. Maeve, where are you?"

Cheeks flushed, but smiling, I raise my hand and wave as heads all turn to scan the crowd for me.

"As many of you know, we bought the camp earlier this year and moved right before camp started," Dad explains. "And we were given a far more exciting summer than we ever could've imagined!"

I feel so connected to everyone now, giggling and making inside jokes during the ceremony. I hate that so many of them will be leaving by the end of the hour.

Mom and Dad explain some of the fun events we did during the summer, like Fright Night and rec.

"Now, we're going to give out charms," Mom announces, walking across the stage in the Great Hall. Resting on a little wooden stool is a box with tons of little plastic baggies. Mom pulls out a handful of them and walks back across to stage by Dad.

"These are courtesy of a very special couple with a history at this camp," Mom informs everyone, holding up one little baggie as an example. "Thomas and Elise Hart have been so kind as to donate towards getting our campers and counselors charms that they can collect and keep in a shadow box or on a charm bracelet. There is a design for each year that a camper or counselor has attended Camp Swallowtail. So, without further ado, George will read out the names of all our first years."

A general murmur of excitement rustles through the crowd. I raise my eyebrows. I had no idea Thomas and Elise would want to donate anything to Camp Swallowtail. I guess after seeing Hayes come back to life, they wanted to give something to the camp. After everything ended, there will always be hurt in their life for their little girl, but if what happened with Hayes is truly possible, there's hope for Cora after all.

Name after name is called and the audience applauds as campers and a few counselors make their way onto the stage to accept their new charm.

"Adeline Bennet," Dad reads, looking around. Addie gets up, red hair swinging behind her in a ponytail and walks across the stage to take the charm from Mom, who hugs her tight and says a few things to her quietly. Addie's parents hold up phones to video and clap loudly when Addie walks off the stage and back to her spot by Isla.

"Can I see the charm?" I lean forward.

Addie shows me the pendant. It's sterling silver, in the shape of swallowtail moth, with a Roman Numeral one etched on the thorax of the bug.

"I like it!"

Pleased, Addie leans back in her chair to admire the piece.

My parents begin to call up all the second-year campers, and I watch Charlie go up and accept her charm happily. I zone out a little with all the names, until I hear "Maeve Everbrill!"

I glance up, stunned. I get up uncertainly and see all the girls in my cabin whoop and cheer excitedly.

Second year? I guess, technically, it *is* my second year, but I thought that my parents would count this as my first. My name wasn't called with the first-years, which made me assume I wasn't getting a charm.

But I stumble over to the stage where Mom hands me a charm and hugs me tightly. Applause rings in my ears and the bright lights dazzle my eyes. The baggie feels cold in my hand and I study the charm on my way off stage. Year Two's charm makes me laugh softly. It's of a cartoon ghost—the kind that looks like a giant sheet with holes for eyes. But the ghost wears a happy smile and has a Roman Numeral two on its belly. I show everyone when I sit down and clink my charm with

Charlie's matching one.

Kiara goes up for Year Three, receiving a charm that resembles a campfire.

Lena goes up for Year Four, gaining a s'mores charm.

Emily gets the fifth-year charm, a kayak.

The Year Six charm portrays a half-moon, given to Madysen.

The years continue until Year Eleven, which belongs only to Isla. She beams when she receives it and races off the stage to show us immediately. Her charm depicts a friendship bracelet around a Roman Numeral eleven. I glance up at Mom and she winks at me. I know she requested this design specifically for Isla because of what a good friend she has been to me.

The ceremony wraps up as Mom and Dad announce the dates for next year's summer session and invite everyone back again. They give instructions for leaving and ensuring all the medication, special food, and luggage has been picked up.

"At Camp Swallowtail, we don't say goodbye," my parents say in unison, sad smiles across their faces, like they remember this little closer from their time as campers.

"We say, see you later!" Everyone in the audience erupts, clapping and standing up to hug each other. It's a closing word I've never heard before, but it makes me smile.

Mom and Dad leave the stage and the ceremony concludes. The Misty Monarch girls hug Isla and me goodbye and rush off to find their parents, promising to see us next year. The whole room is a blur of bodies in movement and tears and laughter among other emotions.

I spot Mom and Dad in the midst of all the chaos, standing by Hayes in the back. I shuffle through the crowd toward them, just in time to see Mom passing Hayes a charm of his own.

"For me?" He looks at her with wide eyes.

"You and your sister have been here longer than any of us," Mom says with a sad smile. "The least we could do was ask your parents to find a design to order for the two of you."

Hayes glances at his feet. "There's only one of us."

Dad shoots me a meaningful look. "We don't know about that forever. She could always come back."

Hayes holds up the charm. I peer at it beside him.

It's fashioned into the shape of a polaroid photo, with the year 1996 inscribed at the bottom, like a caption.

A gasp escapes his lips, and he looks sincerely at my parents. "Thank you. So much."

He reaches for the chain around his neck, bare of any charms, and slides this new treasure onto it, clasping it back around his neck.

I pull mine out from underneath the neck of my t-shirt, smiling at him.

"Maeve!"

I whirl around and see Addie barreling toward me. I hold out my arms and she rushes into them, squeezing me tightly.

"I just wanted to say thank you," she says, her voice muffled by my Camp Swallowtail t-shirt. "You've been an amazing counselor and friend. You were always there for me and ready to talk. You never judged me. And that meant the world."

I pull back. "Don't tell anyone, but you were my favorite."

She glows. "You were my favorite, too."

"You'll be back next summer?" I ask. When she nods, I say, "Good. This place needs more people like you."

"Will you be back?" she fidgets with her ponytail.

I glance at my parents, still chatting with Hayes. I smile and lower my voice. "That's the plan. But you never know what life has in store."

She nods as if she completely understands what I mean.

Isla finds Addie and I and hugs us tightly. "Love you two so much!"

Addie squeezes her back and bids us one last goodbye before chasing after her parents, who call her name with a wave, ready to start the drive back home.

Isla pops a hand on her hip and smiles at me. "Look who grew so much this summer. You're really learning how to be free, you know that? I'm super proud of you."

I shrug. "I learned from the best."

She punches me lightly on the shoulder. "Amen."

Hayes appears beside us. "Hey, your parents wanted me to tell you to meet them in their office when you wrap up here."

"You're the new hire?" Isla tilts her head.

He nods. "Was. I guess the summer's over now, right?"

The words stab me with an overwhelming sadness. I meant what I said to Addie—I do want to stay here. But what if this summer was too chaotic and my parents decided it wasn't worth it? What if we move back?

Not now, when I've finally found good friends. When I have a boy that I really like.

I slip my hand into said boy's, and he smiles. Isla raises her eyebrows at me.

"Thanks for the message. I'll be sure to go over when I've said goodbye to everyone."

Hayes nods, still smiling, and squeezes my hand before leaving. His skin is so warm. It feels real and safe.

"What's that about?" Isla demands.

"He's the one I always told you about," I answer honestly. "You thought he didn't exist?"

She shakes her head in disbelief. "I can't believe I missed him. He's so good-looking that he sticks out like a sore thumb among the rest of these weirdos." She gestures towards the guy counselors, bidding their campers farewell.

I stifle a laugh. "See you next summer?" I hope the words are true.

"Sooner," she says. "We'll meet up before then."

I smile. "Perfect."

After a parting hug, I escape the crowd and walk quietly toward my parents' office, wondering what they have to say to me. Memories of this summer play back in my mind. I hate the piece of myself that passionately argued that camp was the worst thing in the world.

Camp is so much more than anything I have ever experienced in my seventeen years of living. It's highs and lows and growing up. It's discovering who you are and finding out who you're not. It's falling for that cute guy who's unlike anyone you've ever met before, only to find out he's not quite who you thought he was. It's discovering friendships and talking them through the tragedies of the past.

It's friendship bracelets and swim bands adoring wrists. It's scraped knees and headaches from dehydration. It's chlorine-coated hair and sunburnt cheeks.

It's ghost stories told around a campfire while the stars twinkle overhead. It's s'mores, gooey and melted on your skin late at night.

It's homesickness that quickly fades because here you are and here is where you feel like you belong. It's your first taste of freedom at such a young age; it's where you learn to be independent and truly yourself.

Camp is early mornings with mediocre food, but pizza nights on Fridays that feel like fancy dinners. It's powdered lemonade mix that never has quite enough mixed in.

It's late-night barn dances and screaming down the zip line. It's night swims with melted mascara and goosebumps across your skin. It's sweat stains and sunglasses and funky tan lines. It's dirt between your toes and bugs in the cabin. It's the songs in between transitions and the promises you make to a million friends that you'll never be able to keep.

It's heartbroken see-you-laters—never goodbyes.

Camp is the piece of you that you didn't know you needed, wished would never end, and never will forget.

Camp is what you make it.

I open the door and find my parents seated by the desk. They look up at me in unison when my feet hit the creaky wood. Quietly, I shut the door behind me. "What's going on?"

"We want to give you an offer," Dad explains, sitting in his chair and leaning forward on his desk, hands clasped in front of him like a businessman. "You did so well this summer, better than your mom or I expected, and we wish to reward you for your actions."

I tilt my head. "I hope you two don't think I only acted rightly because I was hoping to get something out of you. I really did enjoy my time here, even if I'm still surprised to hear myself say it."

Mom chuckles. "We know. We don't think that. But we would like to give you the choice. We admit it was rather unfair of us to make you move here, especially with such little warning. We uprooted your life and your friendships and expected you to just be okay with it.

And although there were some minor moments, you were really very flexible, Maeve. And we're so proud of you for how much you've grown this summer."

"Owning a camp has always been our dream." Dad motions around the building. "This is where we met and fell in love. We wanted to inspire as much magic as we could into the lives of young people, and this was the best way we felt we could do it. But we chose this camp because we had some wrongs to make right."

I nod.

"Your friend Alivia contacted us after chatting with her parents." Mom smiles at me. "And she's happy to have you move in with her for your senior year back in Arkansas if you'd like. You'd be able to finish your last year of high school with your friends and your team. Of course, your father and I would come to visit often during the year when we don't have retreats. We wouldn't miss things like your birthday or graduation."

I go quiet. *Oh.*

When I first moved here, it felt like the world was ending. I didn't think there was any true possibility that I would be able to escape the cards that fate had dealt me.

But now I have the choice. I could stay here and adventure through many more unknowns, like where I'll go to school and who I'll be friends with. Do they even have a volleyball team in a town this small? Camp isn't forever, it's only for the summer. I've only just begun to experience this new piece of my life.

Or.

I could go back to what is familiar and comfortable and safe and finish high school there, with people that I know and who know me.

The thing is, I don't know if I *can* go back. That life doesn't feel like me anymore. I think back to what Isla was saying about the difference between college Isla and camp Isla—where she doesn't feel the freedom to be as carefree as she is here. And I don't want to live like that anymore, because that's exactly who I used to be. I want to bring camp Maeve with me everywhere.

I'm just not sure that's something I can do at home. "Do I have to go?" My voice is small.

Shocked, they look at each other. "Chickadee...you'd want to stay?" Mom whispers. "I think I want to finish high school here. In this town. With these people."

Dad shakes his head, loss for words. "What made you decide that this place is better for you?"

I think of Isla, Misty Monarch, Hayes. I think of the people I want to spend my senior year with. I think of the possibilities and the adventure and everything that will be new. I think of Cora and the possibility that she might come back.

I want to tell her how much it means to me that she chose to save me in person.

I want that. I want to live. I want to *be*.

So, I shrug. "Camp is what you make it."

the end

acknowledgements

Wow, to anyone who finished this book, I wish I could do so much more than just say thank you. To know that I've spent two years on this novel and have people decide to spend their free time reading it is truly incredible. This is what I've wanted to do since I was five years old.

Thanks for making that come true. :)

(And thanks for reading the acknowledgments! They're honestly a very fun part of every novel!)

about the author

Allyson Norris is an indie-published author from Keller, Texas. She is currently studying English at DBU and hopes to pursue a career in editing and writing. She loves psychological thrillers, romance, and classics, especially if she can read them while drinking coffee. *1996* is her debut novel.

Follow on Instagram: @allysonwritesnovels